VAMPIRES
NEVER GET OLD

VAMPIRES
NEVER GET OLD
TALES WITH FRESH BITE

EDITED BY
ZORAIDA CÓRDOVA
AND NATALIE C. PARKER

{Imprint}
MAKE YOUR MARK

New York

【Imprint】
BAKE YOUR MARK

A part of Macmillan Publishing Group, LLC
120 Broadway, New York, NY 10271

Library of Congress Cataloging-in-Publication Data is available.

ISBN 978-1-250-23001-0 (hardcover) / ISBN 978-1-250-23000-3 (ebook)

Our books may be purchased in bulk for promotional, educational, or business use.
Please contact your local bookseller or the Macmillan Corporate and Premium Sales Department
at (800) 221-7945 ext. 5442 or by email at MacmillanSpecialMarkets@macmillan.com.

Book design by Elynn Cohen

Imprint logo designed by Amanda Spielman

First edition, 2020

5 7 9 10 8 6 4

fiercereads.com

The vampire's curse is loneliness. The book thief's life is far, far worse. Steal this book and may your soda always be flat, your ends always be split, your breath always be rank, and your food always be saltless.

To those who are hungry for strange, dark stories.
Also to Julie Murphy and Tessa Gratton
for indulging us when we said,
"You know what we miss? Vampires."

CONTENTS

INTRODUCTION

A Note from your Editrixes:

Vampires are creatures of imagination. Of myth and moonlight. Of terror and adoration. When we sat down to begin work on this anthology, neither of us could recall when we were first introduced to the idea of the vampire. Its presence in our culture is so deeply rooted that uncovering its origins in our own imaginations proved impossible. We could recall the stories we read in school—Bram Stoker's *Dracula* and John William Polidori's *The Vampyre*—and those we discovered later—Anne Rice's *Interview with the Vampire* or Stephenie Meyer's *Twilight*—but which was first? Neither of us could say.

Of the vampires in our collective imagination, which is admittedly Western-focused, nearly all resided in stories about power. Despite rampant queer subtext and outstanding nonwhite examples like Jewelle Gomez's *The Gilda Stories*, the vampires were predominantly men, white, cisgender, straight, and able-bodied, and we were ready for stories that reimagined that default.

INTRODUCTION

With the stories in this collection, we want to prove that there is no one way to write the vampire. After all, a being with the power to shape-shift should wear many faces and tell many tales. Here you'll find vampire stories that expand on and reinvent traditional tellings. Following each story, we, your editrixes, offer brief notes on vampire myth and how our authors are reimagining the tropes we all know and love.

Our hope is that this collection inspires you to investigate the stories that have already been told, the beautiful collection of myths that exist around the world, and we hope it inspires you to dream up your own monsters, to interpret them through the lens of your own experiences. Vampires may not be real, but the stories make them something we share. They are eternal, reborn, and living in our nightmares for all eternity. Because vampires never get old.

We're very happy that you've decided to join us on this journey out of the coffin and into the night.

Cheers,

Zoraida & Natalie

SEVEN NIGHTS FOR DYING

Tessa Gratton

Esmael told me that teenage girls make the best vampires.

It sounded like a line, but he'd already been in my pants so I was inclined to believe him.

He'd found me because of the art pinned to the wall at El Café, where I worked. I'd brought in a few sketches and tried to stick them to the exposed bricks with putty, then cussed until Thomas said if I couldn't figure a way without damaging the wall, maybe I didn't deserve to be an artist. I hung string from the coat-rack to the bookshelf and clipped my art to that. Ten bucks each. I did them when I couldn't sleep most nights, while watching TV with the lights out or after midnight, when I could only see by the streetlamps outside the window. Hard to notice mistakes that way, and I can just rub my feelings into the paper and sell them as dark mood prints. Get it?

I know what I'm doing.

Esmael came in at the end of Thursday, when we're open till seven o'clock, and it was January so the sun was long down. I wasn't there—I prefer to open the café even if I have to be there by five a.m., because I'm alone and just put everything to rights, no cleaning. Flick on the industrial espresso machine, put the stools and chairs down, pick a streaming station, inventory the milk and shit, and wait for Miss Tina to bring the day's muffins. The sun rises behind our block of shops, so light sort of glows up gradually until around midmorning it crests the buildings and hits the east-facing windows across the street and absolutely tears into my eyes, even from all the way behind the counter.

Apparently Esmael got his cappuccino with cinnamon dashed against the foam like dried blood and then held it while he stared at my art. Bought a piece called *howling* and asked for my info to actually commission something. Thomas just told him to find me at opening on the weekend or Tuesday, when I had a late start at school and worked until nine.

He was waiting on Saturday when I unlocked the door at 6:30 a.m. sharp. It wasn't unusual for a regular. I also didn't mind, because that vampire is extremely pretty. Small for a guy, but moves like an athlete, you know, who can spring to action before you realize it. He was in tight jeans and a button-down and a floral vest, and it worked. Really nice, if blanched, peaches-and-cream skin; dark blond hair tucked neatly behind his ears; green eyes. Like, actually green. Ocean-green. Green-like-a-mermaid-tail green. And his hands were so deliberate. He had a weird shiny black ring on his forefinger that seemed to float there when he gestured or handed me cash and when he tucked a ten into the tip jar.

(That was the first thing that caught me like a warning flag.)

Also he was old. Thirty, I'd have guessed, or maybe twenty-five before I saw his eyes, which aged him because he didn't blink or look around much. That gaze just held on to me, or my art, or the register. Whatever he looked at, he *looked at*.

He said he liked my style and asked how I did it—with ashes in the dark, I said—and he laughed softly, not really making an expression. Then he asked if I was interested in having a show at his gallery. If so, I should come by, see the space, and we'd talk.

I got out my phone and said, "I need a picture of you to send to the police if I go missing."

When I held it up he smiled, and Mary Mother, was it a *smile*. I took the pic and texted it to Sidney: *If I disappear this guy named Esmael Abrams wants to show my art at a gallery.* She texted back: *I hope he wants you to put out for it* and a line of eggplant emojis.

♦

The first time he bit me it was right in the groin, and I didn't give a fuck because he'd just ruined me for all other guys. Not all other girls—girls are better at that, especially Sid.

Anyway, I guess there's a vein down there.

♦

This other vampire, Seti, agreed that teenage girls definitely make the best vampires, but not for the reasons Esmael thinks. She said it's because teenage girls are both highly pissed and highly adaptable, and that's what it takes to survive the centuries.

I asked what Esmael's reasons were and he said, "Your art," like it was obvious. He lounged against the tinted window of his apartment, which was the whole floor over the gallery (yeah, he did have a gallery). His robe was silk, and it draped around him in proper vampiric fashion. He reached for the hose of his hookah, took a slow drag, and let the smoke trickle out around his tiny little fangs like a fucking dragon. (It was rose tobacco and apple juice in the base, too sharp for my taste.)

Seti rolled her eyes and her head, too, so her fat henna-red curls dripped down the back of the chaise lounge. She had a foot up on the cushion and another pressed hard to the tile floor; both were clad in army boots. Otherwise she was mostly naked, except for red velvet shorts and a camisole that looked like it was made of spiderwebs. Even the firelight touched her tawny skin carefully, like maybe it would be burned by the contact. I really wanted to have sex with her, too. She said, "Esmael, you're such a Victorian waif." To me, she said, "It's your frontal lobe, not quite fully developed. So you mostly know who you are, but you take big risks for not much reward. And people raised as girls in this shitbag of a country are raised to be adaptable. So you come out ambitious—or useless."

I was pretty sure Seti was from the Middle East somewhere, but a long, long time ago. Her nose was what I imagine the Sphinx's nose should look like, and there was something about her eyebrows. Plus the name she was using. I looked it up and it was some pharaoh's name. She was younger than Esmael, both literally by about a century and by her looks, too—seeming maybe nineteen or twenty. I asked her where she was from and she said her people were gone, so it didn't matter. "I don't waste that story. I'll tell you if you live to be a hundred."

♦

They gave me a choice. Live forever as a child of the night (yeah, Esmael used those words exactly), or forget them and live out my days, however many they might be, under the sun.

The next morning I lay down next to my mom and told her everything, just to talk it all out. Mom always said talking something out could point you in the right direction. By the time I'd explained it all, I was thinking that since I'd made such a fuss about not having a choice about who I wanted to sleep with—born that way, etc., etc.—I'd better take this actual choice, about who and what I wanted to be, pretty damn seriously.

◆

"If you could live forever, would you want to?" I asked Sid as we squeezed through the hallway to our free block. When it was this cold out, we both spent the hour in the auditorium with Ms. Monroe and I usually could get my biology reading done for the week. Then I didn't have to lug that cinder block of a textbook home.

Sid cocked her head and tugged at the rolled waistband of her pleated skirt. I wore the pants option all winter, but Sid said that edging up her skirt so every teacher considered taking a ruler to test the uniform code against her knee was the only thing that made her actually feel Catholic. "Like some Highlander, or a vampire, or in some kind of relativity loop or something?" Sid knew this game.

"A vampire." I didn't bother being casual about it, and I stared at her like I wanted to sink my teeth into her white neck.

Her lips curled in a smile because she liked when I got weirdly intense, said it was my artist look, and she nudged open the auditorium door with her hip. "I think so. Like, a vampire doesn't have to live forever, so you could just live as long as you wanted to. Do you have to kill people?"

(I'd asked Esmael the same question. He'd dragged his knuckles down my bare leg and said, "No, but you *can*.")

I shook my head at Sid.

"Only drawback is the sun?"

We picked a curved row of dingy old theater seats and plopped down far away from most of the juniors sharing our free block. "And holy water and some kinds of magic."

"Magic, huh, so we're not some kind of virus vampires, but the demon kind."

Seti and Esmael didn't seem particularly demonic to me, but I supposed technically it was accurate. "Yeah."

"I think I probably would, but maybe I'd want to wait a few years until I'm legal. And maybe try to lose a few pounds."

7

My eyes widened. I hadn't even thought about that. If the transformation maintained my body exactly the way it was, I'd have this belly and fat around my bra for all time.

I slid down in the theater seat to put my skull against the back and stare up at the ceiling.

"Are you going to live forever with me?" Sid whispered in my ear.

That wasn't part of the choice; the vampires had been clear. Just me, and if I tried to turn anybody for the first fifty years, they'd kill us both. I kissed her quickly. "Of course," I said. "We'll rule the night together and rampage across the world."

♦

Esmael took me for a long walk that night in the Power and Light District, where the bars shared neon and bass between them like a love language. Cold couples and parties of bros dashed from club to hotel to parking lot with breath fogging heavy around their heads, clapping hands over their mouths, wearing each other's coats and laughing and cussing at the icy breeze. I had on a long jacket and a scarf, but Esmael had fed me some of his blood for the first time and I barely felt the cold. That magic heated me from the inside. Seven nights in a row, that was the basis of the ritual. He drinks from me; I drink from him. If we broke it after six, I'd be ill for a few days, then fine. But human.

We walked north from the Sprint Center, through dark downtown buildings until the bars distanced themselves from each other and the locals heading home or urging their little dogs to pee on two square feet of frosty grass outnumbered partiers. I tucked my hand in Esmael's elbow, which he found charming, and didn't mind my boots tapping the sidewalk while his made no sound at all. He was a sexy shadow and could protect me from anything.

I wondered what it would be like to walk this street alone and still be unafraid. No keys pressed through my fingers like brass knuckles, no heightened pulse, and if somebody called me a dyke, I could flip them off no worries—or better, rip out their goddamn throat.

"You're excited," Esmael said softly.

"There's power in it."

"Yes. And danger. You must, if you join us, learn to think not only about surviving tomorrow, but the next decade and century. Make plans, a framework for eternity, and then you can afford to live in the moment. You can seem to be human, but only if you think like a monster."

"What does that mean?"

"There are cameras everywhere and phones listening to us. We survive by never being sought. If someone wants to find you— wants to find a vampire—they will. There is no hiding in this world, no longer, and so you must be a person."

"That's why you have a gallery."

"So that I can pay taxes. I'm in the system."

"Sounds boring."

He slid me his real smile, the one too beautiful for words. "Nothing is boring if you understand it."

"What a line," I managed; I was pretty breathless from that smile.

"Imagine what you can do with a decade to learn. Imagine your art a hundred years from now, when you've lived in Thailand and Germany and New Orleans. Imagine who you can know. What you can experience."

We neared the Rivermarket, where the restaurants were fancier or at least had names with words like *gastropub* in them, and I thought of drawing it all: the angle of light from the shop windows ahead and the sheen of starlight—one was warmer than the other.

Could I draw something like warmth? "It's worth the sun?" I asked softly.

"You learn to make your own sun."

I thought about Thailand and New Orleans, about dancing and twisting my tongue around new languages and new concepts. I thought about all the sex I could have. All the music I could hear. It pinched in my chest.

Suddenly I was crying.

The tears froze a little on my lashes and the smear was cold and dry when I rubbed them away.

Esmael did nothing but hold my hand.

"Take me to my mom," I said.

His sigh was extremely melancholy, but he whisked me off as requested.

◆

I told Mom the ridiculous argument that paying taxes kept monsters alive. That was her favorite sort of thing: finding humor in bleakness. Instead of making jokes for her, though, I complained about the unfairness of life. Wouldn't Mom love all the music of the world and learning every language? It was bullshit that she couldn't come be a vampire with me.

Or instead of me.

◆

The next night of the ritual, after I touched a finger to the blood at Esmael's wrist and dripped it onto my tongue like a designer drug, Seti took me out.

She said, "Esmael is smart, but I know how to live."

We went to a club that was literally underground. It popped up in the caves under the river bluffs sometimes, Seti explained, and I was definitely too young, but she got me in.

I danced and panted, kissed and screamed and let that music

crash through me. She gave me a shot of expensive tequila that tasted like almond candy and let me press up against her like a promise. When Seti dug her nails into my palm I went with her, and I watched her drink blood from a woman's inner elbow while the woman was grinding back against Seti. Then Seti kissed me, lips tangy with blood, and it was a little horrifying, to be honest.

"When you're one of us, that will be the only glorious taste in the world," she whispered later, sprawled on Esmael's bed. "I know it disgusted you. Do you want to be the thing that craves it? You can't survive forever if you hate yourself."

From the chair by the fire, Esmael huffed slight disagreement. Naturally.

I sprawled on the bed, too, my head dangling off and my legs stretched across hers, but I could see him upside down. My pulse throbbed pleasantly in my skull, and in a few other places.

"Why me?" I asked.

"Your art," Esmael said distractedly, staring dramatically into the fire. The same answer he'd given when I asked why he thought teenage girls make the best vampires.

"Ugh," I said.

Seti laughed.

Esmael glanced at me. "I think art should be developed. You're fine now, but as I've said, imagine what you can make in a hundred years."

Suddenly Seti was on her knees, crouched over me. She reached, grabbed my hair, and dragged up my head. Her vivid brown eyes were alight with passion. "Imagine what you can *change* in a hundred years!"

I sat as best I could, still in her grip. Her intensity transferred through her hands into me, and I felt like I was trembling at the edge of something important.

She said, "What are you angry about? We can make it better. We can shape history, because we can do it a little at a time, child. A heart here, a mind there, then another and another—around the world. Having a goal—that's how you survive the years."

"Seti likes to seduce community leaders and write angry blog posts," Esmael said.

He was there behind me, faster than humanly possible.

"It works, you tax-paying stooge," Seti snarled.

His hand gasped her throat and she released me. I scrambled away, but Esmael was smiling. "Socialist whore," he hissed.

I grabbed a quilt from the foot of the bed and went up to the roof as their wrestling deteriorated into sex. It was frigid outside but oh so clear, and the pink in the east, past the rest of the city, wasn't the color of blood at all.

◆

I made a list for my mom of everything in the world that I'd change. It only had one line.

◆

The fifth night of the ritual, Esmael came to the house, a bungalow from the 1920s two streets off from the millionaire tax bracket that surrounded my high school. I was in my bedroom smearing pastels to the light of a few candles that smelled variously of spruce, wassail, and orange juice. He wrinkled his nose in distaste.

"Did Grandma let you in?" I asked, handing him the heavy paper. Most people took my work by a corner, careful not to smear charcoal on their fingers, but Esmael took it like the gift it was.

"No, she is unaware I am here," he said thoughtfully, studying the strokes of black and dark orange. It was a rough pomegranate, cut open in one ragged slash. It bled its thin juice, and five tiny pips lined the bottom of the page, little smears of red pressed there by my pinkie. If the light was better, maybe you could see the ghost of my fingerprints in it. I hoped so.

Esmael's lips parted and he breathed in, smiling tenderly at me. "Very well, my Persephone, come for your next seed."

I held out my hand and he lifted it, licked my palm, and drew a breath that tickled the fine hairs on my arm. He pulled me nearer and kissed my wrist, licking and sucking softly until my knees were weak and I dug my fingers into his hip bone. My art fluttered in his other hand as he settled it upon the bed and bit into me.

After, he held me in his lap as his blood swept through my system.

"You don't have to say goodbye yet," he murmured. "To any of them. Not until you want to. Or not until they do."

That was nice, I thought, knowing I would say goodbye fast anyway. A lingering death sucked. A death you knew was coming— or a goodbye you knew was coming—sweetened everything to the point of pain. Waiting to say goodbye would be just like that. I ground my teeth together to stop thinking about it.

"Do you do this often?" I asked, eyes closed. We were both in my desk chair, and the candle nearest us on the desk smelled vividly like a fresh, unadorned Christmas tree.

"Yes." His arms encircled me gently, supportive and cold. "Most don't live past the first year, but those who do are nearly always young women. You need to live, I think, because of what's been denied you. You're already hungry, every young girl I've ever met has been hungry—that makes the transition easier. You know how to live with hunger. And anger—Seti is right about that. Not just any anger, not old masculine anger, sharpened with toxicity, but true anger, the kind that fills you up like a light."

I said, "I don't feel angry."

"You are."

🌢

I opened El Café the next morning and Sid came in to lean on the counter and flirt over Americanos and last-minute calculus.

When my shift ended, she drove me to school. That time of morning the lot was full, so we parked on a side street and crunched through slush to the main building. "What's wrong?" she asked.

I shrugged. There were so many possible answers.

Sid had a knit cap pulled down over her ears so you couldn't see any of her short hair. Her coat was long and her boots tall, but her bare knees were pink and chapped by the two-minute walk.

"Are you angry?" I asked her when we hit the wide sandstone staircase, stopping her with a gloved hand on her shoulder.

"With you? Should I be?" Her brow lowered.

"No, no, just—just in general. Angry at the state of the world. At, like, systemic oppression and the patriarchy and . . . what a shitbag this country is."

"Sure."

"Sure?" I pursed my lips, pretty *sure* that if your answer was so *whatever*, the real answer was *no*. I charged up the steps and slammed into the door, dragging its weight out and open.

Sid caught up to me. "Is this about your mom?"

I actually snarled, like a fucking vampire. Teeth bared.

"Shit," she snapped, and shoved past me.

As she strode away, the swing of her short uniform skirt very clearly stated, *Well I'm angry now, bitch.*

I thought about Persephone and her six pomegranate seeds. She went with the god of death half the year and for the other half returned home to her mom. The best of both worlds. Maybe that *was* what I was angry about.

🌢

That night, the sixth night, I asked Seti, "What if I *want* to kill someone?"

14

"Do it with a tool a human could use, so as not to draw attention. Have a drink, but use a knife to the throat."

I shuddered, wondering if someday I'd be so old a monster I could say such a thing so easily.

"It's difficult to drink enough blood to kill a full-grown man," she continued, pulling me down the stairs into a speakeasy. "Unless you do it slowly. We rarely get into the big arteries because they're more difficult to control. Too much force and you end up gagging, and blood spray on clothing is suspicious." She touched her finger to my bottom lip. In a sultry voice, she added, "It's best for us when we have to suck a little bit."

I snorted. "Okay, so you don't get caught up in the pleasure of it and accidentally drain somebody dry. What about garlic and crosses and shit?"

"Garlic gets into the skin and blood and can be overwhelming, but it's not dangerous. Crosses, salt, holy water, those types of things can be imbued with magic that disrupts ours, hurting us, but rarely these days. Almost nobody practices that sort of magic anymore. Just general protection spells and the evil eye and blessings."

"Are there, like, slayers?"

"Sure, but you're more likely to be struck by lightning."

"Would that kill us?"

"I bet so."

Seti charmed the bouncer and stole a table, and we perched on high stools drinking smoky cocktails out of little crystal coupe glasses.

"And the sun?" I asked.

"Deadly."

"Why?"

"It breaks the magic, or kills the demon in our blood, I suppose. You won't burst into flame, but all your blemishes and wounds since you died return with a vengeance, and you age. The sun breaks the spell, and you're as dead as you should've been."

15

"Direct sunlight? Or any?"

"Direct, or we'd be toast under a full moon, too."

"Do you ever watch the dawn?"

"At the movie theater."

"I should paint it while I can."

Seti grinned slowly. "So you've decided?"

In that moment, I wanted to run.

♦

When we returned to the gallery apartment, a little boy was there with Esmael. Eleven or twelve, white with rusty-red hair, *cherubic* is what his cheeks are called, and dressed like an adult in tight jeans, polished loafers, a blue button-down with the sleeves rolled to his elbows, and a vivid teal tie with tiny yellow flowers.

"This is Henry," Esmael said, two spots of actual pink on his cheeks, so he was either elated, furious, or *very* full of blood.

The boy bowed at me like in a costume movie and lifted his huge, light brown eyes. Then he smiled, and the fangs that seemed tiny in Esmael's mouth completely overwhelmed the delicate lips of that little boy. "Greetings, miss."

"A little kid vampire!" I couldn't help being rude.

Seti snorted. Esmael touched my cheek with one hand and put his knuckles to Henry's lightly curling hair. "It's a sign, darling: Henry is my oldest living progeny. He came to see me, just in time to speak with you."

"So much for teenage girls being your biggest successes," I said, laughing a little. I was stunned, as well as nervous. Here was such a little kid, who could rip my throat out in a snap.

"People *raised* as girls is exactly what I said," Seti corrected me, grinning. "Isn't that right, Hen?"

The little boy sighed like an old man and went to the sideboard to pour a glass of whiskey.

Esmael said, "I was living as a priest in France in the fifteenth century—within the Church was the safest place for monsters in those days—and served the family of a minor lord. Henry, my lord's fifth child, came in to confess that he was angry at God and terrified to grow breasts and hips and belly like his sisters. He knew he was supposed to be a man, that's what he dreamed, over and over again, even though it was a sin. I said, 'I cannot make your body into that of a man, but I can make you as strong as one and keep you from ever growing into a woman.'"

"I thought it was a miracle, and Father Samuel an angel," Henry said, heavy with irony.

I sat down on the chaise lounge. Henry brought me his glass of whiskey and allowed me a sip. I stared, and then asked a million questions about living almost five hundred years as a kid. He answered some of them.

Several hours later, I let Esmael give me the sixth seed.

◆

I stared at Sid in Biology, feeling extremely old. I'd apologized to her, and she'd shrugged it off. "Make it up to me," she'd said, and I'd promised. But I stared at her, wondering what she'd say and if she'd miss me for long. Would it be like I'd died? What would any of them say?

My mom told me that how people talk about you when you're dead is your only real legacy. I hadn't wanted to hear it then. I wanted more than anything to hear it now.

◆

The seventh night—the last night—I went to the cemetery. It was easy, as always, to sneak in after dark.

Esmael knew somehow, the bastard, and was waiting for me. He leaned against a small granite obelisk several graves away from Mom's. Wind fluttered the tails of his coat and the curls of hair at his temple.

I stopped, hugging myself.

"What's holding you back?" he murmured. The night sky seemed to take his voice and carry it gently toward me.

"She deserved to live forever," I whispered, trying not to cry.

For a long while, Esmael said nothing. Then he only gave me one word: "Deserved?"

"She wasn't angry, she wasn't a bitch, she always tried to help people. I'm nothing like that, so why me, why not her? Anger shouldn't be the key to immortality, you dick. Shouldn't it be compassion or kindness or something good?"

"Seti would say use your anger to make that true. Change the world, she says."

"What do you say, Esmael?"

He stepped closer to me, silent and gray against the night sky. "I say anger is just as valuable as compassion, if it makes art like yours."

I groaned, curling my hands into fists. I shoved them against my eyes until I saw red-sparking stars.

"Tonight," he said, too close now, his words hardly more than a breath. "Tonight is the last night. If you come to me, all I have will be yours. If you do not, you'll never see me again. Though I cannot promise I won't look for your art, out in the world."

I opened my eyes, but he was gone.

◆

Back in September, swaddled in a blanket we'd stolen from the hospital, Mom had said, "You keep me alive, baby." She'd shivered, eyelids paper-thin as she closed them and leaned into the wingback chair. "The things you say about me. How you remember me."

"That's too much pressure!" I'd yelled—actually yelled at her. "Too much responsibility. I'm just seventeen, Mom."

"You carry the world on your shoulders," she murmured, falling asleep. "You all do."

◆

All right, I was angry.

No, I was furious, curled against Mom's headstone, legs up and arms hugging them against my chest. I knocked my forehead against my knees, face scrunched up.

It hurt how much I missed her. Actual, physical pain. What if becoming a vampire preserved that, too? This ache was just *there*, all the time. A part of me, in my bones.

"It'll get rid of the zits on your forehead, but not the fat on your belly," Seti had said when I asked. She was laughing at me. "The magic preserves us as we are, at our most ideal. Sorry you think that chubby roll isn't ideal, but you'll learn better. Trust the blood, the magic. Whatever it leaves you, belongs."

Or what if I transformed and this pain was gone? Like it *didn't* belong? What if the blood magic stripped it away? That would be worse, to lose it.

◆

I opened the gallery apartment door slowly and shoved it with the toe of my snow boot. Esmael waited at the hearth, leaning there like some couture model. Seti lay on her stomach on the bed, legs up, feet kicking slowly back and forth. She smiled at me triumphantly.

I said, "Is grief like anger? Will I take it with me?"

Esmael said, "Come here, and I'll show you, instead, how it's all just love."

That was *definitely* a line, but I believed it, too.

CREATION MYTHS
Or Where Do Baby Vampires Come From?

Zoraida Córdova &
Natalie C. Parker

Like so many supernatural creatures of the night, there are rules around the creation of a vampire. Those rules are rarely the same from story to story. In some traditions, all it takes is a bite from a vampire and, presto chango, you become a blood-sucking fiend! In some, you have to exchange blood with a vampire, in others a curse will do it, and in still others if a wolf leapt across your grave you would rise up as a vampire. The stories we tend to be most familiar with involve some kind of transformation: from human to vampire, good to evil, living to undead. Sometimes the choice isn't up to the one going through the change. What we love about Tessa's story is how the choice is completely up to our heroine and how she doesn't have to make it in an instant, but over a span of seven nights.

If you had the choice, would you want to live forever?

THE BOYS FROM BLOOD RIVER

Rebecca Roanhorse

"It's just a song, Lukas," Neveah says, her voice heavy with disdain. "Nobody believes the Blood River Boys will actually appear if you sing it." She leans a plump hip against the old-fashioned jukebox that squats in the corner of Landry's Diner and runs a bright blue fingernail down the playlist, looking for just the right song to get us through after-hours cleanup.

I lean on the mop in my hands and watch her. She's so confident. So easy in her body. Where I'm . . . not. I'm too skinny, too gangly, too tall. Caught somewhere between a baby bird and Slender Man, if Slender Man were a pock-faced sixteen-year-old boy whose hair wouldn't lie flat no matter how much gel he slathered on it. If Slender Man weren't even the least bit cool.

"Your brother believes," I offer.

She shakes her head. "Honestly, Brandon is the last person in the world who knows anything about the history of Blood River, much less about the Boys."

Her eyes dart to me and then quickly away. I know she's avoiding looking directly at me, as if not making eye contact will mean she doesn't have to acknowledge the purpling bruise circling my left eye. As if not seeing my black eye means I don't actually have one.

But not acknowledging something doesn't make it go away. Most of the time it makes it worse.

"You don't believe in the Boys, do you?" Neveah asks me.

Neveah works here at the diner with me, and she's the closest thing I have to a friend, but even she's not my friend. Not really. She's older than me, almost graduated from the community college, whereas I have another full year of high school. If I were going to classes, that is. I'm pretty close to dropping out. Neveah's smart, way smarter than me. But she's wrong about the Boys.

"Brandon sure knew all the details," I challenge nervously. I don't want to make her mad at me. She's pretty much the only person in this town who even talks to me. But she's wrong. I know it. "Their escape, their hideout up by the old mine, the things they did when the townspeople came for them."

"What about the song?" she asks, eyes focused back on the jukebox. "Do you believe that part?"

"No." That was the least plausible part. But even as I say no, I wish I were saying yes. "But—"

"Shhh . . . Here's my jam." She punches the little white button, and after a few seconds a song starts. But it's not the one I expected.

The slow moan of a fiddle wails from the jukebox, joined by the heavy *thump* of a washboard drum and then a banjo, picked strings as soft as a weeping woman. And a man sings: "*As I walked*

22

by the river, the moon my companion, I spied a young fellow, an amiable lad . . ."

Neveah frowns. "This isn't the song I picked." She slams a hand against the side of the jukebox, but the song plays on.

"He'd the face of an angel but the heart of a demon, and that night he did take the lone life that I had."

"It's the Blood River Boys' song," I say, voice high with excitement. "The one we were just talking about!" I'd never heard it before, but it had to be it. Since when did Landry put that on the jukebox?

A thrill rolls down my spine as the fiddle joins the melody with a minor note, and I'm not sure if it's the music or something else that's making the room feel colder and the night darker out there beyond the thin windowpanes.

"I didn't pick this!" Neveah complains. She slams her hand against the player again. "It just started on its own." She shoots me a suspicious glare. "If this is some kind of sick joke, Lukas . . ."

"He said, 'Wrath is my birthright and woe my first swaddling, blood for my feast as I take what is owed . . . The harvest is coming, and we reap what's been sowed.'"

"I didn't do it!" I protest, laughing. "You did it. If anyone's playing around, it's you."

"Well, *you* make it stop!" Her voice rises, panicky, and I realize she's serious. I drop the mop, letting it clatter to the floor, and take three quick steps so I'm close enough to reach around the back of the jukebox and hit the emergency OFF button.

For a minute I think it's not going to shut off, like we're in some horror movie and the thing has a life of its own, but sure enough, the machine cuts off, just like it's supposed to.

Silences rushes in. The lights behind the counter dip with the electrical surge, the neon signs in the windows blink off and then power back on with a high-pitched whine. And something out in the night howls.

My skin prickles as a solid rush of fear rolls up my back. Neveah and I exchange a look.

"We are never letting Brandon tell us scary stories again," she says, nervously rubbing her hands up her arms.

"Sure thing," I say, absently, eyes drawn out into the night, searching. But for what, and why exactly, I'm not sure. It's just a feeling . . .

Neveah shudders like it's cold. "I just told you that if you sing the song, those freaks are supposed to appear, and then you play it? Don't you think that's a little much?"

"I told you I didn't do it."

"Well, somebody did!"

A shadow passes by the window. Something's out there, moving through the parking lot. Probably a raccoon or a skunk. But bigger.

"Probably Brandon," Neveah mutters.

"In the parking lot?"

"What? No. It was probably Brandon who set up the song." She peers out the big front windows. "What do you mean 'in the parking lot'?"

"Nothing. Just thought I saw animals in the trash." Maybe it was Brandon. Scaring the shit out of us would be his idea of fun. But still. How would he have set it up beforehand? And Landry would never go for that sort of thing. She's pretty uptight about the jukebox.

"I want to go home," Neveah says, thrusting her hands in her hoodie pockets. "This is all too much."

I sigh. I want to go home, too. The night feels sour now, as if the joke's on us and we're not in on it.

She pulls her phone out of her pocket, swipes it on, and types furiously. "Where is Brandon? I knew he should have waited for my shift to end."

"I can give you a ride." Even as I say it, I'm wincing. Maybe it's too much, too presumptuous. Like I said, we're not really friends.

She glances up, and I can see the calculations run across her face: surprise, suspicion, hesitation, and then all that finally loses to her desire to get out of here as soon as possible.

"Okay, sure. Why not."

I grin, strangely relieved. Maybe being rejected for offering her a ride home would have hurt more than I want to admit. It's not that I like Neveah that way. I don't like any girls that way. She knows that. But I'm the town loser. Nobody wants to spend too much time with a loser. It might rub off.

She bends and picks up the mop where I dropped it, hands it back to me. I gesture toward the rag and spray bottle on the counter. "It'll be faster if you help."

She exhales disapprovingly but slouches over to the counter, grabs the cleaning supplies, and gets to work. I start mopping, and we clean in silence, neither of us much wanting to try the jukebox again. But I can't get that song out of my head, and before I know it, we're both humming it.

We realize it at the same time and stop. Neither of us look up, an unspoken agreement to pretend like that didn't just happen, but the horror still lingers on my skin, in the faster-than-normal beat of my heart.

Around midnight, we call it good enough. Neveah helps me put away the supplies, and I let her out the door first, locking up behind her. I pause in the parking lot, eyes scanning for the shadow of movement I saw earlier, but there's nothing there. I tell myself it was probably just a raccoon, like I thought.

◆

My old car putters through the empty streets of Blood River. I wouldn't even own a car if I had a choice, but I need a car to get my mom to her weekly doctor appointments at the hospital in the next town over. That's also why I got the job at Landry's. My paycheck, what little there is of it, goes into paying off this piece of junk, and anything left over goes to Mom's medical bills.

Blood River isn't very big. About four square miles of gridded streets. We're two dozen miles from the main highway. It's one of those towns that was important back when the railroad ran through here and the grain silos were full, but now, with the big interstates and airplanes and nobody growing grain much anymore, people don't come here. Blood River is what some folks would call a dying town. I mean, there's the diner, and the high school football games are pretty popular on Friday nights, and there are a few places trying to draw in tourists for white water rafting or fly-fishing in the nearby river, but the only thing we're really famous for, what gave the place its name, is a massacre.

Not so popular with tourists.

We pass the old graveyard and trail through the empty streets, past overgrown yards and single-story bungalows with paint peeling from the planked sides. I take the corner Neveah tells me to and we roll up to a trailer on blocks and a smattering of dead cars parked haphazard in the gravel out front.

"This is me," she says.

I pull over. We haven't said much the whole ride.

She opens the passenger-side door. The little light in the ceiling goes on, and I can see her face. Her skin is a peachy white, pretty much the opposite of my brown skin, and her hair is a bottle yellow, showing darker at the roots. Her nails are long and bright blue, little rhinestones embedded on the tips. She pauses, one blue-jeaned leg sticking out, the rest of her body still in the car. She looks over at me, bottom lip caught between her teeth, hazel eyes too big.

"What is it?" I ask, wary.

"Thanks for the ride," she says. "I know people give you a lot of shit in town for being—"

"Native?"

"Gay."

We both flush hot and embarrassed. The silence stretches like another lonely block of this trash heap town.

"I'm sorry about your eye," she says in a rush.

My heart speeds up a little, but I frown like I'm not following. "How do you mean?"

"How Jason Winters beat the crap out of you, how he and the Toad Twins always beat the crap out of you. How that's the reason you never go to school. Well, that and your mom being sick."

I stare at her blankly, willing her to shut the hell up.

"I figure that's why you like the Blood River Boys story so much. It's like a fantasy, right? The idea of those Boys coming to rescue you from your shitty life in this shitty town."

My face heats up, the flush creeping down my neck. "My being interested in the Blood River Boys has nothing to do with any of that," I lie flatly. "I just like a good story."

"You sure?"

"Positive."

"Because if it were me . . ."

And I know she is not going to take the hint. "Good night, Neveah," I say, reaching over and pushing her door open a little wider.

She frowns.

"Good night!" I repeat.

She leans back into the car and reaches for my arm. I shrink back. It's an automatic response, not personal, but it leaves her hand hovering in the air. The overhead light catches in the rhinestones on her nails. She pulls her arm back and says, "I am trying to be nice to you. Trying to be sympathetic."

"Keep it," I say harshly, and even as the words leave my mouth, I regret them. But I don't know what her kind of sympathetic means. It smells like white girl pity to me, and I don't want Neveah's pity. I throw a meaningful glance at her trailer, the beaters in her driveway. *You're not better than me*, I say, without saying a thing. *Just look around.*

Her faces twists up, and my stomach slips to my feet like a deadweight. I'm being a jerk and I know it, but I won't take it back.

She nods once and slides out of the car. Closes the door, and the overhead light goes off, casting me into the darkness.

Shame blankets me and I groan, rubbing a hand over my face. Why did I do that? No wonder I don't have any friends. No wonder Jason Winters likes to kick in my face. I'm kind of an asshole.

I wait for her to walk to her door, and once she's inside, I pull out, gravel rolling under my wheels. I'm halfway down the road, trying desperately to not think about what Neveah said, when I realize I'm humming that song again. The Blood River Boys ballad.

Later, after it is all over, I'll wonder if things would have turned out different if I'd said something. Apologized for being a dick, admitted what I wanted and why the Boys fascinated me, how I felt about my mom and everything. Maybe Neveah could have said something, conjured some words or a warm touch that would have changed things. But I didn't, and she didn't, and things went the way they did in our dying town named after a massacre.

◆

The next morning I catch myself singing the Blood River Boys song in the shower. And later as I'm boiling eggs for breakfast.

And again when I'm prepping Mom's medications for the day, laying them out in their little individual bowls so she doesn't have to guess the dosage.

And I know I've got to face a hard fact. Neveah may not believe in the Blood River Boys, but I do. I believe in them with my whole heart. A heart that feels like it's slowly crumbling to dust in my chest, a heart so damaged that I sometimes feel like it's a wonder it pumps at all.

Back last year I figure my heart was normal enough for someone my age. But then my cousin Wallace died of a drug overdose, and my friend Rocky moved away, back to his dad's place in the city, and then, just as the school year started, Mom got sick. At first no one believed Mom's illness was serious, least of all me, but by October she was in and out of the hospital and the doctors were giving her less and less time and then Mom sat me down one night after she had been especially bad, wheezing and coughing through dinner, and told me the truth. She wasn't getting better. In fact, she was getting worse. "This will be our last Christmas together," she said, point-blank, just like that. "You'll be eighteen soon enough. Better get used to being on your own."

But the thing is, I don't want to be on my own. Some kids would, I know. They'd see it as independence. Freedom. And it's not like I don't want that one day, maybe? Just not this year. I mean, I already lost Wallace and Rocky and now it's going to be Mom. And I think that if I'm not careful, I'm going to lose myself next.

♦

"Hey, Landry," I ask, as I lay bacon on the flat grill. "When'd you put that Blood River Boys song on the juke?"

Landry's doing the books in her office, but she's got the door open so she can keep an eye on things, namely me. The cook called in sick, so I'm stuck covering the dinner shift in the kitchen. The diner is so small that I do a bit of everything. Janitor, cook, server. I don't mind. It means more money in my pocket come payday and more meds for my mom, and most people's tastes are simple around here. As long as I can break eggs and dress a burger, I'm good.

"What song?" Landry says, decades of cigarette smoke turning her voice to a grumble. "I ain't changed a song on that box since before Ronald Reagan was president."

"No?" I shrug and grab the next waiting ticket. "Maybe I just never saw it. So that means something's wrong with the juke. Neveah was trying to play her song last night and the wires got crossed. Played the wrong song."

Landry gave a noncommittal grunt. I busy myself with the order and, once it's done, slide the plate through the window for the server to pick up. I ring the bell, and Fiona appears, all smiles. She takes the plate and disappears.

I turn to retrieve the next order and Landry's right there, inches from my face. I yelp in surprise, jumping back a half mile. "Jesus, Landry, don't sneak up on me like that!"

She peers in close. I can see the wrinkles on her face, the rheum that covers her left eye. "That song's only appeared once on that jukebox, and that was before the Finley boy went missing. They say he called it up, and so it came." She narrows her eyes. "You got a hankering to listen to that song?" she asks, voice hard. "Bad things happen to boys who sing that song."

"No," I say automatically. "I was just telling you what happened. I-I don't want to . . ." I brush my hands together, nervous. "I didn't sing that song."

She peers at me some more. "Okay." And then she shuffles back to her office.

"Why do you have it on the juke if you don't want anyone singing it," I mutter, and if she hears me, she ignores me.

◆

I'm closing again, and this time Brandon's on time to pick up Neveah.

"She's in the bathroom," I say, as I unlock the door to let him in to wait.

He answers with a grunt that could mean anything. He was okay the other night when he was talking about the Boys, but now he barely acknowledges me. Like I said, nobody wants to spend too much time with a loser. But what Landry said is on my mind, so I ask.

"You ever hear of somebody named Finley?" I ask, trying to keep my voice neutral.

He's got a wad of tobacco in his mouth, and he eyes me, jaw working like a cow chewing cud. "Dru Finley?"

I shrug. "Maybe."

"Everybody knows about Dru Finley. He used to live here, back in the eighties. Big baseball star. Everyone thought he was going to make it to the major leagues. Then supposedly he snaps one night and kills his mother, father, two sisters, and a little brother, but they never find him or a body. Just his family, exsanguinated. Do you know what that means?"

I shake my head.

"Bloodless," he whispers. "Someone drained all their blood."

"How'd that happen?" I say, my voice breathy.

"Who knows? But the bigger question is what happened to Dru? Maybe he ran when the killers came and never looked back. Maybe he got kidnapped. Nobody knows." He widens his eyes theatrically. "Why do you want to know?"

"No reason. Someone mentioned him today."

31

"Yeah, well, whatever happened, at least he got out of this shit town, right?" He chuckles at his own tasteless joke.

Neveah hustles out from the bathroom. "Ready?" she asks Brandon without even looking my way. I guess she hasn't forgiven me for being rude the night before. Brandon kind of gives me a nod and then he's following his sister out the door.

Once their car is gone, I lock the door again.

The jukebox glows in the corner.

I walk over and stare at the song selections. My heart is thumping, loud in my ears like a warning bell, but I've been thinking about it all day. I have to know.

My guess is that it doesn't matter what button I push, that they'll all do the same thing. So I close my eyes and reach out a hand. Press a random button and wait.

Fiddle, drums, and banjo. And then that voice. "*As I walked by the river, the moon my companion, I spied a young fellow, an amiable lad . . .*"

And this time, I listen. The whole way through. And when it's done, I play it again, and this time I mouth the words, remember the phrases, the rhyme and rhythm of it. And on the third time, I sing.

I let the words come bubbling from my throat, trickling across my tongue and past my lips, and once I've started, they feel like a flood, like the Blood River itself, a force unstoppable and powerful and ancient. And I put everything into it. All the stuff I've been feeling about being alone, the injustice of Jason and his friends bullying me, my mom dying, every scared part of me. My crumbling, dusty heart. And I let it all go.

When it's over I feel wrung out. I hobble over and collapse in the nearest booth, panting. Wishing for a cold glass of water, but I'm too tired to walk over and get one.

And I wait.

And . . . nothing.

I wait thirty minutes, and then thirty minutes more, and there's no movement in the parking lot, no dimming lights, no chill. Just me and some scary stories and my wretchedness. I press my cheek against the cool Formica and let the tears leak from my eyes. After a while, I sit up and use my cleaning rag to wipe the tears away.

I get up, my bones feeling a thousand years old. Make it to the car. Drive the empty streets home. Check in on my mom.

I collapse into bed, no different than I was when I started this awful day.

♦

He comes the next day. I'm back at Landry's Diner. It's late, a half hour until closing, when I notice him. He's in the booth farthest from the door, the four-seater by the jukebox where I'd wept like a little kid the night before. He's wearing a black cowboy hat, which is what I spot first, and a dark denim jacket. He's got boots on, not unusual around these parts, and they're propped up on the opposite seat. They're black, too, and the leather catches the light and makes them gleam.

The brim of his hat is pulled down to cover his face, so all I catch is a sliver of pale skin and a slice of easy grin as I approach him.

"Kitchen closes in thirty," I say when I'm standing in front of him. I'm on server duty because it's Neveah's night off. I hold up my order pad, pen poised.

"Nothing I want is on the menu," he says, his voice a soft drawl. He tips up his hat, shows his face, and I suck in a startled breath. If you asked me to describe him, I couldn't do it. But the curve of his lips, the narrow slide of his nose, the sharp cut of his cheeks. It was a kind of perfection—that much I know.

"Are you on TV?" I blurt. Because no one who looks like this boy has ever come to Blood River before.

He laughs, and even that's beautiful, like the rush of a cold wind on the first day of autumn or the roll of thunder on a hot summer night.

"Naw," he says. "I'm not on TV."

I look over my shoulder, for what I don't know. A witness, a hidden camera. Jason and the twins playing a trick on me.

"You called to me, Lukas," he drawls, "don't you remember? You called me with my song and that dusty heart of yours." He throws out his arm expansively. "You called all of us."

I look behind me, again, and sure enough, walking down the aisle are three more boys, all a little older than me. They're all wearing cowboy gear, hats and boots and broken-in denim, except for one kid who's got on a backward baseball cap and oversized jeans.

"Allow me to introduce my brothers," he says. "This is Jasper, and next to him is Willis. And that there is Dru. And I," he says, with a tip of his hat, "am Silas."

"Are you the . . . ?" But I can't bring myself to ask. I'm afraid if I say it aloud, they'll laugh at me. Or disappear.

"What's good in this joint?" Jasper asks, rattling a menu. He's got a deep voice and some kind of accent I can't quite place. His skin is the same shade as mine, and he's got a head of dark hair under his hat.

"Menu's about the same everywhere we go," Willis says, laughing. His skin's a shade darker that Jasper's, and tight black curls peak from underneath his hat. His voice is high, nervous, and his black eyes flicker around the room.

"That it is, brother," Silas says with a grin. He slaps a hand on the table. "Let's go somewhere else." He tilts his head. "Won't you come with us, Lukas? Come share a meal."

"Me?" I ask.

The boys laugh—well, Jasper and Willis do. The third boy, a

redhead, says nothing. He seems agitated, knee shaking under the booth table.

"I-I've got to lock up," I stutter.

"Then do that," he says. "We'll wait to eat with you."

This makes Willis laugh and the redhead shake his head, but I don't get the joke.

Then they're all moving toward the entrance, languid and graceful as cats. I watch them go, convinced I'm hallucinating and will never see them again once they're out the door. The tiny bell over the entrance rings as they slide out, one by one. Silas is last and he tips his hat to me as he crosses the threshold.

My heart is hammering in my chest and I'm not sure what to do, but I know I've got to go with them. I know it's risky. I don't know them, and they could have bad intentions, but something tells me . . . no, something inside me *knows* that they don't. That they're exactly who I think they are and they came because I called them and I'm meant to go with them if I ever want to be truly safe again.

"Cook," I yell, rushing around the corner of the counter and pulling off my apron. "My ride's here," I shout, hoping he won't remember I drive myself. "I gotta go."

"What about cleanup?" he asks, sounding outraged.

"Not tonight," I say, grinning. "I'll owe you one."

"You owe me about five," he mutters, but I know he'll do it. Despite his protests, I never ask him for favors.

"Thanks!"

I take a minute to rush to the bathroom, check my face in the mirror, wish desperately for another face, less brown, less skinny, less acne-prone, but then I remember what Silas said, that he came because my heart asked him to. I turn on the faucet, douse my face, and run a wet hand through my hair, trying to make it behave, and then I'm out the door . . .

. . . where I run smack into Jason Winters.

"Whoa," he says with his fake laugh, grabbing me by the shoulders. "What's the rush, Lukas?"

I freeze. I can feel his hands, too warm, the pressure of his fingers. I look around the parking lot, frantic. Where are Silas and the others? Where did they go?

"Did you see . . . ," I start to ask, and then remember who I'm talking to and snap my mouth shut.

Jason looks over his shoulder, and now I see he's not alone. The Toad Twins are getting out of the back seat of his blue Chevy truck, laughing and heading our direction. Something catches in my throat. No, no, no. Not now.

"Look," I say, the memory of Silas waiting for me somewhere out there, making me bold. "You can pound on my face another time. Right now, I've got to go."

Jason points over my shoulder, back at the diner. "Says Landry's is open another twenty minutes. Me and my boys just want to grab a quick bite. Surely you can help us with that. I mean, isn't that your job?"

The twins have joined us, Tyler and Trey, and they laugh, that same automatic guffaw they always laugh for Jason. Like having a job is a joke.

"Cook's still there. He can help you."

His hands tighten on my shoulders. "I want *you* to help me."

The way he says it stops me in my tracks even more than the heavy dig of his fingers into my flesh. His eyes meet mine, clear blue like the summer sky, and he smiles.

"I . . ."

"Oh my God," one of the twins says, Tyler or Trey, "he's gonna try to kiss you."

I'm not. Of course I'm not, but my face still burns like it's on fire. I open my mouth to protest, but I don't get the chance.

The punch to my stomach is so swift I don't realize he's hit me until I'm bent over double, gasping for air. The second one comes a moment after, a fist to the side of my face just below where my eye's still healing that leaves my ears ringing. I hit the gravel with a thud, the tiny gray pebbles digging into my cheek.

More laughter, and I brace myself for the kick that's coming.

"Is there a problem here?"

I'm so wrapped up in my humiliation that it takes me a moment to recognize that voice. I roll my head to the side and look up. Silas is there, black boots and jacket and hat and that easy smile.

Jason sneers. "Mind your own business, cowboy," he says.

"This here is my business. Lukas is my friend."

The three high school boys laugh. "Lukas Loser? Well, I know you're lying, because he doesn't have any friends."

Now the kick comes, right to my gut. It's not as bad as it could have been, as it's been before, but it's enough to make me suck in a breath.

"I thought I asked you to stop," Silas says, low and quiet.

"Or else what?" Jason puffs himself up, broad football player's shoulders almost twice as wide as Silas's slim build.

"Or else I'm going to kill you."

I blink, thinking I must have heard wrong. But there's Silas, cool as the evening air and looking unconcerned, like he's not threatening, just stating facts.

Jason and the Toad Twins gape, first in shock, I think, but then like they're gonna laugh. The other Blood River Boys come melting out of the night. Jasper, quiet and smiling, hands stuffed in his pockets. Willis, his eyes bright, and he chants, "Kill you dead, kill you dead," in a breathy, high giggle. Dru dragging farthest behind, his cap turned around to face forward, hiding most of his face in the shadows.

Jason's not a fool. Well, not that kind of fool, at least. He does the math, figures it's four—five if you count me, but I'm sure he doesn't—against him and the twins. He raises his hands.

"Sure. Fine. We don't want any trouble. Just came to get something to eat."

"Eat somewhere else from now on," Jasper says in his low, rumbly voice.

"This diner's closed . . . to you," Silas echoes. "Permanently."

Jason glances down at me, and I must be smiling because his face goes all dark and furious. "Later, loser," he mutters, "when your rodeo-clown friends aren't around." And then he and the twins are making a hasty exit.

I laugh, I don't even care that it makes his retreating shoulders tense up or that I'm definitely setting myself up for a worse beating when Silas isn't around to save me. It's worth it to see Jason get the smallest taste of the humiliation he doles out to me on the regular.

A hand comes down to help me up and I take it. Silas's palm is cold, dry, and icy enough to burn. His skin has a glass-slick feel, his flesh stiff. He pulls me to my feet like I weigh less than I do.

"You all right?" he says, dusting me off. His hands on my body make me nervous, but he acts like he doesn't notice. He looks concerned, like he really cares what happens to me.

"Thanks," I say. "You saved me." And he did, in more ways than one.

He presses a cold palm to my cheek, and for the first time our eyes meet. His are a swirl of color, impossible eyes, eyes like deep pools, a child's kaleidoscope. My breath catches hard in my throat and my legs feel unsteady. Something passes between us, electric and intense. I sway and he steadies me. "Anything for a brother," he drawls, hand still cupping my face.

"Shoulda killed them," Willis says.

"Not now," Silas murmurs over his shoulder.

"He's right," Jasper rumbles. "Now we'll have to hunt. I *need* to hunt. Now."

I frown. "What does he mean?"

"Nothing." Silas smiles at me and I feel a flutter in my chest, like my heart wants to answer him with a matching grin. "We've got to go." He drops his hand and steps away. "See you again, soon, Lukas. You get home. Take care of that mother of yours. She needs you."

"How do you know about my mother?"

"You told me."

"I didn't . . ."

"See you again soon."

And then they're backing into the night, disappearing into the darkness like they never were. My face throbs where I took the punch and I've got a dull ache in my stomach, but I've never been happier in my life. Pretty sure I could float home. But instead I climb into my car and head home, singing that song the whole way.

🜄

When I pull into the drive, there's someone on the porch. My pulse ticks up, thinking it might be Silas, even though I just left him at the diner, but it's a woman. Middle-aged and looking tired, her cardigan pulled tight around her shoulders against the fall chill. She seems familiar, but I can't quite place why.

"Are you Lukas?" she asks, as soon as I'm within shouting range.

"Yeah. Who are you? And what are you doing at my house at midnight?"

"Delia Day, and I'm sorry about the time," she says. "I'm the patient advocate and social worker at the Bennet City hospital."

That's how I know her. And there's only one reason she would be here at this time of night. "My mom?" I ask, my throat tightening. "Is my mom okay?"

"I'm afraid not, Lukas. You better come inside." Her voice is kind. Too kind. It's the voice professionals use when they're about to give you bad news.

I freeze, not wanting to get any closer.

"Is she at the hospital?" I ask. I'm shaking. When did I start shaking? "Can I go see her?"

Delia rubs at her arms. "Why don't you come inside? We can talk about it there."

And I know. Right then I know exactly what's she going to say. And I don't want to hear it, because hearing it makes it true.

I stumble back to my car. Delia Day is calling my name. I make it down the drive, back onto the street. I don't know where I'm going, what I'm running from, what I'm running to. All I know is I'm running.

◆

The funeral is short. Mom was adopted and didn't have any brothers or sisters. After she grew up, she lost touch with her adopted family, and my dad was never a presence in our lives, so it really was just her and me.

And now it's just me.

Nobody comes to the funeral except Delia from the hospital and the county assessor to hand me an envelope I don't want to open and a few folks from the church I don't even know but who seem all right. Landry sends her condolences, but she's at the diner, working.

Once everyone's gone and it's just me and the fresh grave and the twilight of nightfall, he shows up. He's wearing the same boots, the same denim, the same hat, which he holds in his slender hands. The breeze ruffles his black hair almost playfully. It just turns mine into a windblown mess.

"Where's the rest of them?" I ask before he's even close.

He stops next to me, eyes on my mother's grave. "Thought maybe it would be best if it's just you and me."

I look over. Stare at the slope of his nose, the fullness of his mouth. My breath hitches, and he smiles.

"The Boys can be a little much," he admits. "Sorry if they scared you."

"They saved me," I say in a rush. "You saved me."

"Jason Winters won't bother you anymore." He says it with such conviction that I almost believe him. But Jason's been bullying me since I was in fourth grade. He's not going to stop just because a couple of cowboys told him to.

"He'll just wait until you're gone," I say quietly, feeling like I'm disappointing him by saying it.

He looks at me, eyes crinkling. "You really are something, Lukas." His voice is wistful, maybe amused, but I don't think he means it as an insult.

We stand there in silence until I say, "I'm alone now."

"You don't have to be."

It's what I wanted him to say, but I didn't dare hope. I want to shout at him to take me away, get me out of this town, away from the diner and the bullies and my empty house. But instead I ask, "What do I have to do?"

"Share a meal."

"What does that mean?"

He looks down, beats his hat against his thigh. "What do you think it means, Lukas?"

I close my eyes. "How? How do I . . . ?"

He touches my shoulder briefly. "We'll take care of that. Just be at the diner tonight at closing. You come if you want to join us. If you don't, no harm and we'll be on our way."

"You'll leave?" I ask, startled, my mouth suddenly dry. "Just like that?"

"Only if you want. You called us, remember? And we only stay where we're wanted."

Relief floods through me, traitorous and unasked for. I can't imagine Silas gone now. What I'd do. Where I'd go. Something about him makes me feel safe, feel wanted. Feel not so alone.

The wind moves through the gravestones, tossing the leaves around. He slips his hat back on.

"The diner," he repeats. "Closing."

And then he's gone.

◊

I pull into Landry's parking lot at a quarter to midnight. The lights are low, and the place looks locked up, only there are people moving around inside, so I know somebody's in there. I spot a figure lurking by the door and I think it must be Silas, but as I get closer, I can see it's Dru. He's got a baseball bat and is swinging it idly as he waits. I remember Brandon saying something about the Finley guy being a big baseball player, and things click together.

Dru looks at me, long and hard, pale skin cold in the lamplight and dark red hair slicked back. Last time I saw him he was wearing a baseball cap, but tonight he's bareheaded. I shift uncomfortably under his scrutiny.

"Why?" he asks suddenly, and it's the first time I've heard him speak.

I shrug, pretty sure what he's asking. "Same as everyone, I guess."

"We've all got different reasons. Jasper did it for revenge, me because we didn't make state and I thought I wanted to die." He chuckles under his breath, like he can't believe he was ever so foolish. "Willis lost his mind after they killed his wife, and Silas . . ."

"Why did you have to murder your family, though?" I ask quickly, cutting him off. I'm not sure I want to know why Silas did it. What if it's for terrible reasons? Reasons worse that wanting a family, not wanting to be alone.

He blinks. "You think I killed my family? For this?" he asks, incredulous. He laughs a shallow, wheezy laugh. "*Five blood bags, one for each of you and two for me*, Silas told me."

A shiver runs across my neck. "Silas wouldn't say that."

"What do you know about Silas?" he scoffs. "He's taking it easy on you, don't know why, what makes you so special." He swallows noisily, eyes lost in memory. "He didn't go so easy on me."

I frown. "What do you mean?"

Before he can answer, Silas comes to the door.

"You made it," he said, his smile expansive, like I'm on time to his party. "Come on in." He ushers me through the entrance, leaving Dru to follow. I hear him turn the lock behind me. I look back, alarmed.

"So we aren't disturbed," Silas says, arm sliding around my shoulders as he leads me in. "I think you know everyone," he says, gesturing around the diner. Dru with his bat and Willis and Jasper on stools, leaning against the counter.

"Listen," I tell him, voice steady with the words I practiced in the car on the drive over. "I know what this is about. What you are." Thinking of what Dru said moments ago, I add, "You don't have to be easy on me."

Silas pauses, leans his head to the side like he's listening.

I go on in a rush. "I figured it out. What you said about Jason not bothering me anymore, and before, saying you'd kill him if he laid a finger on me again. And I know the stories, about the massacre. And Dru's family." My eyes cut briefly to his. His face is stony, giving nothing away, and for a minute I think maybe I've misunderstood, that what I'm saying likely sounds certifiable, but I barrel on anyway. "And I want you to know I'm okay with that. I'm okay with . . . sharing a meal."

Silas waits until he's sure I'm done talking, and then he smiles. "I knew you'd come around, Lukas. Nothing wrong with going easy on a man who's had his fair share of troubles. Some people just need to ease into feeding."

Feeding. I shiver despite myself. The way he says it makes it somehow more real. But I tell myself that Jason deserves it. He's been cruel to me my whole life, would probably kill me if he had a chance, so maybe I'm just beating him to the punch. And if that means I get to stay with Silas, with the Boys . . .

Willis and Jasper stand up to reveal a body laid out on the counter.

I expect to see broad football shoulders. Annoying chestnut hair. Terrified blue eyes.

But instead I see dark roots, the glint of rhinestones, hazel eyes too wide.

"Neveah?"

I gasp, fall back a step as she whimpers, eyes pleading with me. Willis runs a hand through her hair like he's petting a dog.

"Shhhh," Silas says, holding me in place, his grip like a vice. "I thought you said you were ready."

"Don't hurt her," I say, turning to him. I grasp at his shirt, begging. "I-I thought you meant Jason. Or the Toad Twins. Not—"

My breath catches in my throat.

Not the only person in town who actually tries to be nice to me, not Neveah with her community college and her trailer and her blue nails. Who let me drive her home. Who tried to help.

"We're not going to hurt her, Lukas." His voice is quiet. Firm. And for a minute, I have hope.

"You are."

My stomach plummets. I shake my head no, horrified.

"If you want to join us, you have to share a meal."

"I know! I'm here, aren't I? At the diner."

"That's not the kind of meal we eat, brother," Jasper says. I look over and he's picking at his teeth, his fangs, with a long fingernail.

"Don't you get it?" Dru cuts in harshly. "You either drink her blood and become one of us, or you get to be a blood donor, too. She's a goner for sure, and you're one bad decision away from becoming one. There's no walking out of this."

"Dru speaks the truth," Jasper says, voice deep like the drum in that song. The song that started all this, when all I wanted was for someone to rescue me so I wouldn't have to be alone.

I shake my head. "No, I can't. She's my friend. Anyone else."

"You'd rather a stranger die for you?" Silas asks. "Better for it to be a friend. Cut your last ties. Then you're really one of us."

"I don't . . . I don't want this." But it's a lie. I want it. I want it so bad it's making me shake. But Neveah's eyes are on me and she's crying, tears catching on her nose, pooling on the counter.

"You asked us to come," Silas reminds me, hand warm on my back, breath soft in my ear. I feel his lips against my neck, just the slightest touch, but it sends heat through my body that almost brings me to my knees.

"He's sweet on you, Silas," Willis says with a knowing chuckle.

"What do you say, Lukas?" Silas asks. "We could feast, and then you and I could go somewhere private." His hand tightens at my waist. "You won't ever have to be alone again."

It's everything I want. Because I can't go back to that house, to the well-meaning church casseroles and the empty rooms and the organized pill bottles and everything that the county assessor will be through next week to claim.

"I don't want to be alone," I whisper.

"You won't be," Silas says.

And then the jukebox kicks on and the fiddle is playing and that man is singing: "*He'd the face of an angel but the heart of a demon . . .*"

"Take what's yours, Lukas," he says, "and become one of us."

I take a step forward.

"No!" Suddenly, Dru's there, between us. He swings his baseball bat right at Silas, almost too fast for my eyes to follow. The bat connects with the side of Silas's head, shattering into shards. Silas goes down.

"Run!" Dru shouts, and I take a hesitant two steps back to the door, my brain trying to make sense of what's going on.

Jasper launches himself at Dru, but the redhead is ready, and he thrusts a shard of baseball bat forward, right into Jasper's chest. Jasper crumbles to ash without making a sound.

"Run, you fool!" Dru shouts again, as Willis jumps onto his back and sinks vicious fangs into his neck. He screams as the blood runs, a river as red as his hair flooding across his throat.

Neveah's on her feet. Whatever was keeping her pinned to the counter, fear or some kind of spell, seems to have broken when Jasper disintegrated. She grabs my hand and pulls me to the door. I stumble after her, eyes still on Willis as he rips out Dru's throat. Dru collapses, eyes clouding over to nothing, head flopping like a broken doll's.

I scream. Willis turns toward me, his face no longer that of a beautiful mad boy but of a monster. He takes a step toward us as Neveah unlocks the door and we stagger across the threshold and into the parking lot. Before he can follow, a hand stops him.

It's Silas.

He's lost his hat, and his hair is clotted with his own blood, but his face is whole. Whatever damage the bat did has already healed.

He looks at me, eyes that swirl of oil-slick rainbow that I glimpsed before.

He says something to Willis, who throws back his head and roars, a sound that shakes the diner and rattles the windows in my car right behind me. But he doesn't follow us. Neither does Silas. He just watches.

My hip bumps the fender of my car. I blink. I don't remember crossing the parking lot. Neveah's sobbing and shouting at me to give her the keys. I can hear the song on the jukebox, just a tinny wail of a fiddle leaking out the diner door.

And I realize that I don't want to go. Leaving means leaving Silas. If I drive away now, I know I'll never see him again.

"Neveah," I whisper, but she doesn't hear me over her own pleading. Louder, then. "Neveah!"

"What?!" she shouts back, breathless and terrified.

"I'm staying." I turn to her, let her see me. My conviction. My want.

"I'm staying," I repeat. "But you can go."

I throw her my keys. She reaches for them but misses and they clatter to the ground. With a sob she scrambles to find them, and when she does, she wrenches open the car door and climbs into the driver's seat. I hear the locks engage, and then the engine, and she tears out of the parking lot, barely giving me time to move out of her way.

As soon as she's gone, I have second thoughts.

But I'm here, and Silas is there, just on the other side of the glass.

And I know what I have to do.

He waits for me to come to him.

I open the door, hands shaking. Dru's body lies still at my feet and Willis is panting like an animal, eyes trained on me. But I stay steady on Silas, remembering what he told me.

"I want you to leave," I say, my voice barely above a whisper. It sounds pathetic to my own ears, and I clear my throat and try again. "I want you and your Boys to go."

Silas tilts his head. The jukebox moves on to the next verse. And my heart breaks a little.

"Are you saying we're not welcome here anymore?"

I nod, even though it hurts.

"Well."

He bends to pick up his hat. Plants it firmly on his head.

"All you had to do was tell me so, Lukas." He gestures to Willis, who reaches down and, with inhuman strength, slings Dru's body up around his shoulders. Silas holds open the door and Willis goes through. Silas starts to follow, pauses to look back.

"But you owe me for Jasper," he says, voice hard like it wasn't before, "and I'll have to collect one day."

I watch them go. Watch until they fade into the darkness, until I'm sure there's nothing in the parking lot, not even racoons. And then I collapse.

◆

Landry finds me on the floor the next morning and lectures me about alcohol and drinking too much. But we both know I don't drink, and she makes me a stack of pancakes and an oversized cup of coffee. Workers come to haul the old jukebox away by noon, and we don't talk about it again. Neveah never comes back to the diner, and a few weeks later, Landry tells me that Neveah moved away, got into a four-year college somewhere. Jason and the Toad Twins wash up the next month, exsanguinated. Rumors circle for a while about some weird drugs that must be on the market, and their story even makes one of the prime-time mystery shows, the connection to the Finleys' deaths too strange to ignore. The conspiracy podcasts go wild. They called it "Murder in Blood River," and it causes a sensation for a while, but people have no idea. Not really.

Sometimes I hum that song, especially when I'm studying for my GED or getting the house ready for sale, but I never put my heart into it. I've decided to leave this shit town after all. Head to Dallas or Denver or something. Try to make my own way, see what happens.

I wonder if Silas will ever come to collect on Jasper's death, like he said he would. I know all I have to do to find out is sing for him and mean it. But I won't. Not for a while. Not until I'm ready. And while I wait, I'll dream of a beautiful black-haired boy in a cowboy hat with oil slicks for eyes.

BITES & BLOOD
Or Why Do Vampires Suck?

Zoraida Córdova &
Natalie C. Parker

Let's face it: Vampires are the mosquitos of the supernatural world. They lurk in dark places and move with unnatural stealth, and when you least expect it, they bite. Blood-sucking mythical creatures show up in stories from around the world, from the ancient Babylonian goddess Lamashtu, who consumed the blood and flesh of children, to Indian tales of shapeshifting rakshasas and half-bat, half-human vetala. So why do vampires drink blood? Simply put, blood is life. It is essential to the living . . . and to the dead. There's a reason it's called a "blood pact." In the mundane world and the magical one, blood is everything. In Rebecca's story, Lukas has to take part in an extreme blood ritual in order to become one of the Blood River Boys. The process involves choice but also violent sacrifice. In order to become a vampire, Lukas has to take something that doesn't belong to him.

What would you sacrifice in order to live forever?

SENIOR YEAR SUCKS

Julie Murphy

Sweetwater, Texas, is best known for its energy-saving windmills along the I-20 corridor between Fort Worth and Odessa and for the Sweetwater Rattlesnake Roundup, which is an entire event dedicated to measuring, weighing, milking, decapitating, and skinning snakes. We even have a Miss Snake Charmer Pageant, where each contestant does all the normal pageant things as well as decapitates a snake. Aunt Gemma says the roundup is unnecessarily brutal, but Mama says brutality is the only way to survive a place like Sweetwater. Our little town is more than meets the eye.

Besides rattlesnakes, the thing we *should* be most well-known for is the thing you'll never know us for, and there's one simple reason: the women of my family are really freaking great at our jobs. We're basically like the people who save the world when the world doesn't even know it's in need of saving. Nuclear warfare. Assassinations. Hostile aliens from space. Someone out there is working in a fortified basement to save the world while the rest of us live in blissful ignorance, tapping away on our cellular devices.

The thing my family is so good at extinguishing that the great people of Sweetwater don't even know they exist? Immortals. Leeches. Children of the night. Vampires.

Every year at the roundup, we get a handful of protestors shouting about animal abuse and rattlesnake extinction. That's kind of a bummer if you think about it. Rattlesnakes are little beasties, sure, but it's not like they're crawling our streets by night, hunting for human prey, like some vampires I've met. Vampire extinction, however? Well, just like the title of Mama's favorite song says, "Sweet Dreams (Are Made of This)." One vamp at a time.

My name is Jolene Crandall, and I'm the newest vampire slayer in Sweetwater, Texas. At the age of thirteen, I swore to protect this crusty little town with my life. Unless vampires miraculously go extinct. I might have given the rest of my life to the cause, but nothing in my pledge said I couldn't join the cheerleading team. Watch out, Buffy.

"Ready? Okay!" I shout into my megaphone. "Hey! Hey! Mustangs! Spirit! Spirit! Spirit! Let's hear it!"

Maybe it makes me a cliché, but there are few things I love more than cheering my ass off on a crisp November night beneath a starry Texas sky in some random town where this night, this moment is the most important thing to happen all week. The short, flippy skirts, crunching leaves beneath our feet, and nonstop movement to fend off the chill. It's a frenetic energy I wish I could bottle as a reminder on all the days when the only thing I want is to leave this place and this life. Mama always says to truly love something, you gotta hate it a little bit too.

Behind me, my team falls into formation, and I leave my megaphone with my pom-poms as I backpedal to take my spot at the base of the pyramid. "Hey! Hey!" I shout again, the crowd joining in and the band sounding off as well.

I stand in a lunge as Karily, a petite white girl, steps onto my thick, dimpled thighs, one cheerleader after the other hoisting her higher and higher.

I'm what some people call meaty or fat. My body isn't trim and slender like most people would expect of a slayer. I'm a stout white girl with round hips and thighs and little to no chest to speak of. I get my ass from Daddy and he gets his ass from his mama. I'm the kind of limber that makes a great pyramid base, and my roundhouse kick packs some serious heat. Turns out vampire slayers don't need to be fat or skinny or any particular thing at all as long as they kick ass.

My squad repeats the cheer over and over again until Karily pops up into a toe touch and lands in a cradle. "Goooooo Mustangs!" we shout.

"And it looks like that's the game, y'all," says the announcer over the loudspeakers. "Another win for the Bulldogs at home."

The whole crowd packed into the visitors' stands in front of us begins to groan.

Beside me, Peach lets out a guttural sigh. "How is it *that* hard?" she yells at the football team. "How? We're out here literally attempting death-defying midair stunts and y'all's one job is to run a ball across a field. That's it!"

Peach is my best friend—a short Korean girl with bleached-blond hair and a razor-sharp attitude. Last year she went to the roundup dressed as a bloodied snake and shouted about animal cruelty to anyone who would listen until the sheriff shooed her off the grounds. She's the only one who knows my family is different. Just not how. I loop my arm over her shoulder. "At least we're still the superior species on campus."

She laughs. "Uh, yeah. No contest!"

Landry crosses his arms over the Mustang logo emblazoned across his red-and-white cheerleading uniform. "Uh, yeah. I like to think of the Sweetwater football team as *our* sideshow. Everyone knows these pom-poms are the real crowd-pleaser." He smacks each of his butt cheeks in case there is any question which pom-poms he's referring to.

Wade Thomas, a barrel-chested white guy, turns around from the football team's bench. "You know we can hear you, right?" he says.

"Good," says Peach. "All y'all need is a little more real talk and a little less of people blowing sunshine up your asses."

Wade flexes his bicep and winks. "You kiss your mother with that mouth, Peach?"

"Anyone but you," she pipes back.

The score on the board reads VISITOR: 11 HOME: 48. The only thing more depressing than that is watching Aunt Gemma try to make dinner out of whatever random leftovers we've accumulated from whatever takeout we've had throughout the week.

"That was a close one, boys!" someone yells from the crowd.

I roll my eyes. A close one? Why is everyone so concerned with giving boys like Wade gold stars for doing the bare minimum? You wanna know what was a real close one? That drifter vamp who almost made Wade her dinner last week when he was pulling a solo shift at his dad's gas station. Big, strong Wade, who's been riding the bench for the last two weeks but still has an ego the size of a tractor? Well, he had no idea how close he came to being just another sack of blood.

It didn't matter that I saved Wade, though, because I didn't kill the drifter and then three days later Aunt Gemma found three truck drivers in a ditch on the outskirts of town with their throats ripped out.

"Let's load it up, y'all!" I call out to the rest of my team.

"Roger that, Cap," Landry says, as a few girls from the opposing team whistle at him. Landry is hot. Not just hot for Middle of Nowhere, Texas, but real-life hot. He's a six-foot-tall bisexual dreamboat with deep brown skin and tight and smooth cornrow braids. The whole world has eyes for him, but lately he's only got eyes for Peach—if only she'd notice.

We all gather up our signs, pom-poms, and gym bags. On the bus, I pull on my sweatpants under my skirt and yank my hoodie over my head.

"Hey, Karily," I shout into the dark bus. "Great job on that toe touch!"

"Yeah!" a few other people chime in.

"Thanks, y'all," says her tiny freshman voice from the back of the bus.

Ms. Garza, our faculty sponsor, boards the bus last with a romance novel tucked under her arm. "All right, Ms. Rhodes," she says to our bus driver. "Let's get going."

Ms. Garza settles into the front row with her reading light and book as we rumble down the road.

I sit with a bench to myself while Peach and Landry settle in across the aisle from me, the two of them huddled over Peach's cell phone, watching their favorite beauty guru vlogger unload the details of her very messy and very public breakup.

I'll never know what it feels like to not know that vampires exist and should be feared, but moments like this are the closest I come to the sweet relief of ignorance. In this bus, I'm not responsible for the lives of everyone in a ten-mile radius. In this bus, we're speeding down the road faster than any vampire can move. I love the safety of this bus when we're driving home late at night after another away game, and I can just let my guard down.

Even if I wanted to shirk my duties back in Sweetwater, my anatomy would never allow it. Vampires set off some kind of reaction inside me. My own internal dog whistle. It's like when you know you've forgotten something but you just don't know what it is, or that feeling of waking up in the middle of the night and realizing you didn't write the paper that's due tomorrow. All this energy piles up inside me, and I'm not satisfied until it's released. Suddenly every frustrating hour of training with Mama and Aunt Gemma clicks for me, and every other desire and care fades away until all that's left is my one purpose: protecting Sweetwater.

But here in this yellow school bus, barreling down farm roads, the feeling is gone. Not a bloodsucker in sight.

No one really knows who was here first: Resurrection Home for Wayward Souls or the town of Sweetwater. Or maybe the town of Sweetwater just started as a bunch of wayward souls. Either way, the rules are simple: They don't leave the ground of Resurrection Home, and my family allows them to continue using their glamour to disguise themselves as a Pentecostal youth shelter on the outskirts of town. It's not a perfect compromise, but we've made it work for more than a hundred years.

I like to think of the place as a halfway house or vampire rehab, where bloodsuckers go to learn to control themselves and drink bagged blood from private donors. The only problem with rehab is that only three kinds of vampires come in and out. First, there are the well-behaved vampires, who pass through Sweetwater after a successful stay at the home. Then there are the vamps on their way to the home, searching for one last living, breathing fix. And lastly, there are those who go to Resurrection Home and fail, coming out worse than they went in.

The bus rumbles over the gravel on the side of the road, jostling me awake, and it's only then that I realize I've been dozing in and out of sleep. The bus comes to a halt.

"Looks like the Sweetwater spirit bus," says Ms. Rhodes, as she peers out the driver's window, pointing to the bus parked ahead with its hazards flashing.

The feeling hits me like a brick wall. Adrenaline. Whatever's on that bus, it's not good. And I have a feeling that everything on it is either dead or immortal.

Ms. Garza stands up. "Must have broken down. Maybe we can save them the trouble of sending out another bus."

Ms. Rhodes pulls the lever, the pneumatic door wheezing open into the pitch-black field alongside the road.

I shoot to my feet. "Wait."

The whole team looks at me. This isn't the first time I've popped up in the middle of a crowd or screamed "Stop!" or tried to cause some kind of distraction. If you ask around town, people will even tell you that Crandall women are *peculiar in a special kind of way, but they wouldn't hurt a fly*. (Supposedly.) Nothin' peculiar about us, except that we know more about what's happening under mortals' noses than any human should.

"I'll, uh, come with you." I mean, really, what's Ms. Garza going to do in the face of a vampire? Throw her bodice-ripping romance novel at its fangs? Yeah, I don't think so.

Ms. Garza waves me off. "Jo, you stay on the bus. You think I'm about to let a student off this bus on the side of the road in the middle of Jesus knows where? No, ma'am!"

She jogs down the steps before I can get in another word.

I walk to the front of the bus, hovering by the stairs. Every away game, the town sends one school bus of fans, dubbed "the spirit bus." You don't have to be a student to ride the bus. Shit, I don't even think you need to show an ID. After all, Sweetwater is the kind of place where every face is familiar. So, basically, anyone or anything could be on that bus.

"Back it up. You heard the teacher lady," says Ms. Rhodes.

"Yeah, yeah, yeah," I mutter. Let's hope I'm faster than whatever's waiting for me on the bus.

I watch as she stalks up the side of the road, my breath held. If we were just a little closer, our headlights might stretch far enough for me to see what the hell is on that bus.

It's too quiet. That's the thing about people: Where there's people, there's noise. Vampires, though, their lives stretch over such long spans of time that they crave the things that make time pass. Quiet. Dark. For people, there really is safety in numbers. *Hint, hint, Ms. Garza.*

As Ms. Garza knocks on the door to the other bus, I tune out every noise around me and focus in on her. *Don't get on the bus, don't get on the bus, don't get on the bus.*

She gets on the bus. Of course she does.

Come on, lady.

I decide to count to ten. That's what reasonable people do. They count to ten. *One, two, three, four—fuck it.* I race down the steps and to the other bus, expecting to find sweet, naïve Ms. Garza in a puddle of her own blood, a vampire crouched over her breathless body.

I barrel up the steps and Ms. Garza shrieks as I catch her off guard. Immediately, I throw my body in front of hers.

I glance around, but . . . not a drop of blood in sight.

"Jo, I told you to stay on the bus," she says sweetly through gritted teeth as she elbows her way out from behind me.

"I was—" *Coming to save your life*, I nearly say, but then my gaze catches on the half-full bus of Mustang fans, most of them familiar faces.

"Oh, thank heavens!" says Mr. Bufford, the faculty sponsor for the spirit bus. "Ms. Garza has invited us all to load up on the cheer-leading team's bus. That includes you, Deidra!" he says to the bus driver.

A few whoops come from the back of the bus.

"The city will send a tow truck in the morning," he continues. "Now, students, please triple-check for your personal items. We're not doubling back for any cell phones or backpacks."

Well, I feel colossally ridiculous. I can't shake the feeling, though. I eye each person on the bus, but it's too dark for me to notice if anyone is out of place.

As we file onto the bus, I slide back into my seat, and with more people, we're all forced to double up. Nearly all the passengers from the other bus find seats without me having to give up my coveted half bench until Ms. Garza says, "Oh, here we are! Alma, you can sit with Jolene."

A tall, thin girl with light tan skin and black silky hair woven into a fishtail braid halfway down her back sits beside me. Her skin brushes mine and I suck in a breath, sounding off a hiss. The same glamour that protects the Home from mortal eyes hides the delicate pointed fangs in her otherwise perfect smile. Another perk of the job: I'm immune to glamour.

When I was a kid, there was a small church just outside town that dabbled in snake handling. You know, the kind of assholes who think it's a good idea to toss snakes back and forth to show that God will protect them from being bitten. Sure, maybe there is a God and maybe he does protect people, but I don't think there's anything in the Bible about protecting stupid. One night, Mom and Aunt Gemma went over there to scope things out, and I remember listening from the hallway as they talked in the kitchen. "It felt like a nightmare," Mama said. "Like we were watching a whole bunch of oblivious people dance at the edge of a cliff."

And that's exactly how this feels as Ms. Garza hovers above us in the aisle and Ms. Rhodes fires up the bus. "Jo, this is Alma. She's new to Sweetwater. I had her just yesterday in fourth period for the first time. Isn't that right, Alma?"

"Yes, ma'am," the girl says sweetly.

"Welcome to Sweetwater," I say, spitting out each syllable.

"What a . . . warm welcome," replies Alma, as Ms. Garza settles in beside Mr. Bufford.

The moment we take off and the road noise is loud enough to drown out our voices, I turn to her. "I should kill you."

She laughs, "Excuse me?" she asks. "Where are your manners?"

"You heard me." She's playing coy, but she knows exactly who I am. These instincts I'm gifted with aren't a one-way street.

"Discretion," she says. "Isn't that one of your slayer pillars? I'm sure whoever you call boss would be just delighted to hear you slaughtered one of my kind in a yellow school bus full of mortals."

"You're from the Home," I deduce. "Leaving or going?"

"And how do you know I'm not some passerby? Maybe I'm just slowly draining my way to LA?"

I scoff. "Yeah, on board a Sweetwater High spirit bus?"

She huffs, throwing herself against the back of our seat in a way that is so completely human and familiar that it's unsettling. This thing used to be a person, and my stomach clenches with guilt as I wonder about the person she might have been.

"Or maybe I just miss being among the living? Maybe I just want to be a normal teenager for a night?" she says, her voice girlish.

The silence between us dangles there for a moment, before I let out a nervous laugh. She doesn't make me nervous. Why would I be nervous? I've never been made nervous by a vampire.

But then again, I don't think I've shared more than five words with a vampire. And definitely not one so . . . lovely. I shake my head. A lovely vampire. *Yeah, right.*

She looks at me with piercing clarity. "Wow." Her voice is breathless, and her expression falters a little. "You really think we're all bloodthirsty monsters? Not all of us are crashing through towns like a bunch of pubescent boys on the Internet without parental controls."

"You need human blood to live, don't you? Yes. The end. Besides, you're in clear violation of the Home's agreement."

"You need food to live, right? But you're not out here plowing through every grocery store in sight. You eat meals. You have *prepared food*. Feeding doesn't have to be a frenzy." Her voice is intoxicating. Delectable, even. But I still have to sit on my hands to stop myself from punching her.

"You're not the only one who wants to be a normal teenage girl," I offer, my guard slowly yielding. Besides, it's not like I could kill her in front of all these people.

"Is that how the big scary slayer ended up in a tiny little skirt as captain of the cheerleading team? She just wanted to be a normal girl?"

"How'd you know I'm captain?"

"I can smell dominance," she says.

"Seriously?" Admittedly, there are plenty of things I don't know about vampires.

She lets out a melodious laugh, tipping her head back and exposing her long neck, clad with a plastic tattoo choker, like those you might find at the mall. I remember stealing a package of them from a Claire's when Peach and I were on a field trip to Dallas in middle school.

"Not in the literal sense," she says. "But you seem like the kind of girl who's either in charge or not participating at all."

"Ouch," I say with a genuine laugh. "A little too real."

"Besides, your sweatshirt says CAPTAIN."

I look down at the cursive embroidery above my heart. "Touché."

Her hands settle in her lap as she closes her eyes, leaving herself completely exposed.

I feel like a behavioral scientist, and this is my one chance to truly *know* my subject. A fleeting moment. "Can I ask you a question?"

"What if I say no?"

"I'll ask anyway."

"Of course you will," she says.

"How old are you really?"

She smiles, her eyes still closed. "What if I told you I was hundreds—no, thousands of years old? That would make for a good story, wouldn't it?"

"You didn't really answer the question."

Her smile melts. "My body is forever seventeen. However, I'm eighteen and one hundred and eighty-four days old. Pretty anticlimactic, huh?"

"Meh. A vampire is a vampire is a vampire."

"A slayer is a slayer is a slayer." The disgust in her voice is palpable.

"Hey, I'm still alive," I remind her.

"It's not like I woke up one day and decided to become a vampire. My humanity was violently stolen from me. I'm continuing on, the only way I know how." Her voice is sweet. Innocent.

That's enough to silence me for a moment. "I didn't have much of a choice in my own fate, either, you know." And it's true. As much as I hate to admit it, Alma and I share this one thing in common.

"You don't seem too disappointed by it." She reaches over me, and my whole body tenses in defense as I grip her forearm, prepared to snap it in half. "Stand down, kitty. Just opening the window."

My hold loosens, and she pushes the lever on the window, a gust of crisp November wind funneling in and the stale bus smell immediately dissolving. Alma breathes in deeply through her nose.

A fallen piece of hair from my ponytail dances in front of my face, and Alma takes a bobby pin tucked inside her braid. In one seamless motion, she smooths my hair back, twirling it briefly with her finger, and slides the pin into place. "So tell me, sweet slayer, if you're so committed to your destiny, why are you wasting your time on the cheerleading team?"

I touch my hair where her hand just was, and it takes me a long moment to gather the words I'm looking for. "I'll always be a slayer. Until the day I die. But I'll only ever have these four years of high school. I answered your question. My turn now. You never answered me. Resurrection Home for Wayward Souls. Are you going or coming?"

She sighs. "Being a maker is kind of like being a parent. Anyone can do it, but not everyone should. You could say that the last year has been . . . a learning experience. I heard about the home and figured maybe I'd find what I was looking for there. And then . . ." She closes her eyes and shakes her head, like she knows that whatever she's about to say is so, so ridiculous. "And then I saw your school and I couldn't remember what it felt like to just be . . . a teenager. I got distracted. But don't worry your pretty little head, slayer. Next stop: Resurrection Home. No pit stops. Girl Scout's honor." She holds three fingers up, pledging.

The bus begins to slow as we roll back into town. Since we stopped to pick up the passengers from the spirit bus, the football team is long gone and we're the last group to get dropped off at the school, where a few stray cars sit, spread throughout the parking lot.

"No stops," I tell Alma before I can think twice about letting her go. "I better not see you again."

She winks before darting off the bus. "No stops."

Alma is gone before I can even check to see which way she went so that I can be sure no one accidentally crosses paths with her. I sit perched on the hood of my car, waiting for everyone to slowly trickle out, until Ms. Rhodes drives off to return the bus to the bus yard. Ms. Garza tells me to head home, but it's Peach and Landry who stick around the longest. Finally, after we've rehashed the highlights of the night, Landry digs out his car keys and offers Peach a ride. Peach studies me for a moment before making me pinky swear that I'll text her when I get home. One day I'll give her the answers she deserves, but for now I appreciate her treating me like a normal girl who should be cautious of men at night and other things that go bump in the dark.

After they leave, I wait a few more minutes for any sign of Alma before pulling my keys out of my backpack and unlocking my car.

I shouldn't have let her go. All I can think about is those three bodies Mama and Aunt Gemma found. If I'd just been faster or stronger than the vamp who almost took out Wade, three more people would be alive.

With my back to the dark parking lot, wind tickles my neck, and I whip around to find Alma less than an inch from me. Loose wisps of hair blow across her face, brushing my cheeks. In one swift motion, I grip her neck with one hand and spin her around, pinning her to my cherry-red Dodge Neon.

"I told you to go back to the academy. No stops." I yank her forward and slam her body against the car once more for emphasis, then reach through the open driver-side window for the stake I always keep in the side of my door.

"I don't respond well to authority," she hisses, and calmly grips my wrist. I see the vampire in her now. It's in her stance and the way her whole body is ready for a fight. She runs her tongue over her fangs. "Besides, I have a proposition for you."

I press the pointed end of the stake to the spot just above her rib cage, the spot I know so well. "I don't negotiate with vampires."

She swallows and her throat rolls against the palm of my hand. "Give me senior year. All I want is the senior year I never had. The minute I accept my diploma and walk across that stage, I'm gone; if not, I'm fair game."

I study her closely, searching for the loophole. "Why senior year? Senior year sucks. You've got a whole eternity to relive senior year. Why Sweetwater?"

"You try living an eternity as a high school junior. Forever wishing you were a senior." She eyes me playfully, like I'm not about to shove a chunk of wood through her not-so-beating heart.

Well, that does sound awful. I guess.

"Besides, I like it here. I like . . . the people."

My grip on her throat tightens, and for the first time her eyes widen with discomfort.

"When I walk through the gates of the Resurrection Home, I know . . . I'll change. Everything will change. I still feel human now. But once I'm there . . . among my own kind . . . I won't be the same. I want to do this while I can still appreciate it. And if I get wind of any vampires stepping out of line, you'll be my first call."

"If you touch a single living human before graduation, my word is null and void."

She rolls her eyes. "Fine."

"How will you get blood?"

"The same way I have for the last year and a half. Blood banks."

We only have one blood bank in Sweetwater. She'll have to be discreet.

"Senior year," she says again. "That's all I want."

There's so much to consider. Mom. Aunt Gemma. The blood supply. Other vampires passing through. But Alma's words ring in my ears. *My humanity was violently stolen from me. I'm continuing on, the only way I know how.* If a slayer had been around to save Alma, she'd be a normal high school senior right now and none the wiser. Like Peach. Or Landry.

I let go of her throat and pull away the stake. Her whole body sags against my car. My fist tightens around the stake as I hold out my other hand to shake on it. This is going to be a shit show.

Alma takes my hand, but instead of shaking on our deal, she pulls me to her, our lips so close I can taste her cherry lip gloss. "I'd rather kiss on it."

My lips brush hers, and within seconds, I'm using my hips to pin her to my car for completely different reasons than I did just moments ago. Her hands grip my waist, using my cheer skirt to pull me even closer.

Inside me, endorphins sound off like pop rocks in a bottle of Coke, like a perfectly timed cheer on a crisp night. Turns out kissing a vampire can feel just as good as slaying one.

THE SLAYER
Or When We Say *Vampire*, You Say *Slayer*!

Zoraida Córdova & Natalie C. Parker

Like the vampire, the vampire slayer has seen many iterations over time, from Van Helsing to Buffy Summers to Blade. While there are many ways to kill a vampire, the slayer is the vampire's human counterpart, the balance to its supernatural strength, speed, and senses. The slayer, whether supernaturally chosen or not, has learned the vampire's secrets and knows how to stand in their way or stake them dead, whichever the case may be. They aren't always cheerleaders, but they do tend to be thin (or vibrantly muscled!), cisgender, able-bodied people. In Julie's story, we travel to high school, where a fat slayer girl meets her match in more ways than one. And it's that beautiful tension between vampire and slayer that makes their relationship to die for!

Which chosen one are you? Vampire or slayer?

THE BOY AND THE BELL

Heidi Heilig

It is a gusty night, dark and chill, with the wind rustling so loud in the leaves that Will nearly misses the delicate chime of the bell.

An incongruous sound in the graveyard—at least so late at night. Under the bright light of day, the church bells toll high noon or to call the parishioners to worship . . . or to announce the arrival of a new occupant of the boneyards. But this sound is not the deep brass tone of the carillon. This is smaller, almost petulant. The sound of a servant's summons—a sound that would have made Will jump in a past life.

But that's all over now.

So he stops instead, standing deliberately still in the deep shadows among the trees edging one side of the yard. It isn't easy. Though his body is still, he can't slow his heart. The longer he waits, the higher the risk of being caught—caught and caught out, with his shovel and his barrow and the calluses on his hands. It is especially dangerous tonight, as the burial is so fresh—relatives might have stationed guards to run off body snatchers like himself. But he'd rather face recrimination by an angry citizen—or even a beating from a grieving relative—than respond to the bell.

Ting a ling ding, ting a ling, ting a ling. The smell of the turned earth is so strong it's like a clod of mud lodged in his throat, and the chill of the churchyard wind slips icy fingers through the worn patches of his jacket. But when he hears the bell, a part of him is back in the big house on Cherry Street. The rustle of the leaves sounds too much like the swish of his old skirts as he runs, and on the wind he can almost hear the high, thin sound of Mrs. Esther calling his name—his old name. A name he'll never answer to again.

Will's racing heart is not only due to fear of discovery.

His lip twists; he grits his teeth. He shifts his shovel on his shoulder. At last, the bell stops ringing. As the sound fades, Mrs. Esther's voice fades as well, and Will can breathe again.

The wind has torn the tattered shroud from the sickle moon, silvering the graveyard, tarnishing the shadows. In the light, the source of the sound is immediately apparent. A little brass chime shines like a tiny beacon atop a wooden scaffold erected above the fresh mound of earth. There is a string attached to the bell that loops through a pulley and disappears down a tube leading to the coffin below.

A strange contraption, but Will recognizes it. One of those new devices—an "improved burial case"—meant to alert the living in case the unfortunate occupant of the coffin has been mistakenly buried alive. Will has only seen them in pictures before, drawn on chalkboards at the university where he trades his midnight cargo for a spot standing in the back of the amphitheater where the dissections take place. For the last few months, the medical college has been aflame with talk of live burial after a string of tragedies across Pennsylvania.

The first reported case was a young girl who fell to a new

strain of consumption—wasting away in a lethargic swoon, growing paler and paler until the blush of fever on her cheeks resembled blood on snow. When even that faded and her body grew cold, her parents entombed her in the family mausoleum. Their grief was still fresh when her younger brother fell into the same stupor. Weeks later, when they opened the mausoleum to inter him beside his sister, she flew out in a wild rage, red-eyed and cringing from the sunlight.

Some called her survival a miracle, but it was quickly apparent that her vivisepulture had driven her insane. At least the family was able to afford placement at Kirkbride's Asylum in Philadelphia, where all the rich send their mad. And of course her brother was spared the same fate. But rumor has it he was still affected—either by his illness or by his sister's entombment. He woke from his swoon, but in the weeks since, he suffered a loss of appetite and a habitual insomnia—at least, according to the doctor that treats him, who lectures twice a month at the college.

Other rumors of live burial had cropped up in the intervening time, some of them so wild they were clearly fiction. A body dissolving into smoke, a wolf wrapped in a burial shroud fleeing an open tomb. Dozens of coffins reported empty when they'd been dug up to check—but Will knows the reason for that.

Still, students and teachers alike bandied about the stories of live burial over beer or breakfast. The more enterprising among them dreamed up solutions and drafted patents, from glass lids to shovels stored at the foot of the coffin, to personal bell towers, like this one. There was even a design with a pantry containing marzipan, tinned fruit, sausage, and brandy, as well as a full set of serving ware. But only the rich can afford such expensive precautions. Much less costly to ask a friend to cut off your head before nailing shut the coffin.

Of course, with the rest of the country wild for that novel by Stoker, that request, too, might raise more than a few eyebrows. Discussions of the fanciful book—and the idea of the vampire— swept through the university as well, though the students took it much less seriously than the problem of live burial.

Will understands why. The century is ending, and with it, old ways of thinking. Of being. In the clear and steady gleam of electric lights, superstition turns to foolishness; in the crucible of the combustion engine, false beliefs are burned away. And under the scalpel and the microscope, the human form is revealed to be much closer to animals' than to angels'. In the secret spaces, man has discovered cells, not souls. Death has become final; there is no such thing as eternal life. As a metaphor, live burial is much more relatable than the story of the vampire.

Ting a ling, ting a ling. The summons comes again, bringing Will back to the present. He narrows his eyes. The ringing is too insistent to be the wind: There is someone moving in that coffin. Someone desperate to get out. But despite Will's growing fascinating, everything in him rebels against responding. His old life was dead and buried, and he'd scraped too hard, spent too much, gone too far to have to jump at the sound of a bell.

Then again, there might be a reward in saving a life. Especially one whose family could afford such a pricey coffin. And with a little bit of cash, maybe Will could afford a new coat, a proper shirt, a pair of trousers without so many stains. The thought makes Will's heart leap—after all, so often the clothes make the man.

And with a new suit, who knows? He might be able to claim a seat in the lecture hall—something in the front row. Where Will could actually see the dissections instead of the backs of the other boys' heads. Where he could watch the anatomist uncover the mysteries he wanted so badly to solve: How do bodies work? And why?

Besides, isn't this the first part of being a doctor? Saving lives?

Still, Will can't bring himself to move until the bell goes quiet. The clouds close like curtains around the moon, cloaking his trek from the pauper's graves to the green swale beside the church. Proximity to God, like burial precautions, is just another commodity reserved for the rich. The fresh grave makes a mounded scar on the grass, topped with that little bell tower above the headstone: MAXWELL THADDEUS HAWTHORNE, 1880–1899, BELOVED SON.

Behind his eyes, Will can see the boy. They'd only met once—if you could call it a meeting. Mrs. Hawthorne had brought her son along when she'd come to call on Mrs. Esther; Maxwell had tormented the cat while Will had waited on the two women. Mrs. Esther's high-pitched call was still worse than Mrs. Hawthorne's praise—"*What a good girl you have!*"—but only barely.

Ting a ling, ting a ling. Deliberately, Will averts his eyes from the bell, studying the stone instead. It is surprisingly modest for the scion of the Hawthorne family—but of course it is only temporary. This part of the cemetery is dotted with elaborate statues—the broken columns of lives cut short, the weeping angels of unending grief, the covered urns representing immortality. Whichever Maxwell was meant to have, it would take time to carve. Will the mason return the down payment if the grave's occupant asks for it himself?

Will stifles a laugh. As though Maxwell Thaddeus Hawthorne would stoop to speaking directly to a tradesman!

At last, the ringing stops. With a grunt, Will swings his shovel off his shoulder, slicing through the earth with the sharp steel blade. The grave is fresh; the soil is soft. It's a perfect night for grave robbing, dark and bitter, the cold keeping honest folk indoors with their curtains drawn. Keeps down the scent of rot, too. Typically, Will has a strong stomach, but every month or so he's plagued by ill humors: a twisting cramp in his gut, a sapping of his energy.

Tonight the effects of the catamenia are particularly strong, and it isn't long before Will is sweating. Still, over the sluggish tide in his belly, the blood in his veins sings as he lifts and turns, lifts and turns. He finds his rhythm to the beat of his heart. He is acutely aware of the sheer strength of the fist-size muscle, clenching as it pumps his blood through vasculature as complex and branching as the roots in the earth. In any dissection it is the heart that fascinates him most. The first organ to develop—the seat of the soul—or so they say, those who believe in souls. The one that tells us what we want—who we are.

Is Maxwell's heart pounding just as hard? Not with effort, but in fear? Is claustrophobia creeping in along with the terror of mortality? How long has he been waiting? Does he pray as he pulls the rope? Rich or no, Will begins to pity the boy in the box; still, he stops digging each time the bell rings.

Will can tell the exact moment Maxwell Thaddeus Hawthorne hears him: The bell starts jangling as though possessed. Once more, Will takes the opportunity to catch his breath, leaning the shovel against the headstone and pushing his knuckles into the small of his back. Eventually, the cramps ease and the bell stops, and Will takes up the shovel again. But he nearly drops it when he hears the voice in his ear.

"Hurry up!"

Will steadies himself against the edge of the grave; the voice had only come through the air tube.

"Are you there, man? Why have you stopped?"

The tone is even more imperious than the words. For someone who's been buried alive, young Mr. Hawthorne sounds more annoyed than terrified. The bell chimes again, and the pity dies in Will's chest. For a moment, he considers leaving Maxwell Thaddeus Hawthorne to spend the rest of the night trying to dig his own way out. But the lion's share of the work is already done. Why throw it away out of spite? Swallowing his pride—and reminding himself of the front row in the lecture hall—he presses his mouth to the tube and speaks, "This pipe looks rather narrow. Best to conserve air."

"*Beg pardon?*" Maxwell Thaddeus Hawthorne replies, in the tone of a man who has never had to conserve in his life. "*This coffin is the finest on the market.*"

Will's lip curls. Only the rich could be more concerned about public opinion of their burial than the burial itself. At least he has stopped ringing the damned bell. "Regardless," Will grunts, returning to his shovel. "It's built to support survival, not conversation."

"*How would you know?*"

"I'm a doctor," Will replies. The claim slips out—more hope than truth. "Or rather," he adds, "I aim to be."

"*Do you?*" The voice echoing up the pipe sounds delighted. "*Is that how you found me? You were going to steal my corpse for anatomy class?*"

Will falters at the accusation. Body snatching is not technically illegal—the politicians know it is a necessary side effect of the advancement of science, and there are plenty of wealthy doctors who can afford to pay them to look the other way. But the practice is wildly unpopular, especially with the poor, who are at the greatest risk of being anatomized. Will himself has carted plenty a pauper from the clay fields to the amphitheater—watched their flesh mutilated, their bodies made a spectacle, each of them robbed of the only rest they were ever guaranteed.

Of course, few resurrectionists are bold enough to take a rich man's body. Is that why this particular rich man seemed to find the threat of anatomization so entertaining? Is it a scintillating brush with the reality of the commoners? Might he be game enough to play along further? "An account from a victim of live burial will be far more interesting to the students," Will says as he resumes digging.

"*An account?*" The amusement in Maxwell's voice falls away. "*I'm not about to be paraded before a lecture hall or be plastered across the papers.*"

"The papers will get wind of it anyway," Will says—after the fanfare of a high society funeral, a miraculous resurrection will be hard to hide. But the voice that comes up through the pipe is flat.

"*Not from you.*"

Will's shovel strikes the coffin lid with a hollow crunch—the prize at last. But he hesitates, stomach twisting. Maxwell's reply sounded almost like a threat. The wind rushes by; an owl shrieks in the dark.

"*Surely you understand the importance of discretion,*" Maxwell adds then, his tone changing once again. Desperate now—and promising. "*Can you imagine being made a spectacle? People pointing and staring when you pass? Having conversations where pleasantries can barely hide the prurient curiosity in their eyes?*"

Will's gut cramps again—not with his humors, but with a sympathetic fear. "I can."

"*I'll make your silence worth your while,*" the voice replies eagerly. But Maxwell's pale fingers are already worming up through the split wood of the coffin lid. "*Just get me out of here!*"

Will tosses his shovel onto the grass and kneels in the hole to help pry apart the coffin lid. He is more careful than usual; still, Maxwell cringes away from the splintered edges of the boards—from the clumped earth falling in through the jagged opening.

With other night parcels, Will's habit is to sling a rope under the corpse's shoulders and haul the limp body through the hole. But Maxwell can clamber up on his own once the hole is large enough.

Gingerly, he unfolds, brushing a speck of dirt from his lapel. "What took you so long?" the boy demands, with less gratitude than Will had hoped, though just about as much as he'd expected. In the tight space of the narrow hole, his closeness is unsettling—or perhaps it is the stark differences between them. Maxwell is taller, of course. And his grave suit alone is expensive enough to pay for a year at the college, while Will's threadbare flannels had cost a dollar at the secondhand shop, and that was before they were covered head to toe in mud.

Will puts his palms flat on the lip of the grave and pushes himself upward till he can perch there. He feels better being able to look down at the other boy. "Got you out as fast as I was able," he says, his stomach cramping again. "It's backbreaking work."

Maxwell curls his lip at the word *work*. As he does, the moon peeks out again, making the boy's teeth gleam, wet and white. The sneer is repulsive, as is the pale face—too handsome. As though it had been carved of marble, like one of the statues scattered around the churchyard. "You should have brought help," Maxwell says.

"I thought you preferred discretion," Will reminds him. Better than to mention that help costs money. "It's important in my line of business."

"To be sure." With a dismissive look, Maxwell holds out one smooth, uncalloused palm. "Lift me out of this hole."

Will raises an eyebrow. But if he refuses to act like the boy's footman, Maxwell will likely remember the insolence more than the intervention. Gritting his teeth, Will takes the boy's hand. Then he draws back with a shudder. "You're cold as death!"

Maxwell stiffens for a moment. "No surprise there. I've been lying in that box for hours."

The boy holds out his hand again, impatient, but Will hesitates. He has handled more than his share of corpses, and there is something too familiar about the clammy touch of the boy's flesh. So

76

this time, when he takes Maxwell's hand, he doesn't haul him up out of the grave. Instead, he presses two fingers against the blue-white wrist.

"What is this?" Maxwell says, trying to pull away, but Will has strong hands from digging. He probes and pushes, searching but not finding. "What are you doing?"

"Checking your pulse."

At that, Maxwell wrenches away, but it's too late. Will's examination might have been cursory, but the diagnosis is falling into place—the pale skin, the bright teeth, the notable lack of a pulse. The recent spate of live burials—but no. Those bodies were dead after all.

Will's mind is racing—not with the price of improved burial cases and the thought of a front seat in the lecture hall but with memories of the raucous laughter of the students in last week's dissection. The corpse had come in two bags, rather than the usual one, and upon lifting the head to display the muscles of the throat, a whole head of garlic had fallen out on the table. Will had laughed too, then. It was all superstition. Fear and folklore were fit for novelists, not for doctors. Or so he'd thought, before he'd wrapped his hands around Maxwell's lifeless wrist.

And if the myth of the vampire is true, what else? Does a soul exist inside the cell? Is there a God to hear the church bells ringing?

Will's own heart is pounding so loud it sounds like he's listening with a stethoscope. He stares at the boy in the grave, trying to resist the impulse to scrub his hands on his filthy coat. "What are you?"

"I might ask you the same thing." Maxwell lifts an eyebrow, and the sneer is back. His teeth look very long. Not the pinched-gum rictus of a corpse but the long and pointed canines of a predator. "I'm fairly certain the college doesn't let *women* practice medicine."

At the word, Will's eyes go wide; his stomach twists at the

wrongness. He is repelled all over again. "I'm not a woman," he says through his teeth, but Maxwell only grins.

"I can smell it, you know. The blood." Maxwell shrugs as Will's stomach twists again. "It seems as though discretion might benefit you more than me."

Ting a ling ting—the wind touches the bell, and the shivering leaves sound just like the rustle of skirts. Or is that only an echo in Will's head? And now instead of the seat at the front of the hall, Will sees himself on the table, his body an object of curiosity, the other boys pointing and staring. "You can't tell anyone," he says, and though the wind is gusting past, he feels as though he is the one in the coffin, the air running out.

"I *can't*?" Maxwell cocks his head, as though he's never heard those words in his life. "Perhaps I won't. It might be useful to know a doctor."

The tone of his voice is grating—the way he dangles the word over Will's head. *Perhaps*. Mrs. Esther used to do the same. *Perhaps you'll sleep after the party; perhaps we'll get you a new dress at Christmas; perhaps you'll eat after the guests have gone.* There is a bargain in it— but what does Maxwell want? Will hadn't read Stoker's book, but he'd heard enough about it to know the boy had nothing to fear from illness. "What for?"

"My meals," Maxwell replies simply. "I need to eat, girl."

"My name is Will." His voice is a growl—he spits his own name through his teeth. "And if you think you'll be drinking my blood, you're sorely mistaken."

"Your blood?" Maxwell shudders. "I prefer something cleaner. Finer. The asylums at Kirkbride's, perhaps. The place is clean, and the blood is blue. And no one will believe any . . . complaints."

"I don't plan to work with the mad," Will says, but Maxwell only smiles.

"Change your plans," Maxwell says, so casually. "Or risk being locked up along with them for your *confusion*. And who knows? I'm told my kind can change form. Bats. Wolves. Mist. Surely the form of a man is not out of reach. Perhaps if you serve me well, you'll have the body you really want."

Perhaps. The word echoes in Will's head as Maxwell reaches out once more, and Will cannot tell if it's for help climbing out of the grave or to shake on a devil's bargain. The young doctor has handled liquifying fats, putrefying organs, long hair that sheds in clumps from rotting skulls, but his entire being recoils at touching Maxwell's hand. Damn the money—damn the suit—damn the front row in the lecture hall. "I have a man's body," he says. "And you can get yourself out of the damn hole."

Will draws back his legs, but Maxwell's hand darts out faster than a blink. Manicured nails sink into the flesh of Will's ankle; his hip pops as the rich boy yanks him back down, halfway into the hole. Will kicks himself free, scrambling backward over the lip of the grave as a shower of dirt rattles on the lid of the hollow coffin.

"A man's body? Maybe in your barrow." Maxwell sinks his pale fingers into the soil, crawling out of the hole like a spider. Will stumbles backward, tripping over his shovel. Pain shoots up his back as his tailbone hits the grass. Maxwell crawls toward him, eyes flashing red in the moonlight. "You cut your hair and don your tattered trousers, but you can't trick me. Under the dirt and the sweat, your blood smells just like a—"

The sentence ends in a wet burble as Will swings the blade of the shovel into the boy's pale throat. Maxwell's hands fly up to the wound as he falls backward into his own grave—those soft, unblemished hands, now stained by thick clots of blackened blood.

Nothing living bleeds that way.

Roaring, Will hacks at the neck with the shovel—once, twice, thrice—till at last the head is severed. Just like in Stoker's book. As the corpse finally falls still, Will's chest heaves. Has anyone heard the shouting? Or seen Will cut off a rich man's head with a shovel? He considers running, but then the wind picks up. *Ting a ling, ting a ling.*

Will won't run at the sound of a bell.

And this body will certainly be of interest at the university.

So despite the fear pricking his spine and the cramps twisting his stomach, Will climbs back into the grave to wrap the rope under the corpse's shoulders. He hauls the body out of the hole and stuffs it into his sack, dragging it back to the wheelbarrow he's left in the trees. He has to make a second trip for the head. As he lifts it by the hair, Will regards the alabaster cheeks—now even more statuesque in their stillness—and the white teeth, like the canines of a dog. What was it Stoker's novel claimed? A single bite could spread the infection, transforming a living man into a vampire.

Will regards the teeth, considering such a transformation.

But as he stands there, he can feel his heart beating—that powerful organ, the seat of the soul at his center. The thing that tells him what and who he is.

A man. And a doctor. And he aims to save lives, not suck them dry.

So he bags the head and tosses it into the barrow. Breathing hard, he carts his prize to the university, stopping every so often to listen—to make sure that the sound of the bell is only in his head.

Ting a ling ding, ting a ling, ting a ling.

BURIAL TRADITIONS
Or Why Didn't People
Triple-Check Dead Bodies
Before Closing Up the Casket?

Zoraida Córdova &
Natalie C. Parker

There are so many old superstitions about how to ensure someone didn't become a vampire in the grave! For example, you could bury someone facedown, stuff a clove of garlic in their mouth, stake them to the ground, or even decapitate them. Talk about *extreme* funerals. But the Victorians took those traditions to a whole new level. In some cases, they buried their loved ones with a bell in their hand and a tube that extended down into the coffin so that if the person woke up, they could ring the bell for help. To be fair, they did have a small (very small) problem with burying people they *thought* were dead but who were actually still a little bit alive. They also had a problem with body snatchers, or "Resurrection Men," who slipped into graveyards under cover of night to steal recently buried corpses to sell to medical schools. But only the wealthy could afford any kind of safeguards. Heidi's story takes all of these ideas and makes them extra creepy by asking the question: What if the person ringing the bell isn't a mistakenly buried human but *actually* a hungry, entitled vampire?

In what other ways are vampires a symbol of privilege?

A GUIDEBOOK FOR THE NEWLY SIRED DESI VAMPIRE

Samira Ahmed

Vampersand™

Salaam, namaste, and hello, dear one.

Stop.

Whatever you do, DO NOT GO OUTSIDE.

Sit down.

Close your eyes. Rest your mind. [See: Meditation 101: Tips, Tricks and Tools for Beginners.]

Now take a breath. (Not literally, but we'll get to that later.)

You're confused. Your memory is foggy. It feels like day, like you should be getting ready for school, but you're not at home. You're in a dark, windowless shanty or a warehouse. We know. We put you here. We saved your life. (You're welcome.)

All your life you've been told not to listen to strangers. And let's face it, this is about as strange as it gets. But trust us. The only thing you have to lose is yourself.

Let's start again, properly.

Congrats! Mubarak! Badhaaee ho!

You're a vampire now. Welcome to the afterlife!

We wish we could bring you barfi and gulab jamun and other sweets and ring your neck with jasmine and rose garlands, but there's no time for that.

Besides, your neck probably smarts or itches a little. Last night is a blur. You don't remember where you slept. Your last clear memory is of that fair-skinned British tourist—you know, the Angrez who asked you for directions or advice on the best place to get "chai tea" (it made you wince, but you didn't correct them because who has time for that) or maybe how to pronounce the drink they were holding in their hand in "Indian," and you mouthed, very slowly: *CO-CA CO-LA*. Is it coming back? Good. Hold on to that—you'll remember more soon.

You're also probably panicking because you stayed out way past your curfew and your ummi is going to kill you. Good news: Technically, you're already dead! This may well undermine the ferocity of your mother's threats. (Hahaha that's a joke—it's not like something as banal as death could spare you from her wrath for breaking curfew. Please.)

Bad news: Since you have to avoid the sun (yeah, that part is true) you're probably going to be spending a lot more time at home with your parents, who are going to be muttering under their breaths about karma or destiny or how you'll likely never be a top cardiac surgeon now because no hospital schedules quadruple bypasses in the middle of the night. Lawyer is out, too, at least for now. (No one wants an advocate who can only work after sunset. The courts aren't even open then.) Fair warning, there's probably going to be a persistent parental chorus of *ay ay ay* or *tobah tobah tobah* to express their shame and definitely a lot of *but how will we ever show our faces in public again?*

You're probably wishing your last meal as a human was a mouthful of delicious biryani, instead of, say, that too-watery, slightly suspect pani puri (or whatever your preferred name for the stuffed and crisply fried dough balls that define our street food) you had at that slightly shady food stand on Juhu Beach or Sultan Bazaar. You're a local; you should've known better—there was no one in line! But you figured you'd chance it because your khala jaan's intensely spicy chicken vindaloo is nothing if not a surefire way of developing an iron gut. Foiled again.

We get it. You're confused. We were, too. Once. A long, long time ago. In a galaxy far, far away. Kidding! We're not aliens. You have to lighten up. You'll learn that a sense of humor will serve you well as you journey into your desi vampire afterlife. Just like it did when you were a regular ol' human desi.

A galaxy far, far away.

Sigh. Need a moment to reminisce about young Luke Sky-walker, our first white-boy crush, which persists even though he's old and gray and we're still unwrinkled beauties. A love like that never dies.

Sorry. Too easily distracted by visions of Luke taking us in his arms and swinging us across that giant chasm to escape advancing Stormtroopers.

Where were we? Right. We were just like you! We also wished our last human night had been spent at the Taj Lake Palace being showered with rose petals like a catered-to, overly soft tourist (who thinks they're experiencing the "real India") instead of shopping for a new lota for our nanni's water closet. Not saying that's exactly what we were doing. That's just an example. But picking the perfect brass water vessel for personal hygiene is critically important. And someone has to buy them. You may feel invincible, but FYI, you still need a lota.

No matter. You're immortal now! The world is your Koh-i-Noor (even if the British stole it). And of course you have questions, especially since your sire dumped you. He didn't wait around to, oh, you know, take any personal accountability or explain himself or maybe even apologize for violating every rule of vamp-etiquette. The bastard.

We normally like to be organized about this sort of thing, but in our experience, there are immediate burning questions every baby vamp has, so let's get a few out of the way to put your mind at ease:

Am I Dracula now? No, duh, that dude was pasty as hell. Your melanin doesn't magically disappear because of vampirism.

Do I have to give up eating dosas and chaat because drinking blood is my only sustenance? Likely, but there's still hope. [Click here to jump to What Should You Eat?]

Can I still live at home? Obviously. You're what, seventeen? Eighteen? And you're not married, right? So where else would you live? Are you trying to give your mother a heart attack? Well, another one? But don't worry, your homestay is not forever. [SEE: Hamara Ghar: New Homes for New Vamps] Once you get your vamp legs under you, you can fly.

Can I fly? Only on commercial flights, but not suggested.

Oh, wait, did you mean fly like Superman? No, obviously not—you became a vampire, not a Kryptonian.
Do I sparkle in the light? Seriously. No. The sun will kill you. Dead. Poof. Vanished. Stay out of it.
[We're also here for your specific questions. Tap to chat.]

You might be cursing your lot in life right now, but no reason to despair; it's not a tragedy. This isn't *Mother India*. What do you mean you haven't seen that movie? It's a classic. No matter, you have all the time in the world to catch up on movies you've missed. Literally. Hello rewatch of all eighty-plus Shah Rukh Khan films. Treat yourself.

Anyway, we digress. (If you dare to call King Khan a mere digression.)

This handy pamphlet is your field guide, your road map, your cookbook. We are here to separate the myth from reality.

Vampires, zindabad!

WHO ARE WE?

We're not trying to be existential here. Though, an overnight transformation into the "demonic" undead is nothing if not cause to have an extended discussion about the nature of existence, but there's time for that later. Also, please note, we take umbrage at the use of the word *demonic* or *demon*. It's marginalizing, belittling, and plain wrong. The West can keep their stratifying terminology; we come down 100 percent on the anti-species caste system side. For now, we're going to live in the realm of the literal. Figuratively speaking.

Call us Gumnaam.

That's right. Anonymous. But not *that* Anonymous. We won't dox you. Unless you really, really deserve it. We're a collective. Think of us as your cool aunties who are always ready to lend you a two-thousand rupee note. Except in this case, rupees are advice. We're not actually going to give you any money. And we're not technically your aunties. We're actually teenagers, like you. But we've been teenagers for decades, some of us even longer, so our pop-culture references are sometimes off. Don't criticize. One day you will be us.

And, no, not all desi vamps are teens. We sought you out. Every time a desi teen is sired, our *Vampersand*™ (*Connecting baby vamps to the community since 2014!*) technology pings your location and someone is sent to move you to a safe, or safer, situation. Because we can't exactly have you waking up at the Gateway of India or the Taj Mahal or the Charminar as a new baby vamp. You'd ravage the place. Now, we know what you're thinking, *I never downloaded Vampersand*™. Of course you didn't. It's spyware attached to every social media app on your phone. Clever, right? We're tech geniuses. I mean, we *are* Indian. Mark Zuckerberg keeps trying to poach our IT people. We may be bloodsuckers, but we're not fascists. Sorry, Zuck. Hard pass.

So here's an important rule. Since the 1975 Paris Accords, International Vampire Law forbids siring of individuals under the age of sixteen. But India's regulations, all of South Asia's really, go further. Desi vamps do not sire anyone under the age of eighteen. The harsh truth is that you are an underage vamp, and an Angrez British tourist likely turned you. Illegally. Ever since Brexit, there's been a surge in illegal sirings. The British Vampire Council can't seem to keep their brethren in order. There are complaints from all over Asia about Angrez vamp tourists flouting the law and taking excessive liberties. No surprise, right? They've always had a problem respecting the sovereignty of other nations. Colonialism: Sucking your country dry and leaving you to bleed out since 1600! And they call *us* vampires.

Things have gotten so out of hand that recently the Black, Asian, and Minority Ethnic (you know, BAME!) British vampires have broken off—formed their own coalition to adhere to international accords, even if their nation fails to. Dare we say it? They've partitioned themselves from the British Vampire Council because of its insistence on policies rooted in imperialism, orientalism, and an unfortunate intolerance of spicy food. You might even cross paths with a vigilante BAME vamp attempting to stop illegal sirings. They're basically badasses with darling accents.

TLDR: Gumnaam is here for you.

We came together when we realized that it's not merely the occasional drunk vamp violating the law; it's a disturbing trend. There had been no new teen vamps for decades, and the ancient ones generally keep to themselves and are, well, sort of like that one great-uncle who always asks you for help with his phone because he downloaded a new OS but also accidentally erased his data and now can't find the thousand blurry pictures he took at so-and-so's wedding.

We stepped into that vacuum! We're here to answer your questions, but more importantly, to be your community. To let you know you're not alone. Desi Vampires Saath Saath.

WHO ARE YOU?

Well, besides a newly sired vampire. You are all different religions, or maybe of no religion. You speak different languages. You're from different regions. Some of you may think your souls have been damned. Some of you may believe you are somehow unnatural.

That you're one of the ancient supernatural creatures of desi myths and faiths.

Let's take a moment to clarify.

You're not a jinn—they're shape-shifters made from smokeless fire.

You're not a rakshasa—a lot of them are shape-shifters, too, born from the breath of Brahma, warriors.

You're not a ghul—okay, they're considered undead, too, but they're more flesh-eating than bloodsucking. Additionally, they have this nifty skill of being able to take the form of the person they've most recently eaten. And they are also shape-shifters! Apparently this whole region is big on the shape-shifting. Alas, you can't do that. Would that we could.

You're not a demon. Remember, we disavow that slur and that theory. Your soul hasn't been devoured by an evil entity—like, you weren't suddenly changed into a billionaire American CEO who thinks he can run a country or a life force–sucking capitalist who flies his private jet to Davos to bemoan global warming and doesn't get the irony. You're a vampire.

You are what you always were. If you were a studious nerd in your human life, guess what? You still are! And good on you for working so hard to pass your higher secondary examination. If it feels all for naught, don't fret! We are working with the minister of education to allow you to sit for the exam, even if there's no college you can go to. Yet. If you were a morning person who loved nothing more than an early wake-up call and sunrise jog, we're so sorry. It's going to suck for a while, and not in a good way.

Vampires are creatures of the night—sunlight is not our friend. Many of us sleep or read during the day or try to organize the hell out of the kitchen spice cabinet before our mamas tell us that the seven-year-old garam masala in some cloudy plastic packet is still good, thank you very much. Or fan our daddis or nannis in the blistering heat with that vintage embroidered hand pankha they've had since before cars were invented. And we can't stress enough how critical your avoidance skills are going to be right now since you'll be in the house all day and will no doubt be dying to evade the various "special" chores your parents have set aside for you. "Beta, since you're stuck inside anyway . . ." is a refrain with which you will become painfully familiar.

We kid, but honestly, a word to the wise: If you were a no-good, useless, shameless dacoit with no respect for your elders in your old life, show yourself out. You're probably going to be worse now, and this community doesn't need any more drama or banditry.

You're an immortal. And that can be wondrous and terrifying at the same time. Your world has turned upside down. Day is night. Many you once loved will shun you. Will call you untouchable. But there is a world for you to discover—one where time is no longer your enemy. Except when it comes to all the mortals you love, who will die of old age.

Correction: Time is no longer the enemy of your personal vanity. It's still a thief. But at least it won't steal your beauty. And, darling, you are gorgeous.

WHAT SHOULD YOU EAT?
Your colonizer.

BUT YOU'RE STARVING NOW
Of course you are. See that thermos next to you? The silver one with the word *Gumnaam* superimposed over a green outline of South Asia? Drink it. Now. It's blood. You are probably both disgusted and intensely attracted to this idea. Vampire life is nothing

if not full of contradictions. So, basically, no different than human life. Trust us, drink it. And we didn't kill for this; it was donated. Voluntarily, by allies.

Just like this handy pamphlet, the thermos came to you through *Vampersand*™ and our incredible blood wallah network modeled on that of the tiffin wallahs.

[See: Relative Nutritional Values by Blood Type]

Hey, it's a six-sigma system. Tif ain't broke, don't fix it. (Don't roll your eyes. The joy of puns is forever.)

BUT, REALLY, LET'S TALK ABOUT FOOD

Many of you are vegetarian. Many of you keep halal. Some of you live life according to the principles of ahimsa: Cause no injury, do no harm. Every living thing has the spark of the divine. Regardless of your religion or to personal beliefs, it's simply a fact that, being in a desi family, you likely approached meals with the virtues of moderation—eat what is simple and natural. Unless it's a wedding, then, obviously, moderation does NOT apply.

We really hate being the bearers of bad news, especially when we're not there to soften the blow with some freshly blended mango lassis or to soothe you with a rendition of our favorite lullaby, "Chanda Hai Tu," but it's the daytime, so we regret we can't be with you. But vampires thrive by killing people. By biting them in the neck and sucking their blood. You've noticed the sharp teeth, right?

You are going to want to do this. And you're also probably fighting it. You're at war with yourself. We understand. It's not fair. You shouldn't have to deny the essence of who you are. You can subsist on animal blood, but every part of you will be drawn to human blood, and one day you'll be feeling extra ravenous and won't be able to fight it anymore. And you're going to feel guilty. Really guilty. We know. We've been there.

A brief pause for this PSA
Know this unbreakable rule: No babies. No underage individuals. No poverty-stricken. No one kicked to the curb and marginalized. Don't do what was done to you.

Remember the desi way of nutrition? Eat what is readily available, doing the least damage to the environment. Is your memory of last night becoming clearer now? What happened? Who did this to you, without your consent? Remember the British tourist? The one who looked extra pasty and probably was dressed in some kind of kurta with jeans and rubber chappals thinking they were blending in? As if.

Now do you understand? Your primary food directive: Eat colonizers first.

Here is a simple, undeniable fact: White British tourists are readily available. To be clear, we mean *British* Britishers: the Angrez. (It's not like *they* think of anyone else as British, anyway. 🙄) Have you ever been to Baga Beach during winter holidays? They're practically tripping over each other at Mackie's Saturday Night Bazaar trying to haggle a poor trinket seller to within an inch of his life. Or the Taj Mahal, during, oh, literally any season, jostling each other to get the perfect "Touch the Taj" snap and somehow forgetting that it's actually a tomb—the final resting place of a queen and her beloved. Imagine how they would react if thousands of desis showed up at Churchill's grave, hungover and complaining about Delhi belly. Obviously that's a hypothetical; we know none of you would go there unless it was to spit on the grave of the man who starved a few million Bengalis.

But we digress.

The Des is teeming with Angrez vacationers, and we suggest that, after a few moments of careful observation, you choose the one who is most obnoxious. The hooligan. The one who is drunker and ruder than everyone else. The one who is heard complaining in a loud voice about how unsanitary conditions are or how uncivilized it is for people to eat with their hands or how the British did India a favor (!) by colonizing her. You know which ones we mean. We trust your judgment.

You might be wondering how you'll go after your victims. That's actually the easy part. Turn on the charm. Promise them a deal. Show them a way to the best bhang lassi shop. Tell them you know the best beedi roller in the neighborhood. Lure them away and let your instinct take over. Have you run your tongue across your teeth yet? Notice your canines feel extra pointy? Voilà! Let your vampire flag fly!

BUT.

The absolute last thing we need is for tourist vamps to overrun India. And, yes, if you bite a human and drink some of their blood, your vampirism spreads (enzymes transferred from direct saliva-to-blood contact) and you've sired them. And, clearly, it is not sustainable if we keep siring more and more vampires who in turn diminish the human population, eventually leading to only vampires, who all starve to death. We wouldn't want that. Especially the Angrez, because then we've just recolonized South Asia with the British undead.

No. A simple rule to follow is this: If you go after one, you must fully exsanguinate them. All five liters. It will not be easy, nor should it be. You've lived your life peacefully, likely nonviolently, until this moment. Even the thought of taking a life may be abhorrent to you. After all, isn't that what landed you in this situation?

Your life violated; your choice taken away. You may not want to perpetuate the cycle. But you may not have a choice.

We cannot reiterate enough: Not completing the task, simply taking, say, one liter to sate yourself, will only ensure a new baby vamp. So you need to kill them. Dead. Think five liters is too much? We suggest working in pairs in case you're worried you won't be able to imbibe the full five. Plus, if you run into any neocolonial British vamps on holiday, you might not want to confront them by yourselves. They often roam around in marauding packs, like their football team just lost and they're out for vengeance. So pairing up is practical. Safety in numbers and all that. The *Vampersand*™ app has a convenient Find Your Friends feature, which we've already turned on for you, so come nightfall, go forth and locate your nearest new BFF. (Want to try it out? Go ahead, just don't actually, you know, go out if it's still daylight.)

One thing we want to prepare you for: Some Angrez tourists are bland AF. These are the ones raised on a national cuisine that includes greatest hits such as beans on toast and where salt is their primary seasoning. (Someone really needs to tell them it's a mineral and not a spice.) Alongside your thermos, you'll notice a small spice packet. Before you drink, we suggest shaking some of this onto your tongue; it will make the blood go down a lot easier. Feel free to change up the spices! Live your best life!

Still hearing the voice in your head saying killing is wrong? But also feeling unable to deny your bloodlust? Don't worry, we're working on a solution—a less human answer to your cravings. A number of your fellow vampires who are alumni of the illustrious Indian Institutes of Technology are working in partnership with the National University of Sciences and Technology in Pakistan to create synthetic blood. Early prototypes proved too acidic or bitter. So our scientists are working night and day (literally!) to perfect their formula. The name of this modern wonder—wait for it: Rooh Afza. It's thick. It's syrupy. It looks like blood anyway. Just don't mix up the original with our knockoff. 😜 And it will be a lot less suspicious in the Vampmarts that will be popping up soon. No need to despair. You will have options soon. But until then, exsanguination is your lifesaver. You're taking one for the team and saving your fellow desis from the truly awful fate of listening to an Angrez tourist try to pronounce *namaste* or *as-salaam alaikum* while totally screwing up the accompanying hand gestures.

MATCHMAKING

If you think being turned into a vampire is going to provide you a convenient excuse to avoid the eternally dreaded question—*Beta, when are you going to get married?*—you are about to be disappointed. Maybe you're not going to have a profile on shaadi.com, but the immortal auntie network is alive and kicking, because being undead never stopped an auntie dead set on getting everyone married.

That's right. You might be a teen vamp, wrongly sired, but there are plenty of middle-aged vamps who've been around for years—imagine having decades to hone the cheek pinch and the art of desi shade delivered like a syrupy sweet ladoo. Imagine being able to deliver the look of middle-aged auntie scorn *forever*. New vamps are feted and fawned over because you represent new blood. New projects. And what greater project is there than matchmaking.

Now, it's true. You're not marriage age. Yet. But a few years from now, in what would be your college years, you'll start getting the questions. Biodata forms with photos of eligible strangers will mysteriously appear on your bedside table or desktop. The upside? You'll never have to worry about someone photoshopping their pic to look younger. *Because we never age.* You're a matchmaker's dream! It won't even matter that you're not a doctor. Even when you're old, you'll still be young and beautiful. And trust us, if you don't find a suitable partner soon, it doesn't deter the auntie network because you're eligible . . . forever! If that thought sends you screaming to the hills, don't worry. There is an ashram in the foothills of the Himalayas, for all denominations, for young vampires who just need to get away. There are even special night runs of the toy train to get you there. We got you.

If you do happen to find your perfect match, then the desi wedding of your dreams can be yours. Unless your dream is Priyanka and Nick's wedding, in which case, sorry, there's no replicating that level of epicness. But there is a whole world of wedding designers and jewelers and florists who are ready to cater to you. Near Chandni Chowk in Delhi and Juhu Tara Road in Bombay are flourishing night markets, hidden from mortal eye by old enchantments held in place by vamp-friendly Mayong tantriks. (Warning: You're a baby vamp, so keep away from the magics. For now. They are powerful and not to be trifled with. You're already eternal; isn't that magic enough?)

Imagine the most magnificent desi wedding you've ever been to—some palace in Rajasthan maybe? A houseboat in Kerala? A colorful outdoor tent in Shimla? Thousands of vibrant flower petals laid out in ombré swirls lining the marriage path. Mehendi so intricate it looks like lace. Zaiwar dripping with gems. All of that can still be yours. If you want it. And only *if*. Yes, the aunties will cajole you, but that's their thing. You still have a choice and it's yours alone.

SO NOW WHAT?
You've got the basics. Food. Community. Marriage. Stay out of the sun. Colonialism is the true bloodsucker, etc. Now what do you do? Like, literally now.

Sidenote

If you don't want to go the traditional route of exchanging biodata through the aunties, **Vampersand** ™ has contracted with <u>TrulyMadly</u> to create a password protected vampire-only community on their site. Your life may feel like it's over, but you can still swipe left or right to your no-longer-beating heart's content.

Find your people. Tell your truth. Live your life.

We don't mean to be flip about it. Well, we do, a little. Trying to soften the blow with sarcasm and bad puns. The thing is, it's hard, living your life. It was hard before this. It's hard now. You didn't ask for this. It was thrust upon you. Maybe, given the choice, this *is* what you would have chosen. Immortality is a hell of a drug. But the fact is you weren't given the choice. And now all you have left is to keep living. Move on. Or find your sire and exact revenge by leaving them to burn in the sun. Stake through the heart and decapitation work, too. So, really, make the best of it, however you choose. We support your choices.

And you do *still* have choices. Your future is not yet written. You have the power to do that. In fact, maybe more so than ever.

Real talk? You still have feelings from before. They don't disappear. Remember what we said? You're not a demon. You're still you. Only more blood-lusting and immortal. But at the core, you are what you always were. And this moment, right now, could be terrifying. And heartbreaking. And enraging. Even if the potential of tomorrow is endless. Even if tomorrow you feel free and can live a life unfettered. Today, something was taken from you that you were not yet ready to give. Family and friends. Loves, old or new. Dreams. All of that will change. Much of it will die. Time marches forward even when you've stopped. Where once you might have felt surrounded, at times suffocated, by your noisy, irritating, nosy, beautiful, loving family, now you are alone. No longer human. Reviled and misunderstood by many. But you are not unloved. You are here. And so are we. We see you. We believe in you. You are enough.

When you leave this place, step out into the late-evening quiet for the first time, reborn. Take in the glittering, crumbling streets around you. Look into the ink-black night. It's dark. And full of diamonds.

And you, dear one, are made of stardust.

VAMPIRISM
Or But Is It Possible That Vampires Are Real?

Zoraida Córdova &
Natalie C. Parker

During the good ol' dark ages and beyond, it was surprisingly easy to mistake a disease for a supernatural affliction. Vampire stories and disease have a close relationship. A bunch of people got sick and died? There is a vampire among us! The body of young Vania didn't decompose during a particularly cold winter? She must be a vampire! Fetch the stake before she spreads her vampirism! A rare disease we now know as porphyria was once known as the "vampire syndrome" because anyone who had it might develop a sensitivity to light and grow pale. They might even crave blood. In the same vein (lol), victims of tuberculosis and the bubonic plague might have been so close to death that they were buried (or thrown into mass graves). Later, not actually being dead, when they slowly rose from their graves, witnesses might claim to have seen a vampire! Samira has taken this idea of vampirism as a disease one step further and paired it with colonialism. If a disease is the presence of something that attacks the body, then colonizers certainly count! (We're looking at you, British Empire!) (Okay, okay, okay, we're looking at U.S. forefathers, too.) In that way, vampires are definitely, 100 percent real.

In what other way might you interpret the metaphor of the vampire?

IN KIND

Kayla Whaley

THE SHADY OAK GAZETTE

Local Father Played Role in Handicapped Daughter's Tragic Death

During Tuesday's record-breaking snowstorm, Grant Williams, 53, reported his teenage daughter's death to police and admitted his role in her passing. The severely disabled girl, Grace Williams, 17, had been wheelchair-bound since birth and was unable to eat, breathe or urinate without medical assistance.

Mr. Williams, a single father and science teacher at Robertson County High, confessed to police that he had administered lethal quantities of morphine early Tuesday evening. He told police his daughter's suffering "had become unbearable" and that she "deserved to finally have some peace."

100

Williams led police to his home, where he had initially intended to bury his daughter before the weather turned. When they arrived, the body was missing from his yard. Police believe wolves living on the heavily wooded property carried off her body before Williams and the police arrived around midnight. By that time, any tracks had been buried by the historic blizzard along with the rest of North Georgia.

"Grace's short life and sudden death is a tragedy for her family and our community, but we can find solace in the fact that she has been saved from a lifetime of suffering," Sheriff Darryl White said in a press conference Thursday afternoon. "We will remember Grace for her courage and her inspiring presence."

Citing the extenuating circumstances surrounding Grace's death, police have decided not to press charges at this time.

My "death" was a gentle affair. Quiet. Rare snow had fallen all day and through the previous night, collecting on pines, willows, magnolias, southern branches unaccustomed to bearing more weight than violent-bright pollen or summer's full bore. As day sallowed into dusk, limbs began snapping in a staggered cascade, like firecrackers, or blood vessels bursting. Above me, my father cried. His tears fell on my face and rolled down my own dry cheeks. I clenched my eyes shut. Listened hard to the sharp breaks in the distance. Felt my heart's jagged beat way up in my ears. My chest refused rising. He cried and cried. He didn't wipe my face. I couldn't wipe my face. The backup generator buzzed. Another branch broke, louder this time. One Mississippi. Two Mississippi. Crack. One Mississippi. Two Missi—crack. One—

The sun rose fast and miraculously hot. At fifty degrees the forest floor had turned to muddy slush. By eighty degrees the ground was straw and red clay once more, the only signs of the unprecedented snowfall being a few zones still left powerless and the half-shouted *can you believe?* greetings from one driveway to the next. He must have planned to bury me, but the snow threw him. Seanan said there'd been a shovel propped against the trunk when she'd found me, a few aborted attempts at holes clustered in front of the magnolia's wide base. Did he case our property in advance, searching for the perfect spot? Or did he know instinctively that he would settle my body snug under the centuries-old tree farthest from the house?

This is how I know my father was flustered: He left my body off-center, angled carelessly askew. Maybe he considered waiting until the melt and thaw to finish. But if he waited, he would have had to carry me back to the house, and where would he have stored me? My bed? The unfinished basement that would surely flood with runoff? The garage that, despite poor insulation, would still be too warm to stop me rotting? No. I needed a grave, and he needed help providing one.

He improvised.

This is how I know my father was desperate: He believed his freezing, shaking hands when he couldn't find a pulse. Probably didn't even think twice before leaving me there and heading for the station.

Seanan didn't need to check my wrist for life, of course. She could smell it on me.

My coma broke like a fever as soon as she latched on to the inside of my thigh. The femoral artery, surrounded as it is by meat and fat, provides the best anchor. You can really clamp down, which means you can suck faster, which means there's less chance the body'll realize it should be dead before the venom can finish recoating the circulatory system. Wrist for sampling, throat for draining, thigh for turning.

I felt her *pull* the blood from my body, the sudden lurch and sway how I imagine a headrush must feel when standing too quickly, only amplified by fangs and intention and finality. Seanan couldn't have known that my heart, like all my muscles, was so much weaker than in most humans. It couldn't pump fast enough for her venom to flood me back to living. Not without some encouragement.

Everything was lurid and pure. No thought, only bright pain and a sense of falling.

Then heat. A mouth full—so much more than a mouthful—of something thick as molasses. The taste of moonlight and brass. Tongue trying to find purchase on teeth or palette, unmoored. I had no body, only this mouth and this liquid mass filling, rushing. I gagged. My throat opened and the flood drained downward. I had swallowed so little in recent years, using a feeding tube instead, but muscle memory took over. My mouth emptied, my stomach bloated with blood and bile, and I lost consciousness again.

♦

"You shouldn't be here," Seanan says behind me. I don't startle at her sudden appearance like I might have before, back when she was the strange loner girl at church and I was the awkward high schooler parked at the end of a pew. We'd never spoken, not once in the three years since she'd shown up alone and aloof one Sunday morning. News of her spread quickly those first weeks, more rumor than anything, as it does in a small Southern congregation where anything new or different is gossip-worthy. She was an orphan, or a runaway. She drank, or dealt drugs. She'd had a baby, or an abortion. Everyone had a theory, all of which painted a ghastly portrait of sin and depravity. Everyone was so focused on their imagined backstories that they missed (or ignored) the obvious: her piety.

I watched her during services. Her devotion wasn't ostentatious in the least—hell, she didn't even sing during worship as far as I could tell—but something in the way she held her hands in her lap, head slightly bowed, her whole body relaxed and utterly at peace, utterly at *home*, convinced me she knew more of divinity than any of us could ever hope to claim. I'd been too afraid to ever greet her. And it *was* fear I felt, not intimidation or embarrassment, but a yearning sort of fright. I suppose that's a contradiction in terms. How can you be attracted and repelled at the same time?

"We talked about this, Grace," she says now, her disappointment palpable as she steps up beside me. "You shouldn't have come again."

My de facto gravesite had looked dispassionately somber on the news the other night. Dozens of people from town had gathered beneath the magnolia where, one week earlier, I had lain in two feet of snow in my blue flannel nightgown, dead to the world. They'd brought lilies and carnations and violets and teddy bears—so many teddy bears, some still with price tags punched in their ears. Gifts for the dead girl. A few of the attendees had carried signs with handwritten messages framing grainy photos of my face: REST IN PEACE or DANCING WITH THE ANGELS or HER FATHER CALLED HER HOME. Our neighbor, a foully sweet woman who insisted on calling me Gracie, had carried that last one. It was my favorite of the signs, as if God Himself had rung a dinner bell and I had dutifully zipped on up to Heaven. As if my earthly father hadn't pumped a shit ton of morphine into my feeding tube instead of my dinner.

At the end of the memorial everyone had been given a cheap white candle, the disposable kind with a paper guard to stop wax dripping on your hand. The vigil had translated beautifully on film: warm pinpricks of light illuminating dark silhouettes against a bruise-blue sky. I'd watched the coverage in Seanan's small living room on mute, shapes moving without sound, a choreography of mourning. One last pan of the crowd had shown a line of people waiting to hug my father, his eyes rimmed red from all the crying.

There is no light now. Seanan says I'll be able to withstand the sun in fifty years or so, once I acclimate. *Not so very long*, she'd said. Shadowed by the new moon, the teddy bears look like alive, watchful things. And the flowers, half a wilt from rotted already, smell gray somehow. I imagine, not for the first time, how quickly they'd catch fire with help from a stray spark. The whole forest might burn before anyone noticed.

Seanan turns away from the display and faces me. "We should go, Grace." It's only been a few weeks, but already I'm learning to read her expressions. Her arms are crossed, head cocked, like she's going for stern, but her eyes give her away: She's worried.

"Have you seen him?" I ask.

"What?"

"Have you seen him?" I repeat slowly, as if to a child. It's churlish, but I do nothing to modulate my tone. "At church? At work? Anywhere."

She sighs, an artificial sound that only draws attention to the prior stillness of her chest. "Why?" she asks.

"This isn't a trick question, Seanan. Have you seen him or not?"

She's dressed for the graveyard shift as we speak: black pants pressed to pleated perfection, a crisp white dress shirt, a black velvet blazer, and her signature ruby suspenders. The occasional flashes of red contrast handsomely with the green felt that lines her card table. She's been running games since the Irish pubs of her youth, seedy backrooms filled with loud men, warm beer, and blue-tinged smoke drifting like fog. Not much different, to hear her tell it, from the casino where she now spends nights dealing blackjack and Texas Hold'em.

"There's nothing for you here," Seanan says gently, reaching for my hand. Her Irish lilt grows heavier as her voice gets quieter. She sounds like a lullaby on the wind. "If you wanted closure or time to grieve, that'd be one thing. But coming here every night, asking about him all the time . . . It's not healthy."

I snatch my hand away, turn my head toward the scent of dying flowers. After a moment, I say, "How many people have you turned?"

"Pardon?"

"How many? Surely I'm not the first."

It's probably a rude question. I'm not well-versed in vampire etiquette yet. The silence thickens, and right when I've decided she won't answer, she says, "A handful over the years. Only in situations like yours."

"Freak blizzards and morphine overdoses?"

"Murder." She speaks plainly, a mere description, but the word pierces through me as surely as her fangs did in the snow. "Even then, turning them is a last resort. I don't make the choice unless the only other option is . . . well. I figure an unnatural life is better than an unnatural death." She shrugs. "Sometimes I'm wrong."

"What, they don't *want* to be saved?"

I face her again. She's staring at the base of the magnolia, too. Past it, maybe. I wonder who turned her all those centuries ago. I wonder if she wanted to be saved.

"That's the thing," she says. "One man's salvation is another's damnation." Her words linger between us, almost tangible in the cool night air. She kneels so we're at the same eye level, which feels condescending somehow, though I know she means to be comforting. "They could still press charges."

I stiffen. "They won't."

"They could."

"If they wanted to arrest him, they would have done it as soon as he walked into that station saying he killed his daughter. But they didn't. They let him go home." My voice rises, not quite to yelling, but the dark has a way of amplifying everything. "There was no police tape around the house. No handcuffs. No questioning the neighbors. They patted his back and offered their condolences. They let him stand at this makeshift memorial and *cry*."

My hands hurt. Why do my hands hurt? I look down to find curled fists. I've dug bloody crescents into my palms. I'm still not used to this new strength. Vampirism is almost the exact mirror of the disease I had in life, strengthening instead of weakening my muscles. I tried to lift my head when I woke after turning and nearly snapped my neck from the utter lack of resistance. I still can't walk, of course. No amount of increased strength will ever stretch out tendons strung taut as tightrope from years of disuse, and thank God for that.

I don't think I could've handled losing that much of myself.

I swipe my palms on my jeans. Blood seeps into the fabric's dense weave, spreading from thread to thread.

"You have infinity ahead of you," Seanan says. "Lifetime upon lifetime. Would it help to focus on that instead? The future?"

She looks so hopeful. Three hundred years old and still her face is gentle and lovely as dawn. How has she stayed so warm for so long when my entire being is frozen solid?

"His original plan was to turn off my oxygen, you know. Said that was the easiest option, just flick a switch and let nature take its course."

"Why didn't he?" Seanan asks.

I turn my palms to the night's meager light: healed, the stain on my jeans the only proof that I can still bleed.

"He thought it would be too hard for him." My voice comes out steady, if distant, like I'm hearing myself from another room. "He planned to let me slowly suffocate to death but didn't think he'd survive it. Morphine was kinder, he said, like going to sleep. 'Just putting my little girl to sleep one more time.'

"Once the drug took hold, I couldn't move. Couldn't lift my hand or turn my head. Every inch of me felt impossibly heavy, like my veins were filled with lead. I couldn't speak, either. Couldn't scream, although maybe that was more panic than anything. The only thought that made it through the haze and the terror was . . ." I take a deep, ragged breath and choke on the burn in my useless lungs. I keep forgetting breathing's optional now. "I thought, *I have to tell him something's wrong. He has to get help.*"

Seanan reaches tentatively for my hand again. I don't pull away. She rubs her thumb over the life line on my palm, where a few minutes earlier there had been four bloody half-moons.

"That's when he told me what he'd done," I say. "When I couldn't do anything with the panic and confusion and rage and fear except close my eyes and try to be anywhere else. That's when he told me."

We stay like that for a few minutes: hands clasped, her kneeling in the red clay, me in this rinky-dink manual chair Seanan stole from the casino that hurts every joint and muscle in my body. Over her shoulder, the teddy bears watch.

"Sunday morning, front row," she says softly, and I realize she's answering my earlier question. "His name was first on the prayer requests. Deacon Bell asked God to grant him strength and comfort in the face of such a terrible loss."

I stare at the pile of tokens left for the dead girl. She feels so far away. Maybe the wolves really did take her. Maybe she fed a whole den of them, kept them warm through the snowstorm. Maybe she's running with the wolves even now.

"What will you do?" Seanan asks.

"What any good daughter would do," I say. "Repay his kindness."

THE ATLANTA JOURNAL-CONSTITUTION

"Mercy Killing" Sparks National Conversation About Caregiver Supports

Following the recent death of Grace Williams, 17, at the hands of her father, Grant Williams, 53, a conversation around the lack of support available for caregivers of severely impaired children has occurred. Grace Williams, who was born with a degenerative neuromuscular disease, was wheelchair-bound and needed intensive, round-the-clock care. Her father, raising and caring for the teenager alone since his ex-wife filed for divorce a decade ago, cited the enormous burden as one of the reasons he decided to enact what many are calling "an act of mercy."

"More than anything, I wanted Grace to have some peace. That was the main thing. Her life was constant misery, and no one can bear to watch their little girl go through that," Williams said recently in an interview with Atlanta's 11Alive News. "But people don't realize how hard it is to be the sole source of care. Trying to hold down a job, put food on the table, *and* take care of Grace? It was exhausting. Unsustainable."

He has talked publicly in recent weeks about the stunning lack of support available to caregivers of children like Grace. While some organizations offer financial help for medical equipment and doctors' visits, there is little in the way of emotional support or respite services.

A few disability-focused advocacy groups have condemned Williams's actions and the public response. "Our sympathies are with Grace Williams, whose life was senselessly and cruelly taken," the spokesperson for All Access, an Atlanta-based nonprofit, told the *AJC* in an email.

"It's criminal, what we put parents through," Williams continued in the 11Alive interview. "Just criminal to expect these parents to sacrifice everything for these poor kids and get no help whatsoever. It's not right."

Williams is reportedly looking into creating a foundation in his daughter's name to address these issues, though he has not yet made an official announcement.

My room tastes stale. The air is heavy on my tongue, like it's already clumping into forgotten dust. Everything is exactly as I left it. Desk a messy pile of books and journals and loose-leaf papers. Apple-cinnamon candle on the windowsill. Humidifier half-filled with water. He didn't even bother to make my bed. The comforter is bunched at the foot, sheets rumpled. You can see the shape of my body on the mattress, a permanent depression from years of sleeping in the same spot and the same position night after night. The sight makes me feel more exposed than if I were naked.

"I'm gonna need some help, if you don't mind." I nod toward my chair sitting in the corner. He also hasn't bothered to unplug the charger, which works in my favor. Probably the battery would have been fine since no one's been using it all this time, but seeing the steady green light that means *fully charged* is a relief nonetheless.

"Of course," Seanan says. "Tell me what you need."

The transfer from awful replacement chair to my trusty friend is smooth. Lifting me is nothing for Seanan, my weight negligible even

110

with the newly added muscle density. She sets me down carefully and waits for instruction. That she doesn't assume what I need, that letting me lead is apparently instinctive to her . . . "Thank you," I say.

We pack a few changes of clothes, some books, my pillows. The rest I leave. It's all replaceable, this dead girl's stuff. With that done, we move into the dining room. All there is to do now is wait. I was worried he might beat us here since he usually comes home straight from work. Well, usually *came* home straight from work, but that was when he had to be here for me. Who knows what his schedule is like now? Maybe he heads to the bar or a friend's house or wherever else people go who don't have somewhere to be. We might have hours to kill.

Headlights glare through the window. Tires crunch gravel on the drive.

Then again, we might not.

"You're sure?" Seanan asks as the car door slams.

Slow, steady footsteps outside. Patient footsteps rat-tatting a worry-free rhythm up the front stairs.

My heart doesn't beat anymore, but I can feel its presence, a great hunk of gristly meat behind a cage of bone. How will I know when I'm scared or excited if my heart can't skip a beat? The doorknob turns and a sharp, bright *something* shivers through me. I'm cold. No more blood pumping to keep the limbs warm. No more sunshine to knock away the chill, not for now. Maybe warmth is overrated. Cold can be bracing, invigorating. Cold can awaken or numb. Cold is the temperature of preservation.

At a certain point, cold can burn.

The door swings wide.

"Hello, Daddy."

When he faints, the crack of skull on hardwood is not unlike that of frozen tree limbs snapping outside a snow-dark window.

♦

He comes to as soon as Seanan leans close, his caveman brain recognizing the danger she represents even from the depths of unconsciousness. His arms flail in their attempt to push away from her, but she just calmly backs toward me. He shoots a frantic glance at the open door.

"Absolutely not," I say. "Not that you'd get far anyway."

"You're dead," he says. He manages to sit himself up against the wall, legs bent toward his chest, as though that will protect him.

"More or less, yeah." My voice is level, purposefully casual. I make sure to lay my hands flat on my lap, fingernails safely away from skin.

"You're dead," he says again. "You're dead. I know you're dead, I ki—" He snaps his mouth shut so hard he bites his cheek. I know because I can smell the blood. Strange, but the tang smells familiar and uniquely him. Maybe my memory stored the scent from shallow cuts and nosebleeds over the years without my noticing.

"You what, Dad? Finish that sentence. What did you do?"

Seanan hovers between us, guarding me from him, or him from me, I'm not sure. Where her expression was all gentleness under the faint starlight filtered through bare branches, now she looks every bit the predator. Dad's attention turns to her, too. An easier conundrum to cope with, I guess.

"You're that loner girl from church," he says, pointing like she's some circus animal smashing into his house unannounced. "The one with no parents. Who are you?"

"Oh, I have parents," she says, laying her Irish accent on thick as gravy on biscuits. "It's just they died back in 1768, you see."

I can practically see his mind trying to understand what's happening. He's not frightened so much as woefully confused. Like maybe he's sleeping. Or concussed from hitting his head when he fainted. I want him present, grounded in the terrible reality of this moment, not drifting where his mind might save him with dreams of hallucinations and easy outs.

"Seanan," I say, eyes still on my father. His beard is growing out. He usually shaves daily to avoid even the suggestion of a five o'clock shadow. The hair is patchy. I wonder why he's stopped shaving. Some strange display of mourning? Guilt? Or maybe he just wants a concrete reminder that he's alive, still moving forward in time.

Seanan raises a brow. The angle of that arch says, *Whatever you need*. I hope she can read me as well as I think I can read her.

"Are you hungry, Seanan?"

Slowly, she shrugs. "I could eat."

I spread my arms. The gesture is so much more expansive than I could have managed in life, my arms lifting off the armrest and swinging wide from the shoulder. It feels wrong. "What kind of host would Grant here be if he didn't offer you some refreshment?"

She stares at me hard for a moment, and I can hear her voice from earlier: *You're sure?*

I glance at my outstretched wrist once. *Wrist for sampling*. She nods, then moves so fast even I can hardly track her.

Dad screams as soon as Seanan's teeth break skin. The sound claws up and down my spine. I've never heard him scream like this. I vaguely remember some yelling matches before my mother left, but I was so small then. They might not even be real memories, just arguments I've imagined to fill in the gaps. This is different. Primal. I have a sudden, desperate need to make his pain stop.

I clench my fists and let Seanan drink.

After what can't have been more than a few seconds, she pulls his arm from her mouth. She's a tidy drinker, only a red sheen to her lips, like lightly tinted gloss.

My stomach turns and I gag.

She's next to me in an instant. "Hey, you're okay. I'm right here." She rubs slow circles on my back as I dry heave. She pulls back my hair, holds a hand against my forehead to stop me giving myself whiplash. I'm not used to this body, this strength. I'm not used to any of this.

"I can't," I whine around a mouthful of acid.

"What the *fuck are you?*" Dad screams from far away. Another room, maybe, or another lifetime.

Seanan keeps holding me while I rock and sob. Vaguely, I notice there's dark, dark red on my hands after I wipe my face. Blood. We cry blood, I guess. How haven't I cried before now?

"Fucking monster!" Dad shouts.

"Back off," Seanan says above me.

He's closer now. I can . . . I can smell the wound. His blood. It smells warm.

He's kneeling now. His breath on my face. Rancid heat. "What the fuck did you do to my daughter, you goddamn demon!"

He reaches for my face with his good hand. The unbitten one. Before he can blink, I snatch his arm down and wrench it backward at the elbow. The bone strains underneath his taut skin. Pearlescent, almost. He doesn't scream this time.

"No," I say. My voice is quiet but no longer level. Even in that one syllable, that tiny perfect word, I hear every biting winter wind that has ever seared skin raw. "You don't get to touch me. You don't get to pretend to care for me."

"Grace, I—"

I twist harder. He gasps.

"What did she do to me? She saved me. She found me and she saved me. What did you do, Dad? Let's talk about that, shall we? Let's talk about what you did."

He's crying again. Tears well and pool and fall down his face. I remember how those tears felt on my own face. How they rolled salty tracks down my skin. I twist harder.

Seanan touches my shoulder. "Grace," she says, "you don't have to do this, okay? Don't do anything you'll regret. Please."

I stare at him hard. "What if I'll regret letting him live?"

She kneels next to me. This time, the motion feels like support, like love.

"Then you kill him."

Dad keens. I've never heard such a sound. Pure, all-consuming fear. It's the sound I would have made as my heart slowed to stopping if I'd been able.

"All I ever did was care for you," he says. "All I ever wanted was to help you. To save you. You deserved mercy."

Suddenly, I know exactly what he deserves. More importantly, I know what I deserve.

"I believe you, Dad. Truly I do." I loosen my grip on his arm, watch the desperation on his face slide tentatively toward hope. I lean in and whisper, "But murder isn't mercy."

I lunge.

USA TODAY

Alleged "Mercy Killing" Victim Alive, Releases Video Statement

Grace Williams, the teenager believed to be the victim of a "mercy killing," has revealed in a recently released video that she is alive after her father's attempted murder.

The video, which multiple news outlets have independently authenticated, shows Grace Williams describing the events surrounding her presumed death. "My father did try to murder me," she says to the camera. "But thankfully, a friend found me where he'd left my body in the snow, mistakenly believing I had already died."

Ms. Williams says that she is currently recovering with said friend in an undisclosed location and that she is not planning to return to her hometown as she fears for her safety.

"My father didn't think my life was worth living so he tried to end that life. He believed he had succeeded. Without my friend's luck in finding me, he would have," she continues. "But he was wrong on two counts. One, he didn't kill me. And two, my life was *always* worth living."

In the media coverage following Ms. Williams's alleged death, Grant Williams was portrayed as a devoted and long-suffering caregiver. The attempted murder was widely called a "mercy killing" and no charges were ever filed.

"There was nothing merciful about my father's actions," Ms. Williams says toward the end of the five-minute video. "I hope everyone who called them such will think about why they could ever believe murder to be a kindness instead of a monstrosity. Why were you so easily convinced that my life meant nothing? Why did no one ask what my life meant *to me*?"

Ms. Williams states that this will be her last communication and urges authorities not to search for her. As she is still a minor, however, a search is indeed underway.

Grant Williams has not issued a response to his daughter's revelations, though he was reported to have been rushed to a local hospital last night with what authorities are calling "mysterious injuries."

A source close to the Robertson County Sheriff's Office said charges of attempted murder against Mr. Williams are "possible but unlikely without the cooperation of Grace Williams." Meanwhile, an online petition calling for Mr. Williams to be removed from his teaching position has reached 50,000 signatures. We will update this story as it evolves.

THE MAGICAL CURE
Or Embodying the Vampire Myth

Zoraida Córdova &
Natalie C. Parker

A good vampire is hard to kill. There are methods, of course: stakes, beheading, sunlight, holy water, a werewolf bite. Sometimes silver will do it. But for the most part, vampires are both impermeable to harm and quick to heal. They possess superspeed, strength, and heightened senses and, in some iterations, can even fly. In many cases, transitioning from human to vampire can save your life à la little Claudia in *Interview with the Vampire*. In this way, vampirism is imagined as a cure for a mortal illness (like the plague!) or a fatal wound. But this is a slippery slope, and we might also see vampirism imagined as a cure for all illnesses and disabilities in a way that alienates the people for whom chronic illness and disability is a part of their identity. Magical cures suggest that the only way to live with disease or disability is to always wish for something else. Kayla's story is in conversation with that very idea—Grace is transformed into a vampire, and while she receives some of those enhanced magical senses, her body remains her body. Being yourself, even when undead, is pretty powerful.

If you were turned into a vampire, what is one thing about yourself you wouldn't change?

VAMPIRES NEVER SAY *DIE*

Zoraida Córdova & Natalie C. Parker

BRITTANY

I honestly don't know why I did it.

There aren't many things I can say that about anymore. I am not impulsive. Perhaps I used to be, but temerity is a luxury of youth. Of mortality.

I have neither.

Maybe that's why I joined Instagram. To feel a connection to the things I've lost. Or maybe I just wanted a hobby and Instagram seemed as good an option as any other. Better, because all I had to do was pick a name and I could be whomever, whatever I wanted to be.

Perhaps I wanted to find a place where I wasn't in charge. Where I wasn't Brittany Nicolette Fontaine, Vampire Premier of New York City. Where every moment of every day wasn't a consideration of power. I suppose it's naive to think there is no power to be found on Instagram, but it certainly wasn't mine, and I enjoyed that for a while.

In spite of being unable to fully participate in the generation of the selfie, I find a vicarious kind of joy in consuming the curated lives of others. There is something soothing in knowing that none of us is exactly what we say. The Brittany I share online is not real, and the truly wondrous thing about this era of social media is that no one expects that she is anything but a myth. A fabrication based on something real. A layer of Chantilly lace over porcelain, sun-starved skin. Like my watery reflection in the tall windows of my apartment.

I step up close, until I am only a breath away from the glass. Even then, the girl who stares back at me is blurred, a series of impressions diffused by the light that sifts up from the city beneath me like cold, pale flames. Beyond a stubborn slip of trees that obscures the roads below, the river winks past. It is a ribbon of darkness trapped between pervasive rows of yellow traffic lights that grow up like crops. A space between spaces.

Before this moment, I'd been happy to exist in that liminal space between what is real and what is not, between what is human and what is not. I enjoyed the freedom I found in constructing a reflection of myself in images of what I saw in the world around me, but looking back now, I can see that I made a fatal error in judgment.

Her name is Theolinda, or @YoSoyTheolinda, to most.

I unlock my phone and thumb over the screen until I'm staring at my Instagram direct messages. Only three people contact me this way. The first is Imogen. I still don't know how she found my account, but she is the youngest of my petits crocs and usually the first to adapt to changing technologies and social patterns. The second, a man who goes by Brad, tosses out generic messages like fishing lures that I never answer because I do not care that he's single and thinks we're soul mates. We are not.

The third is Theo. Her user icon is an image of a crescent moon morphing into a brilliant scarlet flower. I select her name and our conversation spills down the little screen. We've been talking this way since she was barely fifteen and took notice of the one and only selfie I've ever posted. We didn't always talk for long, but after an initial period of pleasantries and the kinds of social exchanges one might expect of a child and an immortal elder, our conversations took a surprising turn.

They mattered.

We discussed life and loss and change. We discussed what it meant to have influence and be influenced. We discussed power and bodies and death.

And then, suddenly, out of the galactic blue, this.

Theo's last message to me perches at the top of the screen. It's an image of a girl in a white dress standing in a dark tunnel. It's blurred, as though the camera gasped at a beam of light, but I can see her light brown skin, her long, black curls tipped over one shoulder, her lips painted in the deepest red.

Across the bottom of the image a message is written in curling silver script:

Who's that girl? Find out tomorrow.
The Root & Ruin (basement lounge) @ 10 p.m.

I hadn't responded at the time. For an indulgent moment, I convinced myself that meeting Theo in real life would be quite beautiful. Despite the vast and considerable difference in our ages, to say nothing of our circumstances, I thought meeting her would be like seeing the sun. And I very much wanted to see the sun once more.

But as I dress in layers of silver and black and pink and draw heavy black lines around my green eyes, as I paint my lips in the perfect shade of winter blackberries, I return to my senses. Theolinda is a girl and a child. She only knows me through a series of desolate cityscapes I've ironically tagged #selfie and through the few words we've shared. She has no idea who I truly am, and learning will only horrify her.

The friendship we've built together is gossamer in the wind, a lovely dream I have enjoyed for too long already. Any longer and it will become a danger to both of us.

With a distant squeeze of regret, I open a new message and type:

Stuck in traffic. Might not make it. Sorry.

♦

THEO: omg love this filter! where'd you find it?
BRITTANY: it's my vampire filter lol
THEO: i know you're joking but do you ever think about what it would be like to live forever?
BRITTANY: sounds lonely

♦

THEOLINDA
"I honestly don't know how I'm going to outdo myself," I say to the empty room.

The Root & Ruin basement lounge is my masterpiece. Truly. Black velvet curtains hang from the wall. The mahogany bar, which was previously covered in cobwebs that rivaled those in my attic, gleams with polish and lavender-scented Mistolin. Although, maybe cobwebs would have worked thematically.

Oh well, there's always next year.

A guy in a black-leather cowboy hat, a velvet vest, and jeans so ripped they don't even count as pants walks in. "Hey, I'm DJ Hex Marks the Spot."

I bite my lower lip to stop from laughing. My eyes must be

ZORAIDA CÓRDOVA & NATALIE C. PARKER

bugging out and I can't afford to mess up the eyeliner that took me three tries to apply evenly. Old guys are so gross. "Mm-hmm. So that's not just your handle. Okay okay okay. I'm Theo. You can set up near the bar. Remember. No pop. No '70s or '80s. Unless it's exclusively Led Zeppelin." I bite the tip of my pointed nails. My gel manicure is white, but the end of each nail looks as though it was dipped in blood. Hey, I thought it was clever, even if obvious. "Although I'm not really sure what Brittany listens to. She likes my music updates, but usually the lady-rock variety—You know what? You're the pro."

When DJ I Will Not Ever Repeat His Real Name flashes a smile, his teeth seem too white and sharp for a second. "I *am* the pro. Imogen recommended me, right?"

"Yeah?"

"Then I gotchu, baby bird."

I laugh nervously. "You do *that*, and I'll go make sure we have ice."

I unlock my phone and shoot off a series of messages. I had to invite my friend Miriam from school because her dad owns the club. But she's nursing strep throat she caught from Andy Jackson III. It was extremely hard explaining to Miriam who this surprise birthday party was for. She was all like, "Vampires are *so* 2005." I have a very detailed scrapbook of the time we went to the *Twilight Saga: Breaking Dawn – Part 2* midnight premiere from fifth grade that says she once thought otherwise. I tell her to feel better, then pull up her dad's last text. I assure Mr. Greenspan that everything is under control and the adult doorman and bartender have arrived (they haven't). But it's early. Mr. Greenspan owns four nightclubs and bars on the Lower East Side. The Root & Ruin is the least popular one, which is probably why he let me have the basement bar, which is pretty much unfinished and has that New York smell of cement, mold, and a dash of pee. But black velvet fabric stapled to the walls makes it look like the vampire den I dreamed of Brittany having.

I rip open a bag of plastic vampire teeth and spread them around the bar. As the DJ dims the lights, some of them glow in the dark. The bartender arrives—a surly guy who looks like Oscar Isaac if Oscar Isaac had been dipped in the same vat of radioactive whatever that turned the Joker's hair green.

"You the boss, niña?"

"Only my dad calls me *niña*," I say, and he laughs. "I'm Theo."

He shakes my hand. My dad always taught me to look someone in the eye and never be the first person to let go. I wish I could implement that at my school with teachers who seem to look through me. Then again, my dad comes from the generation of immigrants who think that everything is fair if you just work hard enough to die for it, even if you're undervalued and underpaid. Me? I have dreams. Big ones. A solid handshake can't hurt, I guess.

"Listen, the doorman flaked," Latino Joker says, scratching the tattoo on his left bicep. "Want me to call Mr. Greenspan?"

"Actually . . ." I hold up my phone. My dad also taught me to never lie. Never steal. Never sin. I failed my catechism for a reason. But there are some things my Ecuadorian dad can't teach me. Not in this city, not in my school, and definitely not in this bar. "I was just messaging with Mr. Greenspan and he said everything's cool."

With that settled, I turn my attention to the finishing touches. A rusty candelabra hangs precariously from the low ceiling. It looks like a safety hazard, something out of a haunted mansion. Using a step ladder, I plunk battery-operated tea lights into each candle holder. When I'm finished, I step back. The ceiling makes a strange groaning sound, and I hold my breath for a second, waiting for it to come crashing down. But it's all good. The DJ kicks off the music—something with heavy bass and deep guitar.

"*Now* I've outdone myself," I say.

"You sure have," says a young woman I recognize right away. The kind of ice-blond hair that reminds me of a cotton swab. She's got killer cheekbones and lips that would make most makeup tutorial accounts jealous. Her dress is all lace, like on the cover of this really old record my mom has of some woman named Stevie Nicks. There's a white lace choker around her slender throat, and she walks like someone who is used to owning a room.

That's the pose I've tried so hard to capture in my photos. Sure, I get four thousand likes just standing with the Brooklyn Bridge in the background, but I definitely don't *own* anything like Imogen does. I will, someday.

"You must be Imogen!" I say. I clear my throat and lower my voice. "I'm Theo. Glad you got my invite. We're just getting started."

"Aren't you . . . adorable." She's about five foot seven, just shy of being taller than me. Her eye color looks a little unreal, a marbled blue and hazel. My whole body tenses when she gets five inches from me. I have the immediate instinct to take several steps back. But you know what? I've gone to Catholic school and private school my whole life. I have seen meaner, richer, bitchier girls, and I stay put.

I spin in my black baby-doll dress. It's a little over-the-top, and tighter than the cheap online picture promised. But I was going for more of a Wednesday Addams look. "Thanks. I like the look. Very retro."

For the first time, I notice another group of women standing around us. How did they get in so quietly? Three brunettes and three redheads with skin so white it looks like it could glow in the dark, like the fake teeth on the bar. One of the girls picks up a pair and jams it into her mouth. She nearly doubles over with laughter.

"I'm curious," Imogen says, tapping her finger on her chin. "How did you and Brit meet?"

It's hard to explain to some people that I met one of best friends on the internet. My mom doesn't understand why I spend so much time on my phone. Why I can't just have friends in the neighborhood or at school, other than Miriam. There's always been something that doesn't click for me. It's like looking at photos of myself might help me figure out who I really am. I know some things: I'm the daughter of Ecuadorian immigrants. I'm an A student. I'm going to take the world by storm someday, somehow. And when I love people, I will ride or die. That's why I have such few friends.

Brittany was a happy accident. Sometimes she'll say the things I'm feeling without me having to explain myself. Sometimes she lets me vent about Genie Gustavson writing nasty names on my gym locker (and then threatens to have her *taken care of*). That's what this whole party is about. Thanking Brittany, because she won't even take the time to pamper herself. She's in college and all she does is take pictures on days when it's dark and rainy. #Vampstagram is our inside joke, and this Imogen and her friends might laugh it up, but I think this party is the best idea I've ever had.

So when she asks how Brittany and I met, I shrug. "Around. She's so secretive, though. You're literally the only person who's ever tagged her in a photo."

"Yeah, she's camera shy." She sashays over to the bar and winks at me. "Come have a drink."

My mom is the best hostess I know. She spends all day making food—rice, pernil, hayacas, potato salad, just the works—then showers and puts on a pretty dress. Alcohol *never* passes her lips, but she's all smiles. I am not my mother, and we drink the bloody mimosas I came up with.

As the music thrums, making the walls and ceiling vibrate, more people pour in. More women who've powdered their skin to the shade of death. One woman is in a lime-green dress and platform shoes. She leads an older woman by a leash and takes up a cushion seat.

Okay, that's new. Maybe she thought it was one of those kink bars, or whatever they're called.

She brushes the woman's hair back and exposes her neck. They look like the time Ricky Ramirez and I had to pretend-kiss when we were Maria and Tony in our school's rendition of *West Side Story*.

A white girl who must be younger than me shoves a cigarette in her mouth. She looks like an extra from a blink-182 music video. "Ugh, I remember when this city was alive."

Oooooookay?

I dive deeper into the club, where people seem to have multiplied. A couple of women are making out on one of the love seats. Red wine is spilled on some of the napkins. Should I have gotten black napkins?

I change my trajectory and go to the front of the bar, where three young guys who look like they took a wrong turn from Williamsburg are clustered.

"Is this BYOB?" one of them asks, bringing out a flask from the pocket of his flannel shirt.

What does he mean, "bring your own booze"? There's literally a full open bar!

They catch sight of me standing near them and one smiles. He's the youngest of the three, with dark eyes and close-cropped hair, like he just got out of bootcamp.

"You new?" he asks, slightly confused.

"Not any more than you are," I say. I don't want to make a

big deal that I'm technically two months shy of graduating high school.

"Where's the guest of honor, anyway?" one with a handlebar mustache asks. "I've got a bone to pick with her. She's got to loosen the reins on this vampire curfew."

"You're telling me," the young guy mutters. His muscles flex when he takes the flask from his friend. He doesn't drink, though. "I know Imogen is still pissed, but that's another story."

"Imogen wants to turn every model that catches her eye. That's why we didn't sign the petition."

"Wow you guys are really into this RPG stuff," I say.

I'm about to shoot Brittany a text when her name lights up my screen. I reread the line where she says she won't be able to make it. Oh, no. *Un*acceptable. I text back without looking and pocket my phone.

The guy with the crew cut looks at me with suspicious curiosity. He grins and it gives him the appearance of a wolf. "Want?"

Do I want a drink out of a flask from a strange, but objectively hot, boy at the party where I'm the hostess and the guest of honor hasn't shown up or texted me back? I grab it and drink.

The liquid is warm and slightly thick. Metallic. I feel my gag reflex at work. Blood. That's definitely, 100 percent blood. The tiniest sip pools on my tongue and dribbles down the corner of my mouth. Before I can wipe it off, the boy drags his thumb along my chin and brings it to his lips.

Gross.

When he smiles again, taking the flask back, I see teeth. Not the neon canines decorating the bar. Real, sharp ones, so sharp I know they'd break skin at the barest touch.

Maybe, just maybe, Brittany wasn't lying.

Maybe, just maybe, I'm in the center of a basement full of vampires.

♦

THEO: how come you only have one selfie?
BRITTANY: i think i'd rather take pictures than be in them.
THEO: i used to think that if i took enough pictures, i'd learn
    to love myself more.
BRITTANY: have you?
THEO: i dunno. maybe i'm getting close.

♦

BRITTANY

I didn't choose to become what I am.

I was made during a lawless time of vampires, when consequence was a thing only for mortals. I was hardly older than Theo when I met my—well, I've never quite determined what to call him. *Sire* is hardly the right word, though it bears some piece of the truth. In two hundred years, I have failed to find a word that encompasses both the immaculate violence of his actions and the transformative power I found in their aftermath. Offender. Trespasser. Malefactor. They all lack some piece of the horror I experienced during the attack and after.

He may have been the catalyst of my transformation, but I was the architect. Every choice I made thereafter was a response to his opening argument. If his argument was something along the lines of being more powerful than me by virtue of his sex and his circumstance, then I have been crafting my answer ever since. Not everyone I bite becomes like me. I have to choose. I *get* to choose. And over the years, I have chosen women like me. Women who were told they were less than, unworthy, weak. Women who were hungry for the world. Women with fangs. My petits crocs.

My phone chimes softly, reminding me that it is 10 p.m. and I am missing an appointment. I dismiss the reminder without looking at the words.

There's an unfamiliar feeling spreading beneath my ribs. Not hunger, but something close enough. As I button my frock coat to my chin and step out onto the streets of New York City, I push Theo and the disappointment she is surely feeling now as far from my mind as I am able.

I may not have chosen the path of the moon and shadows, but I did choose New York City. One hundred years ago, I left the windswept valleys and rolling mountains of Virginia for the frenetic energy of a city. It's easy to become a drop in the ocean when the ocean is so unimaginably vast.

I turn away from the river and aim for the park. We don't hunt here. We used to, soon after it was established in the late 1800s, but I outlawed it decades ago. Now hunting here would put us all at great risk. There are too many eyes on this park, too many stories birthed from its rolling hills and dark corners. Anyone who hunts here now will be expelled from the city.

I don't have many rules. Just a few. Each is meant to protect my flock from a world that seems increasingly capable of understanding creatures like us and accepting that we are real. But the most important is this: No siring.

The city may seem large, but that could change in an instant. We must add to our ranks with care and exquisite intention. Anyone who disobeys this edict won't simply find themselves expelled, but very dead.

I slip around the reservoir and my feet crunch against the gravel as I cut south, ghosting past the sandy-faced obelisk, illuminated from all four corners. Soon I leave the park behind, crossing the swift current of Fifth Avenue and diving into the clutches of the city.

A girl with dark, frenzied curls emerges with a laugh from a building directly ahead of me. Her mouth is red and her eyes are an autumn-leaf brown that reminds of me of Theo. It takes me a second to realize it isn't her, but I've stared too long. The girl's smile falters suddenly and she flinches as if something whispered into her ear: *Danger*. Her expression shutters when she catches my eyes, and she turns on her heel, swiftly moving away.

That unsettling feeling in my ribs expands again, that not-hunger hunger. If I were still human, I might have a name for this feeling. Unease? Frustration? Guilt? Something that puts me at odds with myself.

"Hey! Let go!" The voice of a young woman rises above the constant refrain of horns and engines and steam.

I find her immediately. She's leaving a bodega on the corner, her arms full of groceries. Just behind her, a young man stands too close, his eyes as wide and wild as his grin. It's a look I recognize. I have seen it on the faces of so many men over the years. It is an expression of sheer delight, of near-ecstatic joy at knowing his actions are wrong and unstoppable.

The young woman takes a brisk step forward, tugging the edge of her coat from his hand with a scowl and a curse. She hurries away and looks back only once to ensure he does not follow. Laughing, the young man steps back into the shadowy corner of the bodega, where he waits for his next victim.

He does not have to wait long.

The hunger that is not hunger expands again and I move in front of the young man. He blinks, certain I was not there a moment ago. To him, I slipped from between the shadows, a dream and a wish.

"Follow me," I say, letting my voice sink into my chest like the purr of a lion.

"Yeah," he says, eyes wide and helpless now, following the

tether of my voice into the narrow alley where shadows are eager to receive us.

I find the shallow depression of a doorway, perhaps the back entrance of the bodega, and I stop.

"This will hurt," I say, and he only nods in wonder. "Unbutton your jacket and don't make a sound."

He smells like lemons and sweat, and when I bite him, I relish his shiver of pain. Blood coats my tongue like the first juicy bite of a strawberry. It is tart and sharp and earthy all at once, and I drink until that strange not-hunger begins to recede.

The young man does not make a sound, and I do not drink recklessly, only enough to sate my appetite.

"There," I say, digging a handkerchief from my pocket and dabbing the corners of my mouth. "Now go home and stop being such an entitled brute."

He nods, eyes still wide even as he scampers from the alley.

Just then, my phone buzzes in my pocket. I swipe past the lock screen to the message waiting for me. It's from Theo.

So . . . did I mention this is a surprise party and all your friends are here? Feels important to say that lol

For a moment, I think I've misread the message. My mind considers all the ways it couldn't possibly mean what I think it means. Theo could not possibly have called together the vampires of New York City to throw a surprise party for me.

Could she?

And then all at once, I know the truth.

I run.

❦

BRITTANY: i'm going to ask you a question. and you don't have to answer.

THEO: i love your dire voice, b. okay. ask me.

BRITTANY: is there anyone who knows the real theolinda?
THEO: i'll answer if you will.

◗

THEOLINDA

The bathroom of the Root & Ruin has a single exposed lightbulb hanging from the ceiling. I sit on the grimy toilet seat after scrubbing my tongue. It's a good thing I carry an emergency kit in my purse—bandages, mints, mini-toothbrush, Midol, ibuprofen, TUMS, a hydration tablet that crumbles to Pixy Stix dust, lip gloss, three colors of lipstick, an emergency hundred-dollar bill, ID, pepper spray, and a pocketknife.

I wet a napkin I got from Latino Joker and dab it on my cheeks and my neck. Oh my God. Brittany is a vampire. Her friends are vampires. That's why she doesn't take pictures. That's why she joked about it being a "vampire filter." I knew it was too cool to copy. But these people, they're not cool. They're dangerous. I should have trusted my instincts when it came to Imogen.

Can they smell my fear like sharks? Was that cute boy testing me by giving me blood? I pop another mint to get rid of the metallic taste, but the ghost of it is still there. I take long, deep breaths.

Okay okay okay. I can handle this.

Can I, though?

I could barely handle when I got into The New School instead of Columbia. I could barely handle when my brother used my library book for rolling paper. This is just—not how I expected the night to go.

Brittany owes me an explanation.

Then it hits me—I've spent the last two years texting with a vampire. She could have easily found me. Drunk my blood and all of that vampiry stuff. Why didn't she? There were so many times when she could have met me at one of the places I recycle for photos. God, I'm a stalker's dream and that's the first thing I'm changing starting tomorrow.

Brittany could have killed me at any moment. Instead, she talked to me. Instead, she was my friend.

Then why isn't she here?

I take another breath. I toss the napkin on the floor and look in the mirror, which is surrounded by decades of graffiti.

"I am Theolinda Cecilia Romero de Reyes and I have too much to lose." I tug at the corners of my eyeliner to smooth out the smudges, reapply my lipstick, and walk back out into the party.

The music is deeper, like a metallic heart that beats at a steady, rhythmic pace, and everyone here seems to have been waiting for me to show myself.

"We were getting worried," Imogen says, standing from the love seat.

The girl in the neon bandeau dress has blood on her clothes. The older woman on the leash is slumped over at a strange angle, not moving, and even though Imogen is talking to me, all I can think is *I don't want to die. I don't want to die.*

"Where is Brittany?" the guy with the mustache asks.

"How should I know?" I say, trying to sound much braver than I actually am.

I can feel the tension building as every vampire in this place turns toward me and I back up against the bar. There's a soft groan and I turn to find the bartender slumped between two vampires, eyes rolled back as they drink from each wrist. I shut my eyes and let out a yelp.

"Where?" the boy with the wolfish grin asks. "It'll be better for you to tell us."

"Is that why you came?" I shout. "To yell at her?"

There is a consensus of shrugs and nods.

"You're all horrible!" I say. "It's her birthday."

"Don't you get it?" Imogen asks. "Brittany has no birthday. Brittany hasn't aged for two hundred years. And I'm starting to think that neither will you."

Imogen is behind me before I can blink. Her hand is cold around my neck. I reach for the hairspray in my pocket. She does *not* get to bite me. I take aim, shut my eyes, and press down hard. Imogen screams and shoves me hard against the bar.

The vampires closest to me begin to cough. Others get ready to lunge. Using the distraction, I scramble to my feet and climb on top of the bar. If I run across, over a dead body and two drunk vampires, and if no one manages to grab me, I can make it to the exit.

Shoot your shot.

I get ready to run. Pale hands grab at me, the steady bass of the music pulses against my eardrums, and I know in this moment there is no running. No breaking free. There are no more photos or yelling at my brother or advice from my dad or hearing my mother complain about how no one helps her with laundry, and if I live, I promise, I promise I will help her and do my chores and turn my A- into an A+.

A hand grips my ankle and I fall. I'm on my back, kicking and thrashing against a sea of hands and teeth.

Then it stops.

I sit up. The door is open. The music is gone. Between the mob of vampires and me is a girl with long, black hair. Her wine-dark lipstick is carefully drawn and her fangs are bared. I take a moment to note Brittany's fitted frock coat, the dark gray leggings beneath that slip into black knee-high boots, and the surprising hint of pink blooming around her wrists.

"Surprise question mark?" I say, and for a moment I swear she wants to laugh.

Then her eyes shift and narrow, slicing across the room like a blade. A rough growl leaves her lips, "*Mine.*"

"You have no right—" Imogen starts.

"Defy me," Brittany says. A few vampires move behind Brittany, cowing their heads. But the rest stay behind Imogen.

"I'll do one better," Imogen says, her moon-pale skin shimmering when it catches the faint light. She lifts her skirt and drags out a wicked-looking dagger.

"Cheap trick," Brittany says, and then lunges.

The two women meet in a fury of fists and blocks, but, empty-handed, Brittany is at a disadvantage. I swing over the bar and search for something she can use as a weapon. I find a tiny knife for cutting lemons and a hammer.

"Brittany!" I throw the hammer, and she catches it without missing a beat, blocking a brutal jab of Imogen's knife just in time. They fight as though they're dancing, each movement as smooth and practiced as if the whole thing were choreographed. It's so beautiful, I can't look away.

"Grab the girl!" someone shouts.

"Oh, me," I say, connecting the dots way too late. "I'm the girl."

I climb back on top of the bar, searching frantically for a safe place to hide, but before I can do anything, Brittany leaps. With one hand, she grips the candelabra and swings. The ceiling groans in protest and I hear something snap as she strikes out with one foot to kick the vampire coming straight for me.

"Get out of here, Theo!" Brittany shouts as she lands.

"I can't leave you!"

I can't explain why I do it, but I run for Brittany instead of for my life.

I see the horror on her face before I know what's happening.

The ceiling shrieks above me as the candelabra comes crashing down, and a sharp pain pierces my neck.

◆

THEO: what's the best birthday gift you've ever gotten?
BRITTANY: i don't celebrate.
THEO: if you did, tho, hypothetically. when were you born?
BRITTANY: hypothetically? i was born april 27th

◆

BRITTANY

The candelabra presses against Theo's neck, and I know before I pull it off her it that it has pierced her skin. I toss it aside as though it doesn't weigh as much as it does. It clangs loudly as it lands, and Theo whimpers. I kneel at her side, gently lifting her head into my lap. There is a smear of red on her chin, and she looks up at me with tearful eyes.

"It's nice to meet you," she says with a humorless smile.

"Sorry I was late." My voice is distorted, as though squeezed through a sieve. I press a hand to the wound on her neck, attempting to staunch the flow of blood, but this is a death wound. There is no time for anything but a swift goodbye.

Imogen stands near, her focus pooling around me like the blood beneath Theo's neck and shoulders. But the room is still. Theo is not my kill but she is my catch. And vampires in my city always respect the catch.

Blood warms my lap. It spills onto the floor in a constant stream, pooling beneath Theo's head in a way that reminds me of a scarlet flower. I focus on that and not on the dying, gasping girl in my arms.

"You're actually a vampire," Theo says, and in her eyes I see questions and theories and so much more than she's able to say right now. She only has a few words left. She chooses two: "Make me."

The not-hunger feeling crouched beneath my ribs returns. It

expands and expands, ballooning painfully inside me. And, suddenly, I have a name for it: sorrow.

"I can't," I answer, knowing the eyes of my peers are upon me and this is a precarious moment. "Theo, I'm sorry. There are rules."

"Remember that question you asked me? Forever ago," Theo says, voice growing weak. "The answer is: you."

How is it possible that a girl I've never met before in my life feels as close to me as my own sister? I cannot let her die. I cannot let this be her end.

I raise my eyes to the ring of vampires surrounding us and I growl, furious and feral and more certain than I've been about anything in my long life.

Then I lower my mouth to Theo's neck, and I bite.

🜂

THEO: if you could go anywhere in the world, where would
  you go? don't think just answer.
BRITTANY: the future.
THEO: that's not a real answer.
BRITTANY: isn't it?

🜂

THEOLINDA

I take the elevator from my floor to Brittany's penthouse. After the accident, after I asked her to turn me, I discovered a lot of things. First of all, Imogen is a jerk, but that's obvious to anyone with or without a pulse. It's been four months, and I'm still dying. Turns out it's a slow, pretty painful process. My body is shutting down and it's a whole mess. But—I have an undead tutor. Even if she's going to have to face a trial for turning me despite the baby vamp ban of 1987 and the whole undead civil war thing that's apparently also my fault.

There are still things I need to figure out. How to convince my parents that night college classes are the thing for me. How to be around them without wanting to murder them. Kidding. Not really. It's hard.

I didn't think it would be easy. Some things will take years to figure out. For instance, how will I manage not casting a reflection? I guess I did want that vampire filter, but it's a mixed blessing. I practice taking my photo in the mirrored reflection of this elevator. Maybe in two hundred years I'll have to deal with aliens and they'll have a cure for vampirism or a phone that puts Apple out of business.

I won't hold my breath. Though I could if I wanted to.

The elevator lets me into Brittany's penthouse. She has a movie theater *in* her apartment. She has everything she needs to never even leave the house.

But I remember the word she used to say to me. *Lonely.*

No more.

She hands me one of the glittery matching tumblers that I bought for us. I can't really look at blood yet, even though I'll have to get over it to survive.

"You know these movies won't teach you anything," she tells me, and hops onto the couch.

"I know, but literally the only vampire movies I've ever seen are the *Tw*—"

"Don't you dare."

"Shut up, it is perfect, okay. Per. Fect." I plop beside her and take a sip. I'm starting to be able to taste minerals, diets. This person really liked sodium.

I miss popcorn. I miss butter. I miss sunlight. I miss so many things and I've only just started. My life ended. My new life has begun.

At least I won't have to go about it alone. I have my Best Friend Forever, and that's a promise made in blood.

THRALL
Or "These Aren't the Vampires You're Looking For . . ."

Zoraida Córdova &
Natalie C. Parker

There seem to be two kinds of vamps out there: those who lure their prey and those who chase them down. There is something downright terrifying about . . . well, all of them, but the idea that someone can convince you to willingly offer your neck for a quick bite is quite unsettling. Vampires are at the top of the food chain, and, like all predators, they have to learn how to hunt without depleting their food supply, which is . . . um . . . us? lol. Psychic powers seem to be how they manage this, and a gentle kind of mind control often shows up in vampire folklore, from Dracula to *Sesame Street*'s Count von Count (though, to be fair, he can only hypnotize you). But what it comes down to is some kind of influence. In this story, Zoraida and Natalie (oop, that's us, your benevolent editrixes, hi!) use this vampire myth to let Theo and Brittany think about what kind of influence they have on the human and vampire worlds.

What kind of influence do you want to have on the world?

BESTIARY

Laura Ruby

It was day 212 of water rationing, and Lolo was acting like a bear. Or rather, wasn't acting like a bear at all.

"Come on, Lo," Jude said. "You have to eat something." She stood inside Lolo's enclosure in the Bezos Family Arctic Tundra exhibit, holding a chunk of hot-pink flesh in one gloved hand, a bucket of the same stuff at her booted feet. Lolo, draped like a wet rug over a boulder in the middle of a greenish, oily pool, emitted a long-suffering sigh. They'd been promised tankers of fresh water to bathe the animals, but so far, the tankers hadn't arrived.

Jude's sigh was as long-suffering as Lolo's, her skin almost as ashen and dirt-streaked as Lolo's fur. She stomped to the edge of the pool and waved the hunk of flesh over the algae blooms. "It's salmon. You love salmon."

It wasn't salmon. Oh, the man who'd sold it to Jude at the docks claimed it was salmon—Wild! Fresh!—but the flesh was far too pink and rubbery. Possibly it was dyed shark meat. Or the remains of some twisted catfish the man had hauled out of the farthest reaches of Lake Michigan, away from the prying eyes of patrols. Whatever it was, it should have been enough to coax Lolo out of her sulk. If anything was going to coax her out of it.

"Listen, Lo, no one wants to see a skinny polar bear," Jude said. "You're going to make the children cry."

Lolo yawned.

"Yeah, yeah, I know, what children?" All the zoo's regulars— parents pushing double-wide strollers, teenagers taunting the animals and one another, couples too in love or in lust to notice they were sharing their first kiss in a miasma of hippo dung—were too busy boiling gutter water or waiting in line at the supermarket for the next shipment of bottled water.

The animals were thirsty. The *people* were thirsty. And that meant—

"Jude, what the hell are you doing?"

She didn't have to turn around to know that scratchy, cranky voice. Diwata was the closest thing Jude had to a boss. At least, she was the only one left who dared to question Jude. The rest of the employees and the volunteers were too weirded out. They had reason to be, though not the reason they thought.

"What does it look like I'm doing?" she said.

"Like you're trying to get yourself eaten by a polar bear."

"Lolo doesn't even want to eat her salmon."

"Probably because that's not salmon," Diwata said.

Jude gave up on the "salmon," dropped the hunk of overly pink flesh into the bucket with a plop. "Lolo's depressed because her pool is dirty. We need fresh water."

"Don't we all?" said Diwata. She stood in the doorway at the back of the exhibit, her tanned, weather-beaten face cross-hatched with so many lines she looked like a map to everywhere and nowhere all at once.

"Maybe it will rain," Jude said. Diwata grunted. Overhead, the weak November sun had just cracked the horizon, scraping the sky a grumpy purple.

"Maybe it will rain for so long that we won't need some jerk to turn on the water; we'll have plenty of our own. For free."

With an elbow, Diwata shoved the heavy door open wider. "And maybe rainbows will shoot out of my ass while we're building an ark. Come here before Lolo decides to bite off your arms."

Lolo snorted, tiny ears twitching in amusement. Lolo thought Diwata was hilarious.

"I brought you some coffee," Diwata said.

Jude nudged the bucket with her foot. "This isn't salmon and that isn't coffee."

"Well, it's all I got," said Diwata. "You want it or not?"

She didn't, but this was Diwata. Jude left the bucket for Lolo just in case and trudged across the habitat. Diwata took a step back to let her through the door, then kicked it closed behind her.

"What did I tell you about climbing into exhibits with the predators?" Diwata said, handing her a soggy paper cup.

"I don't know. Something about claws, something about teeth, blah blah blah." For show, Jude took a sip of the coffee, winced. She used to love coffee, even the fake stuff. She used to love a lot of things.

The coffee cup had the name MOJO JOE printed on it. Next to that, someone had scrawled *Jood*.

Jesus.

"How much did this cost, Diwata? And what's it made out of? Whipped jellyfish? Toxic slime?"

Diwata punched in the code to lock the door to Lolo's exhibit, jabbing at the keypad harder than she needed to. "Don't try to change the subject. One of these days you're going to get hurt."

Ha. "I'll be fine."

"I don't understand how you're so sure."

Jude rarely told the truth, but she did now. "I talk to the animals, that's how."

Diwata waved at the cell phone sticking out of Jude's front pocket. "That's what happens when kids are raised by video games and Disney movies. Why do you carry around that old thing when the other kids have ports in their brains?"

Jude shrugged. She had no interest in the latest tech augments. And she didn't need the phone. But her mother was somehow still paying for it for reasons that remained a mystery to Jude. Sometimes Jude liked to press the HOME button, liked to hear the phone say, "Ask me anything" and make random suggestions:

> *What is today's date?*
> *Google the War of 1812.*
> *Will you get me a table for three tonight?*
> *What are the symptoms of bird flu?*
> *Will you find Brett?*
> *Give me directions for home.*

Jude said, "How do you know I don't have ports in my brain? And who are you calling a kid?"

Diwata slurped from her own cup, smacked her lips. "You can't be more than sixteen, so yeah, I'm calling you a kid, kid."

Jude opened her mouth to lie or maybe blurt another truth, but Diwata was already marching through the tunnels behind the habitats, where many of the zoo's inhabitants were still waiting for someone to release them to their outdoor spaces. Silently Jude greeted them, pressing cool fingertips to the glass. *Hello, Jonas, Hello, Victor, hello, hello, hello.* She knew their calls and their smells and their boredom, the beat of their hearts. And because many of the animals were ancient, she knew their aches and pains, too, felt them thrumming in her own body. A bad hip. A cracked hoof. Sore gums boiling with infection. Memories of a slow-moving herd in the desert, the blast of the gun that changed it all.

Over her shoulder, Diwata said, "It's a school day. Why are you here?"

Diwata was also ancient but sneaky-fast, motoring along as if on wheels. Jude jogged to keep up. "I'm taking a gap year."

"You do those after you graduate, not before."

"If I went to school, who would help you with all the critters?"

Diwata grunted and kept marching. They'd been having this exchange ever since Diwata had taken Jude on as a part of the cleanup crew—just another pair of hands to sweep up after the stroller moms, just another drugged-out teenager who wouldn't know honest work if it slapped her upside the head. And then came the morning after . . . well, the morning Diwata had found her curled up with the lionesses Olive and Nell, the three of them sleeping in a pile like kittens. Instead of calling the police, Diwata promoted her. And she'd protected Jude when management wanted to know why the hell some "goth-witch addict" was feeding the rhinos and the crocs by hand. Did the girl have a death wish? Did Diwata want them to get sued?

Jude did and Diwata didn't, but then the rationing began and none of that mattered anymore.

"So," Jude said, "who's next? The penguins? The seals?"

"They're all next. Them *and* their habitats. We've got to get everything in this place cleaned up."

"With what? Mojo Joe?"

"With whatever we can find. The shindig's this Saturday."

"Shindig," Jude repeated.

"Don't tell me you forgot."

"How could I?" Jude said. She side-eyed the little gaggle of suits taking pictures of the various habitats, drawing up plans on their tablets. Party organizers hired to put up lights and tables and decorations. One of them, a young, dark-haired man with coppery skin, stared at her so boldly and for so long that Jude flipped him off. He laughed and took a picture of her, then pouted when he got nothing but a blur.

Diwata said, "You should come to the party."

"Right."

"Seriously."

Jude stopped walking, almost tripping over herself. "No way in hell I'm going to a 'shindig' for the asshat who turned off the water."

Diwata stopped walking, too, turned to look at Jude, one gray and fuzzy eyebrow arched. "It's the board's position that the asshat didn't technically turn off the water; he simply raised the price of said water."

"That's the same thing when no one can afford it."

"Either way, they're not going to say no to the CEO who could turn *on* the water, you get me?"

Though she wasn't in the least bit cold, Jude rubbed her bare arms. "Is he going to turn it on now so that we can clean the place? Where are the water trucks we were promised?"

"And they're not going to say no to all the cash he's giving them," Diwata went on. "He's renting the whole damned park for a whole damned day. There will be fancy bands and fancy food and hundreds of fancy people. When was the last time we had that many people here at once?"

"This is a public park. As in, for the public."

"That's cute. This place is no more public than the water is."

Diwata was right, Diwata was always right. Long ago, the zoo used to be free, but now it took twenty-five dollars to get in, more for parking. At the Safari Café, french fries cost eight dollars, a bottle of water ten. Now, just past dawn, the zoo was cold and deserted, a stray napkin twitching under the café tables, moved to dance in the chilly lake wind. But the place wouldn't be much more populated at opening, or at lunch, or at dinner. There would be no laughing crowds of children piling into the Macaque Forest, no families bursting from the Lionel Train Adventure, and the AT&T Endangered Species Carousel would twirl around and around all by itself, imagining the species that might join it one day, if there was anyone left to carve a polar bear or cast a tiger.

The old, fruitless anger rose in her, souring her guts. Though she'd pay for it, Jude drank down the rest of the coffee in one long pull, crushed the cup in her fist. It didn't help. Only one thing would, but she wasn't doing that ever again.

She tossed the crushed cup into the nearest trash can. "Score," she said. The flies and the ants and the other insects burrowing inside the garbage protested with the bug equivalent of *WTF, we're trying to eat here!* But Jude had too much practice to flinch at language only she understood.

Diwata's face went soft anyway, the lines smoothing out. "Listen, kid. Maybe this party won't be so bad."

Jude hated when Diwata felt sorry for her. She scratched at the phone in her pocket as if she suddenly had to answer a call, take a meeting, make a reservation. "Stop."

Diwata sighed, sounding a lot like Lolo. Old and sore and disappointed. "I just meant that maybe there will be some people for you. Young people. Not asshats." Her eyes cut to the young man with the copper skin and then came back to rest on Jude's face. "I know you don't think so, I know how much you love Lolo and Olive and Nell and the rest, but you've got to find your own pack."

"Lolo is my pack. Olive and Nell are."

"I'm talking about humans, here."

"Humans are animals, too," said Jude.

"Knock it off." Diwata waved a veined and gnarled hand. "Everybody needs someone."

"I have you."

"That's not what I mean and you know it. Find some girl-friends. Find some boyfriends. Find some *friend* friends. Have some fun. You must have had fun once, right? You remember what that feels like."

She did.

There was an animal that threw up its own stomach to distract predators, but Jude couldn't recall which it was. Diwata was the furthest thing from a predator and the closest thing to a pack that Jude had, but Jude vomited the Mojo Joe all over their boots anyway, one more mess they had to clean up.

◆

Find Disney movies.
How many days since I've eaten?
When did all the ice melt?
Play some blues.
Are we there yet?
Text Brett I'll be late.

After a long day of feeding animals, mucking out stalls, and scrubbing what they could with the little water they had left in the zoo's rainwater catchment system, Diwata and Jude tucked in the critters, locked up the gates. Across the street from the zoo, security guards welcomed rich residents into grand buildings with solar panels on the outside and marble foyers on the inside as Jude and Diwata trudged the five blocks to the nearest bus stop. Because of low ridership and competing fleets of self-driving cabs, the city had axed all but a few bus routes. That meant that the buses were always packed with people. They waited as first one graffiti-covered bus and then another drove right past the stop. Diwata unzipped her army coat, reminiscing about how frigid Chicago falls and winters used to be—"So cold your breath froze in the wind! Snow up to there! Everyone in coats so puffy they looked like bears!" Now, the sky was the same angry purple as it had been at dawn, the air dry enough to electrify Jude's hair. When she tried to smooth it down, she zapped herself, jumped.

Diwata laughed. "We're a pair."

They were. Diwata, pushing seventy, hunched and small in the olive drab jacket her wife had gotten while fighting in some war or another, and Jude, pushing infinity, gangly and tall, in nothing but a ragged T-shirt and jeans, long black strands of hair sticking to her moon-pale cheeks. Another woman, still wearing a surgical mask due to the last bird flu outbreak, joined them at the stop, only daring to look at them once. When Jude grinned at her, the woman's eyes dialed wide. She hurried off without waiting for the next bus, boot heels hammering the sidewalk.

"That was mean," said Diwata.

"All I did was smile."

"Uh-huh."

They waited another ten minutes in silence. But no matter how long the bus took, Jude wouldn't let Diwata wait by herself, and Diwata had stopped objecting the day she'd scooped Jude out the Lion House—an unspoken pact. Most of the time, Jude's fear-lessness alone was enough to ward off would-be muggers. Most of the time.

A third bus lumbered by without stopping. Outside a bodega, a stooped old man held out an empty cup to customers coming and going. "Something to drink, ma'am? Sir?" Even when the people shook their heads no, the man said, "Bless you."

Diwata said, "What if you could do something about all this?"

"All *what*?" said Jude. "What do you think I could do?"

"I don't know."

There was a lot Diwata didn't know. She didn't know that, not too long ago, Jude lay down in the woods, hoping to feed hungry coyotes with her own flesh. She didn't know Jude had waded into the lake and tried her best to drown. Diwata didn't know what the lionesses had done to save her.

Finally, the bus rumbled up to the stop. Before she got on, Diwata said, "You want to come with me? Vivian's making chicken adobo tonight. Not fake—the real thing."

"Rain check," Jude said.

At this lie, Diwata nodded, and then she climbed aboard. Jude watched the bus drive away and started the long walk home. Head down, hands jammed into her jean pockets, she dodged commuters and messengers, students and criminals. The occasional dog barked frantically at her—*Not food, not food, NOT FOOD*—until she murmured that they were safe, that she wouldn't hurt them or their humans.

"Girl," said a Latino kid with a faint pubescent mustache, dragging his mutt away from her shoes, "you're seriously creepy."

"Right?" she said.

Night fell over the city, and still she walked. This was the only thing that had carried over from before, this night-walking. It used to be she walked so that she didn't have to go home to the little house in Jefferson Park, the brick bungalow that was so adorable on the outside and so awful within. Her mom needed her dad but her dad needed his oxy; their fights could be heard for miles. Jude started drinking in middle school to dull the punches and drown out the noise. Later, she used boys to pass the time. When the country was gripped with bird flu terror and the boys' parents kept them home, Jude found herself in basement clubs with other lost souls, daring Mother Nature to take her best shot at them. Hers came in the form of another boy, prettier than Jude ever was, shiny and gold. He told her he loved her. And he had, in his way, though his love had ruined them both.

Also a ruin: Buckingham Fountain. The city didn't have the water to spare to keep it operational, so the basins sat empty, the sculptural dragons as thirsty as everyone else. The pretty golden boy had had a thing for magical beasts: unicorns, basilisks, griffins, chimera, and other creatures of all kinds.

"*You're* the magical beast," she'd told him.

"Yes," he said, pushing her back onto a dirty mattress. "Yes, I am."

Now, the lights from the buildings downtown stared at her like so many yellow eyes: *What if you could do something about all this? What if?*

Some questions you can't ask. The familiar queasy thirst clenched her stomach, pulsed at the root of her tongue. If she didn't keep moving, the thirst would permeate the air like a perfume, call to the people around her. They would come to her whether she wanted them to or not, offer themselves, even if their eyes rolled in confusion and terror as they did.

So she kept moving, the proverbial shark in the water, swimming so as not to die. As if she could. But she didn't make eye contact with anyone, she didn't linger anywhere long enough to reveal her desperation. An hour went by. Then two. The crowds of people dwindled to nothing. Jude was left with only the cataract moon, a murky smear in the sky.

She heard the man long before she saw him, so much more desperate than she. Though she could have sidestepped him easily, she didn't bother. He showed her his knife, a sad little thing, and demanded her money.

"I don't have any," she said.

His eyes got a hungry look that she had seen before. "You got something." He tried to drag her off the path to take what he could. He didn't appreciate her loud bray of laughter, the flick of her wrist that sent the knife flying.

"I'm going to hurt you for that," he growled. And charged.

She grabbed him by the sweatshirt, spun him around and around until he squealed in queasy protest. Then she pulled him in close, let him see the shiny daggers of her teeth, let him smell the desiccation on her breath.

"If you want," she said. "I can give you something to scream about."

He did not want.

She thrust him away, left him panting on the pavement. He was no special kind of beast. And neither was she. She ended up in the same place she'd begun: the zoo. She scaled the outer fence and then coded into Lolo's indoor enclosure. Lolo was sleeping in the man-made cave in the corner. Jude crawled inside and snuggled against Lolo's chest, her big bear heart ticking off the minutes till dawn.

◆

When did the Florida Keys disappear?
How do augments work?
How long can the human body survive without water?
How much blood loss is too much blood loss?
Play whale songs.

Morning came, and with it two water trucks.

"We were promised *five* trucks," Jude said.

"Don't look a gift horse in the mouth," said Diwata.

"What does that even mean?"

151

"Means that you should go to the Raptor House. Raul needs help with Peaches. Something about her wing."

Peaches the snowy owl had a bit of an attitude. Which was putting it nicely. Peaches would take out your eyes if you weren't careful. Raul wasn't careful. Raul—skinny Raul, brown skin gray with fear or just neglect—was running around the raptor enclosure, swearing, as Peaches flapped brokenly after him.

"Get out of there, Raul," Jude said. "I'll do it."

"Thanks," said Raul, ducking out of the habitat. "She almost took a chunk out of my face."

Inside the raptor cage, Jude answered the bird's cries of *PAIN, PAIN, PAIN* with "Shhh, shhhhh. Calm down, you silly monster." Peaches let Jude pick her up, examine the bent wing. She had no idea how the bird could have injured it. Jude remembered the golden boy telling her about the caladrius, a white bird that would eat the sickness out of a person and then fly away, healing that person and also itself.

Peaches tucked her head under Jude's arm. Jude said, "Poor girl. What kind of sickness did you eat?"

"Whole world's sick," said Raul, watching through the mesh. "What's that got to do with a broken wing?"

"World's broken, too," Jude said.

"Same thing."

Behind Raul, two party organizers appeared. "Hey! Hold up the bird so we can get some photos!"

"She's not a turkey and this isn't Thanksgiving," Jude said, cradling Peaches closer.

"Oh. She's hurt." It was the dark-haired, coppery-skinned guy, who looked much younger than Jude had thought he was.

"So?" said the white guy next to him. He had his finger on the side of his neck where his computer implant connected with the piece in his ear and the lens in his eye. So, augmented then. And another jackass. "Shit. These pictures aren't coming out." He pressed the side of his neck again. "Shit."

"Come on, man. Leave her alone," said the coppery-skinned guy. His eyes were large and dark and wet. "Sorry to bother you, miss."

"Miss?" said his friend, incredulous. "Jesus, Sanjay. She's knee-deep in bird poop."

"Hello, Sanjay," Jude said, and smiled.

He should have been scared, everybody was scared. But Sanjay didn't seem scared. He said, "Maybe we'll catch you later?"

"Maybe," Jude said. Her voice sounded strange, even to her.

◊

Launch Photos.
Should I bring my umbrella?
Tell me the story of Judith.
Play my dance mix.
Text Brett I'm on my way.

Later, Jude found herself back at Buckingham Fountain, perched on the back of a stone dragon, as if it could fly her to a place where she made sense to herself, where she could scare people when she wanted to, where the thirst wasn't drying her to a husk.

And because she sat there far too long, they came. The girls. Five of them, stumbling through Grant Park, a gaggle of teased hair and short skirts, pleather shit-kickers and crappy tattoos. Jude's heart ached along with her stomach. Not so long ago, she might have been one of them, lost and lonely, declaring herself a bad seed before anyone else could do it first.

"The fuck you looking at, bitch?" said the leader, a big, solid girl with white skin and striped hair.

"The stars," said Jude. "You?"

"Listen to this one," the stout girl said. "What are you smoking? You got weed for us? You got candy?" The girl inched closer, pulled in by Jude's thirst.

Jude licked her dry lips. "You should go home, if you have one."

The girl spread her arms, "This whole city is our home. Maybe *you* should go."

Jude had thought about leaving so many times. But where would she go? And who would take care of Lolo and Olive and Nell and the others? Who would watch over Diwata? The world might be dying, but shouldn't she stay around, even if the only thing she could do was to ease the pain a little?

"Hey! I'm talking to you," the stout girl said. The other four girls crowded behind her with a chorus of "Yeah, bitch" and "We're talking to you, bitch."

"I'm not smoking anything, and I don't have candy for you," said Jude.

The stout girl laughed a stout laugh, sidled nearer. "What about that phone in your pocket? Someone will pay a few bucks for that." She was so close now that Jude could have traced the lines of her muscled thighs, thick and firm under fishnet stockings. The pulse quickened at the girl's white neck, the blood beckoning from beneath the skin.

"Really," said Jude. "You should go while you can."

"Go?" the girl said. "I don't . . ." A crease appeared between her brows, betraying her.

"Hannah?" said the girl farthest away. "What do you want us to do?

"Do?" said Hannah. Hannah's feet lurched her forward. She was nothing but a rabbit, nothing but prey, beautiful in her sacrifice.

One of the other girls plucked at Hannah's arm. "Are you okay?"

Hannah shook off the other girl, chest heaving, wild eyes not leaving Jude's. "I feel you," she breathed. "Your teeth."

"What the hell are you talking about, Hannah?" said another girl, and then watched her own shoes in horror as she took a step toward Jude.

To Jude, Hannah said: "I'm . . . I'm ready. Please."

Jude reached up and laid her hand on Hannah's cheek. Hannah turned her head. Jude leaned forward, thirsty, so bloody thirsty, but Hannah was thirsty, too. All these girls were.

The space between Jude's shoulder blades itched, then burned, pain so deep Jude couldn't reach it even if she tried. She could take Hannah, she could take them all, but what would it change?

"I thought I was ready, too," Jude said, tearing her hand away from Hannah's warm skin. "But I wasn't. Nobody is."

Hannah shook her head, blinked. She took a step back, then another, dimpled knees quivering. "You touch me again and I'll beat the shit out of you."

"Yeah," Jude said. "Of course you will."

◆

Will it be hot today?
Will it be cold?
Who is near me?
Are you coming?
Are you here?

The party organizers ramped up their organizing. Dozens of people descended on the park, hanging lights and banners. More trucks came—some with water, others with chairs and tables and linens. Jude did her best to ignore them, only lashing out once, when one

of them, a middle-aged white woman with fluffy hair and augments, suggested that Lolo be moved to her indoor habitat during
the party. "That thing looks half-dead already," she said.

Jude said sweetly, "Better than being all the way dead, wouldn't
you say?" and threw a chunk of "salmon" at her fluffy head.

"What's gotten into you?" said Diwata.

"Nothing," said Jude, which was true.

"You need a break," Diwata told her. "Go home. Come back
when you're acting like yourself."

Acting like herself? And who, exactly, was that? Her night-
walking took her northwest, all the way to Jefferson Park. The
house was just as she remembered it, a little bungalow nestled
among dozens of other little bungalows. She circled around to the
back of the house, jumping up to the porch roof. Through the window, she watched her parents sleep. Her mother had one arm flung
across her face, covering her eyes, her father was slack-jawed and
snoring. She opened the window and stepped inside. Pill bottles
littered the surface of the nightstand, and the room smelled like
stale smoke.

But she must not have been as quiet as she'd hoped, because
her father's eyes opened. "Judy?" he said, in a voice thick with beer
and drugs and sleep. "Is that you?"

"No," she said.

He struggled to sit up. "What are you doing? What time is it?"

"Late. Early. Depends on your perspective."

"Huh?"

"Never mind."

He rubbed his eyes. "You look horrible. Are you sick?"

The whole world is sick. "Are you?" she asked.

"My back," he said. "You know how it is. Hey, you got any
cash?"

It had been a year since she'd been here; you'd think he would be more surprised to see her. Happy, maybe. But this was not the place for happiness. For a brief moment, Jude wanted to flip the bed, dump them both on the floor. She wanted to tell them about love and thirst and what both had done to her when her parents weren't looking. She wanted to tell them about the golden boy, the one who had worshipped fairy-tale beasts, the one who was a beast himself. The things he had taken from her: will and blood and humanity.

But she wasn't here for any of that. "Ask Mom for the cash," she told him. "She's still paying for my phone."

"What? How?" He shoved at Jude's mother. "Wake up, you bitch. You been holding out on me."

Her mother rolled over. "Fuck off, Mike."

"Judy just told me."

"Fuck Judy, too."

Jude left them to their inevitable brawl and crept into her old room, surprised to find it the same—clothes strewn all over the bed and the carpet, old lipsticks gathering dust on the dresser. She found a duffel bag and scooped a bunch of clothes inside. Then she shouldered the bag, slipped out the kitchen door. She walked to the zoo, arriving with the sun. She put the leather bag in her locker and started her morning routine. Diwata came and helped her put out food for Lolo. Lolo showed no interest in the food, but she loved the bucket it came in and put it on her head like a hat. When Diwata told her she looked ridiculous, Lolo whined and growled until Jude put the bucket on her own head.

While Jude and Diwata and the rest of the zoo staff released the animals into their outdoor habitats, an army wearing identical black T-shirts descended upon them. The T-shirts said B'S BIG B-DAY BASH, and the people wearing them zipped around the property in golf carts, delivering food and drinks to cafés and food stands. Watering trucks came from every direction, and the zookeepers were told to water the animals and "Perk these babies up!" A moving van rolled up and parked between the Wild Things Gift Shop and the Lion House. The T-shirted people set up a stage and then hauled outdoor furniture from the truck and set up chairs and couches around portable fire pits. Hundreds of thousands of tiny lights adorned both trees and cages, meticulously placed by men wearing gloves and stilts. Dozens of security guards watched over people and animals alike, their fingers pressed to the feeds surgically installed behind cauliflower ears, their eyes filled with suspicion and sociopathy. One of them grabbed Jude by the arm just as she went to water Olive and Nell.

"Hey! Where's your ID?"

Jude looked down at the man's hand, resisted the urge to rip it from his body, bite off the fingers one by one. Instead, she fished her peeling badge from her front pocket.

"Here," she said, and smiled.

The man rocked on his heels, mumbled, "Sorry," and let go. "I . . . I'm sorry."

"I know," she said.

Inside the lion habitat, Olive, the smaller and leaner of the two lionesses, rubbed against Jude's knees. *Monster girl*, Olive purred. Nell stood on her hind legs, put her paws on Jude's shoulders and licked Jude's face. *Favorite girl*, rumbled Nell. *What did you bring us today?*

Jude tried to ignore the T-shirts and the security guards as she hosed down the lion habitat, as she petted the lions. Olive and Nell lapped up the water in big, greedy gulps.

"Good kitties," Jude told them.

A T-shirt said, "Hey! Goth chick! I need to get some good shots to put up on our social feed. Maybe you could find your furry friends a toy or something?"

"I'll try," Jude said.

Right before the guests of honor were due to arrive, Jude met Diwata in the employee locker room. Diwata gazed at her, astonished.

"I almost didn't recognize you. Did you comb your hair? And what are you wearing?"

The clothes she had gathered from her old room, her old life: short skirt, fishnets, pleather shit-kickers. "I remembered what you said. That I could do something about all this. I thought maybe I'd meet some people."

Diwata was quiet for a long moment. Then she said, "Since when do you listen to me?"

"Since now, I guess."

"Okay. You look . . ." Diwata tipped her head, considering.

"What?"

"Young and desperate. You'll make a lot of . . . friends. If that's what you want."

Jude didn't answer, sipped at the bottle of water Diwata had handed her. She wondered why Diwata wasn't drawn to her the way others were, but then, maybe she was, in a different way. Diwata had saved her. Jude had thought she was paying back the kindness by walking Diwata to the bus stop every night, but now that seemed silly. That was not what Diwata had asked her to do.

"Come with me?" Jude said. "I'm a little nervous."

"I don't believe you," Diwata said. "You're not scared of anything." But Diwata motored ahead of Jude the way she always did, plowing a path through the throngs of guests, most already drunk and rowdy.

Diwata grumbled, "Any of these jackasses even *looks* at my animals the wrong way, there will be hell to pay."

They reached the big tent in the middle of the main mall, where the birthday boy was holding court like some kind of king. He was middling tall, with stiff, graying hair and a ruddy face, a small, selfish little mouth like a lamprey's. He had a bottle of beer in one hand, and he gestured broadly with it. All around, other ruddy-faced men laughed along with him, or toasted him, or slapped him on the back. "Happy birthday, BK! You're the man!"

Diwata and Jude found some seats by the bar and waited. Across the room, Sanjay stood with a bunch of other party organizers. He waved at her, his big, wet eyes making him look even younger, like a fawn in a tangled forest. She hoped he wouldn't be afraid of her, after.

"You never told me whose blood it was," said Diwata.

"What?"

"When I found you with Olive and Nell. There was blood all over the place. Remember how long it took to clean?"

"Oh. That." Jude had offered herself to the golden boy she loved and, in turn, he'd offered her to some magical beasts he loved more. She was meant to be the toy, but she'd become something else. Something with claws, something with teeth, blah blah blah. A different kind of beast. She'd taken the first bites, but she'd let Olive and Nell do the rest.

Diwata tapped the bar top. "I just want to know if he deserved it."

"More than I did."

There were other people who deserved it, so many others.

It wasn't long before the birthday boy's eyes found her, young and desperate and so, so thirsty in her fishnets and her skirt. He made his way over.

"Hello, ladies," he said. "Are you having a good time?"

Diwata grunted, but Jude said, "I'm having the greatest day of my whole life."

The man's tight mouth stretched into a grin. "Can I get you anything? Beer? Water?"

For the first time, Jude relished her thirst, the power of it. She felt the itch between her shoulder blades, where the wings would burst from her back at the first bite.

Jude smoothed the skirt over her thighs. "Water would be lovely, thank you."

BATS
Or The Cutest Misunderstood Flying Rodents

Zoraida Córdova &
Natalie C. Parker

It's hard to imagine talking about vampires without mentioning nature's most goth little rodent, the bat. But bats haven't always been part of vampire lore. Yes, Count Dracula shape-shifts into a bat in Bram Stoker's *Dracula*. But he can also travel in moondust particles and shape-shift into a wolf, dog, and fog. So why doesn't Dracula change into a bunny or a butterfly? It isn't just that those creatures are super adorable and lacking in the "has fangs" department. One theory is that Spanish conquistadors brought stories of blood-drinking bats from the Americas when they returned to Europe, introducing a whole world of terror to their home continent. Blood-drinking bats are clearly only one step away from blood-drinking humans or monsters, right??? Unfortunately, in the real world vampire bats won't give you immortality—just rabies. The same way witches have feline familiars, the connection between supernatural creatures and animals is so strong that they occasionally become them. In Laura's story, Jude was transformed against her will and it left her angry and isolated, but she finds her footing among the beasts.

If your vampire self could shape-shift into a creature, which would you choose?

162

MIRRORS, WINDOWS & SELFIES

Mark Oshiro

invisibleb0y
June 5, 2018

~~Do you know what it's like to be invisible?~~
~~Do you know what it's like to not see yourself?~~
I made this because I have no one to talk to. That's not me being melodramatic, either. I have been reading the words of others for so long, but it's time for me to speak.

My name is Cisco.

(Deep breath.)

I'm a vampire.

(Cliché, I know.)

And I'm all alone.

Well, there are my parents, but I don't feel close to them most days. And not in that corny way you probably assume, either; they think of me more as an anomaly than anything else. I am not supposed to exist, and yet here I am! Shoved out into the world, an impossibility, and I don't even get a choice in the matter.

I made this because maybe it'll help my life be a bit more bearable. I don't know. I don't really have any grand plans for it. I just need to talk about how I haven't seen myself.

Literally.

I don't know what I look like.

Pretty sad, right?

0 Comments
6 Notes

invisibleb0y
June 6, 2018

There are rules. I can't break them. My life is a gift, I'm told. Vampires don't breed, according to my parents, who normally are my only source of information on my kind.

So these rules are there to protect me. To keep me alive and safe. To keep me away from the other clans, from the vampires who will do terrible things to me if they know I exist. I'm too unique and too special. Vampires are territorial, sure, but Mami and Papi assumed the worst was coming, because . . . well, I'm not supposed to be real.

So they hid us away, far out in the middle of nowhere, and I've known the rules for my whole life.

The Rules

1) I'm to be supervised at all times. Seriously. No time away from Mami y Papi. I've broken this rule for brief periods of time—maybe a few minutes here and there—but they

are seriously always around. I don't even get to hunt by myself. It's too risky, even though we're so isolated from others, because someone might find me. They might find out I exist. That's the worst possible outcome for my parents: that I'm discovered, taken, dissected, studied, that the very knowledge of my existence will bring heartbreak and death to us all. So we live in an abandoned farm outside of . . . well, let's just say somewhere like Blythe. Or Sheridan. Or Freeburg. We're always in the middle of nowhere. Sometimes there are a few scattered homes, but generally? Nothing for miles and miles.

And *still* I'm not allowed out of their sight.

2) No photos of any kind. No evidence in the world that I exist. Which means . . .
3) No unsupervised Internet usage. Papi stole an old school computer years and years ago, and we sometimes get lucky enough to siphon off a nearby signal. A quarter mile or so down the dirt road from us right now, there's another house. No clue who lives there. But they've boosted the signal for whatever reason, and their connection is probably real shitty because I'm using it every time it reaches us, particularly on clear days.

But I find moments when my parents aren't paying attention. When they're occupied. When I can go to all the sites they'd say no to. They don't want me to read any of the unsavory things people say about vampires. Too much misinformation and propaganda, apparently.

I know how to erase my browsing history, though. Mami y Papi aren't that savvy, so they have no idea how to stop me. So I've read a lot about "us." What the world thinks of vampires. You all have weird ideas of what we're like. But I don't feel any different knowing all the myths and rumors. Is it really so bad just to *know*?

4) Then there are the little things. The things they tell me are true and I believe them because I haven't found anything online to counter it all. So: no silver.
5) No wooden stakes. (As if I'm going to stake myself? Okay.)
6) No mirrors. Apparently, they used to be backed with silver, and even if they aren't anymore, old habits die hard with vampires. No risks taken, no rules broken.
7) No interaction with any humans who are not a meal, either immediate or planned. Do you realize what that means? I have never had a conversation with one of you. Not a single one. Oh, I've spoken to humans, but it's usually as they're fading away and I'm thanking them. Otherwise? Nothing.
8) No *anything*.

Okay, maybe that last one isn't an actual rule. But it feels true. My life is ordered and safe. I don't think I've done anything dangerous since I was born.

It is exactly as boring as it seems.

ThrowawayOne: first
8 Notes

invisibleb0y
June 8, 2018

I shouldn't exist. Isn't that a fucked-up thought? But it's not a thought. It's who I am. I wasn't joking about the whole breeding thing. As far as I know, there hasn't been a child born to vampires . . . *ever*. Papi sat me down when I was real young and told me the whole story. Vampires have been around for a long time—maybe longer than what you would consider "humankind"—but the only way for new vampires to exist is to sire a human, to turn them into one of us. But then, despite the impossibility of it all, Mami became pregnant, and then I popped out nine months later. Just like a human.

But I'm not human.

I'm something else.

It's cool, I guess. I can run really fast without getting tired, and I can see super far. I can't turn into a bat; Mami said she doesn't know where that myth about vampires came from. Even though I rest during daylight, I don't get sleepy like you—just tired. It's more like meditation than anything else.

I wish this felt more like a superpower.

Because it's turning into a curse.

They left the clan the moment they found out Mami was pregnant. We disappeared up north in Appalachia, then headed west. We don't move as frequently anymore, at least not since we found out how desolate it is in the desert. And so I'm stuck here. No real way to do anything but learn about the world instead of live in it.

I'm a secret.

I'm an impossibility.

I'm so fucking exhausted by it all.

0 Comments
7 Notes

invisibleb0y
June 10, 2018

You know what I did this morning?

I waited.

There's a moment as dawn arrives when light can fill a room without hurting me. I've only felt daylight once, when I was a kid. I was curious. Can you blame me? You've probably tested your parents' boundaries before.

Okay, maybe not like this. I won't forget the way the sun pierced through my skin that first time, sank deep into my bones, poisoning me for days. Mami brought me an old man, someone near death who lived alone, and I drank him completely dry to accelerate my healing. Even then, I was nauseous and sweaty for a full week.

Never again.

But I've found a sweet spot. I'm so close to making it work. There's one brief moment as the sun rises in the east and is blocked by the branches of the willow tree outside one of the windows that's not boarded up. It's just the essence of light, and if I turn my face toward the window, it's there. In the computer screen. The color of my face. A brief reflection of it. There's no real shape there; it's all blurry and rounded, and I haven't made out any details yet. I don't know if that's because we have no reflection *anywhere* or because it's just a terrible surface. But I'm determined to see myself.

This is what occupies my time some mornings, before the sun is too bright, before we all descend into the cellar we lock from the inside.

NoOneKissesLikeGaston: Ooooh, creepy. Love this. What a cool story!

4 Notes

invisibleb0y
June 12, 2018

I did something reckless today.

And I feel alive.

I told Papi that I wanted to lie on the roof and watch the stars. I'd read about a meteor shower appearing over the desert that night, which wasn't a lie. He said I showed "initiative" by wanting to explore more of the world, and he smiled at me, and it made his dark, bushy mustache wiggle on his wide face. I got a funny feeling in my stomach, a tickling sensation, and I liked that.

Some days, my parents are not that bad.

Papi did not join me at first; he said he'd be out later. I climbed up to the roof in a few leaps. From the top, I could see for miles in every direction. It was a clear night, cool and quiet, and I could hear the coyotes far in the distance if I focused, blocked out everything in my mind. My hearing has always been better than my vision.

But tonight, there was a flicker. A flash a quarter mile to the east.

"They are too close," Mami told me once. "We leave them alone. We do not hunt nearby." I had no idea who lived there, but I knew what that flash was.

Headlights.

I made for it without another thought. I leaped off the roof and rolled right into a run. I had never pumped my legs faster, never used the power of the last feeding so intensely, never felt the desert air rush over my face like that. I focused on the location of that flash, and seconds later, I stood just outside the property.

I had to be quick.

Darting to the building, I peered inside the closest window, let my eyes adjust to the lack of light.

Nope. Not there.

I rushed to the back door, aware of the sounds of the man inside shuffling about. There was some metal device on the roof, and I wondered if that was how he boosted his wireless signal so far out from his home.

Again, I peered inside.

His home was cluttered, full of scraps of metal, wires, motherboards, and other sorts of electronic paraphernalia. But not what I was looking for.

I spun around, saw my home in the distance. Terror rose from my gut, and I imagined my father climbing up on the roof to join me, discovering that I wasn't there, realizing what I had done. *Faster, Cisco!* I told myself.

A light came on in another room. I heard water running. It *had* to be there.

I crept around the east side of the house, toward the tiny window where yellowish light burst forth. Jumped up and put my fingers on the windowsill. Went still, quiet. Then pulled myself up as slow as I could, hoping the man inside wouldn't notice me. I squinted, trying to block the light out and—

No mirror.

He had no mirror in his own bathroom.

I let myself fall and landed on the dirt without a sound. I was darting away from the man's house when I heard the squeak, the sound of a rusted hinge.

I spun around.

No one was there.

But it blew in the wind. *The door to the mailbox.* I ripped it open.

An envelope.

I pulled it out. *Jairo Mendoza.* And an address. An address! Oh, how had I never thought of that?

I said it over and over and over and over and over and over, and as I ran back home, desperately hoping my parents had not yet come to check on me, I repeated it.

I was on the roof seconds later, and when Papi came to join me, he said nothing for a while.

"This is nice," he told me.

"Yeah," I said.

I have an idea. I don't know if it'll work.

NoOneKissesLikeGaston: Okay, now I'm hooked. When does the next chapter come out? You should be posting these on AO3.

CanIScream: It's not fanfic. Only fanfic belongs there.

NoOneKissesLikeGaston: I think it's a good story regardless. Almost feels real lol

15 Notes

invisibleb0y
June 14, 2018

I did it.

I did it.

It was so much worse this time. I had no meteor shower to use as an alibi. We had just finished my lesson on some boring part of America. I hate when my parents try to teach me history because . . . well, usually they'd been there. At least for the last couple hundred years, that is. They trade giggles and knowing smirks, and they make secret references to things, and it frustrates me. They never tell me any of the good shit! They just stick to the high school textbooks they'd stolen, occasionally making comments about how "inaccurate" the text is.

It's another way I live a separate life from them. And they designed it that way. My whole life is designed.

So when Papi said he was going to run to the school again to see if they had an Algebra II book, I told him I didn't need algebra because I was a vampire. He thought it was pretty funny.

He still went.

Why? Why do they want to me to learn about stuff I'm not allowed to experience? Why should I care about history and math and science when they won't let me experience the world?

After Dad left, Mami wandered over to where I sat, my back pressed against the wall, irritation running through me. She said she was going to head down into the cellar for a few minutes. "Be right back, mijo," she said, running her fingers through my black curls and kissing me on the forehead.

I knew it was my only window of opportunity.

I ran. Even faster than the other night. I headed straight for Jairo's home, and when I reached his back door, I froze.

I'd never done anything like this.

I raised my hand to the doorknob and slowly turned it. It made no sound. I pulled on the door and peeked around it. No humans. No one. I moved silently then, stopping the door from slamming, and drifted from the kitchen into his room.

He was asleep.

And it was so hard. I had not fed in two months, and while my control was decent, I could hear him.

Thump, thump.

Thump, thump.

THUMP, THUMP.

So loud.

So . . . delicious.

But I had a reason to be there. I moved to the small bedside table, and I grabbed his wallet, fishing out two credit cards.

I was gone seconds later.

Home not long after that.

Reading a news website when Mami came back upstairs.

"Anything interesting happening in the world?"

I shook my head. "It's all the same."

She sighed. "We're low. You want to come hunting tomorrow?"

I nodded. "Sí, Mami." I started to say something else, but she cut me off.

"Juntos," she said. Frustration roiled in me at the reminder: never alone.

Mami stared at me, and in her eyes was the same infantilization as in her voice. She was in control. I couldn't choose for myself.

"Okay," I muttered. My face burned. "Together."

She ruffled my hair, and her touch sent rage down my spine. "When you're grown, we'll talk about it."

Then she was gone.

She was standing just outside the room, mere feet from me, when I used Jairo's credit card to order a digital camera, one with excellent low-light capabilities.

I'm going to do it. As soon as it arrives at his house, I'm going to do it.

NoOneKissesLikeGaston: how am I this invested in a stranger

ToEachTheirOwn: why do u write with all those sentences on
    one line each

6 Notes

invisibleb0y
June 14, 2018

What do I look like?

Is my nose sharp? Wide? I've felt it before. I think it flares out at the sides. What about my brows? My ears? I don't really have anything to compare them to. Are my eyes dark? Light? What do my curls look like? I know how they *feel*, but that's not the same. Papi is the one who gives me haircuts, only a couple of times a year, and whenever I wrap my curls around my fingers, one side always feels shorter than the other. But I can't see for myself. He says it looks fine, and once again, I must defer to what my parents tell me. I get no choice of my own.

It's going to happen.

I'm going to see myself.

IAmJustLikeYou: I'll help you. I promise.
4 Notes

invisibleb0y
June 15, 2018

My ambition gave me energy on our hunt tonight.

We were miles and miles from home, far to the south. Papi said he knew of a small settlement that hugged the mountains out that way, and he was certain that we could find someone. Someone no one would look for.

We'd been running for ten minutes or so when we passed it. Tucked next to a grove of mesquite, it glimmered in what little moonlight there was. I slowed, and Mami was the first to notice. "Cisco, vámonos," she ordered. "We have a long way to go."

I walked to the edge of the small oasis, to the lake that rippled in the slight breeze. I leaned over the water's edge. Saw the outline of myself, a shadow and vague shapes, my face twisting in the gentle waves. It wasn't a full moon, but would I be able to see more of me if it was? I had a couple of weeks to find out.

I would come back, I told myself. A backup plan, just in case.

I ran with my parents. I couldn't stop thinking about that water and my shimmering, blurry reflection.

NoOneKissesLikeGaston: So, you didn't *really* hunt, did you?

MiseryBusiness: I just found this blog. Wow, this is such a cool project. Wish I'd thought of it!

7 Notes

invisibleb0y
June 16, 2018

I've been reading about other lives for so long. I have devoured stories here from people all over the world, who are dealing with things that are arguably worse than what I'm going through. But I still feel empty most days, as if all I can do is pour myself into the lives of strangers. I want to be fulfilled someday, too. I'm tired of looking into the windows of your homes and your families.

I want someone to see *me*.

Papi told me that I spend too much time on the computer. That I need to listen to him and Mami more, that they know the world better than anyone else. I just smiled at him. What am I supposed to say to that? They haven't "lived" in the world in seventeen years. We've been self-exiled outcasts since I was born. How could they possibly know more than anyone else?

I have to do this. Papi just made me all the more certain of that.

NoOneKissesLikeGaston: We support you! Lmao listen to me, I sound obsessed.

MiseryBusiness: People always tell me I spend too much time online. Maybe if the outside world was better, I'd spend more time in it.

CallOfDuty92301: Why do you guys like this melodramatic garbage? 👎

12 Notes

invisibleb0y
June 17, 2018

I ran to Jairo's house today. There was a brief opportunity for it. I'm getting good at finding these flashes of time, and our hunt from the other night gave me some much-needed energy. We caught a man peeping in to another man's home, and I fed for nearly an hour on the culprit. I felt no guilt as I drained him; that was nice. Some days, I do feel guilty when we have to cut a life short. But we thank them for what they give us. Their sacrifice allows us to live.

Mami laughed when I sat back and belched. She looked at my face for a long time, and it wasn't like the other day. "Estás creciendo," she said, and her eyes were warm. "Maybe you *will* get to hunt on your own."

I perked up at that. "¿De veras?"

She shook her head. "Not that soon. Once we know you can be trusted. Once we know you'll follow the rules."

"Haven't I been?"

"Yes," she said. "But we need a few more years just to make sure."

So . . . never.

That's what she meant, right?

We took the other man with us. Turns out he lived alone, and he didn't make much noise.

There was no mail at Jairo's house today.

Maybe this was a terrible idea.

0 Comments
6 Notes

invisibleb0y
June 18, 2018

Do you know what it's like to be trapped?
    Walled-in. Unable to escape.
    I don't see how I'm ever getting out of this.
    Sorry. There was no delivery again. Today sucked.
    Ha ha. I wish that was as funny as I hoped it would be.

NoOneKissesLikeGaston: I'm sorry. :(
3 Notes

invisibleb0y
June 19, 2018

They found me.
    I'm such a fool. I should have known it was too easy. I should
have known it was all too good to be true.
    They thought I was hunting on my own. They were *proud* of
me. That's why they followed me, at a distance, watching me as I
dashed away from home, out into the lonely desert.
    They thought I was ready to be something else.
    Instead, they observed me as I approached the house.
    As I made straight for the mailbox, not paying attention to
anything else.
    As I flung it open.
    Pulled out the package.
    Tore at the edge.
    And Jairo Mendoza raised his shotgun.

Aimed at me.

I heard the flint strike, then saw a blur, a flash, and then a bang, and Mami had Jairo on the ground. She shrieked something fierce as she ripped out his throat, one fluid motion, a spray of blood soaking the thirsty sand.

When she rose, her hand was gone. Just a stump where it used to be.

She'd taken the buckshot for me. And there I stood, ashamed, the digital camera box in my hand, and Papi was screaming at me, the same thing over and over.

"¿Qué hiciste, Cisco?!"

What did *I* do?

Mami fed, ravenously, completely. Jairo Mendoza was gone, emptied in minutes, and she panted as she began the regrowth process. It would take days. It would be painful.

"We did this to protect you, mijo," she said, the redness falling down her own throat, over her now-stained camisa. "You were supposed to follow the rules. Why? Why did you do this?"

I had nothing to say to them. I couldn't explain it then, and even now, sitting in the dark, I have nothing.

They buried his body far away. They said we should be fine, but we would most likely need to move soon.

The sun is coming up.

I have to go.

NoOneKissesLikeGaston: Come back! We're listening to you!

ThrowawayOne: This is still going?

MiseryBusiness: Damn, is this thing real? I feel weird about this whole thing. Maybe it's some real kid going thru something? I dunno.

19 Notes

invisibleb0y
June 24, 2018

I still have nothing to say.

He's dead. And it's all my fault.

NoOneKissesLikeGaston: You did what you had to. Please
   come back!
TrueAnneRiceFan: man, this blog is gay
ToEachTheirOwn: @TrueAnneRiceFan who says that anymore
   in 20-gay-teen?
18 Notes

invIsIbleb0y
June 29, 2018

I went back to the lake today.

The moon was full, and I had not left home since they caught
me. I told Papi y Mami the truth this time: that I needed to get outside, even just for an hour, or I was going to explode. I think they
could tell how sad I felt, how much I regretted what I had done.
"Una hora," Mami said. "Then be back right here. ¿Entiendes?"

I nodded. "Lo siento."

I have said that a lot lately.

I knew one of them would follow me. I knew they wouldn't
leave me alone. They didn't trust me.

So I stood at the edge of that shimmering beauty, and I was
disappointed to find that I looked exactly the same.

Blurry at the edges. Undefined. Shapeless.

This was such a pointless exercise.

Which is why I thought I imagined him at first. I looked up at the figure on the other side of the oasis, and I thought maybe he was another saguaro cactus, tall and quiet.

But then he moved forward.

Stepped to the edge of the lake.

I could see black hair, shining in the light of the moon.

He raised a hand to me.

I returned it.

I looked north, where I expected to find Papi watching me, but he wasn't there. Maybe he was hiding again. And if so, had he seen this person gesture at me?

Then: A ripple. A wave. Something drifted through my body, light and tingly.

I turned, focused on the young man.

He *smiled*.

The wave passed again, and I took a step forward, the edge of my shoe now in the water, and whatever this feeling was, it tugged me forward, closer to the boy.

And then . . . he was just gone.

A wisp of dust kicked up in the spot where he'd stood. He had moved so fast, and . . . was it possible? Was he another one of . . . *me?*

Another vampire. It seemed so bizarre; I'd been kept away from others my whole life, and sometimes, they were just a myth. A tale. An exaggeration.

Maybe that's what I feel like to all of you. Just a story.

I walked back home. Mami was standing at the doorway, caressing her hair. She was nervous. She was always nervous around me now, as if I'd make a sudden move and disappear on her. Any trust was gone, but even worse? It seemed like any *hope* she had for me, for my growth, had vanished, too.

"You look tired," she said.

"Do I?" I said. And I indulged myself. "What do I look like, then, Mami?"

She examined me, her eyes tracing my face, and I wanted to know what she saw. Did she see that I was frayed at the edges? That I was drowning in guilt?

"You're beautiful," she said. "But you frightened me. Made me scared I was losing you."

"I'm sorry," I said.

I noticed she had not answered my question.

"The rules are for a reason," she reminded me. Then she walked quickly into our home.

Fuck their rules.

CanIScream: damn you, I'm so invested in this story. Can you
   update more than once a day lol pleeeeeaase.
53 Notes

invisibleb0y
July 9, 2018

I find any excuse I can to get back to that lake these days.

I want to see him again. I want to know what that sensation was. I want so many things.

So I've been every night since that first night, and he's never there.

Maybe I did imagine it. They say guilt can do messed-up things to your mind. And I can't get the image of the spray of blood out of my head, even though I've seen blood more times than I could ever remember. But Mami had never killed someone like that. Not *ever*.

It all hurts so much. Like the biggest pile of the heaviest rocks is sitting on my chest and I can't shake myself free.

You probably won't hear from me for a while.

NoOneKissesLikeGaston: Please come back. :(
68 Notes

invisibleb0y
July 16, 2018

He's real.
  He's real.
  I wasn't imagining it.
  HE'S REAL.

BrujaBorn: Wait, what do you mean? Come on, man, give us
  another post!
127 Notes

invisibleb0y
July 17, 2018

I'm sorry, I didn't mean to leave all of you with a cliff-hanger there.
Mami came into the room, so I had to close the tab and pretend
like I was doing some research for Papi's silly history lesson that
night.

  By the way, where did you all *come* from? I'm surprised anyone
is interested in these pointless rants, but . . . welcome.

  I still can't believe it. I'm not alone.

  There are others.

  He was there this time, and when he appeared at the edge of
the oasis, I almost didn't believe it. After trying so many times,
why now? Why *this* time?

  I felt him before I saw him. I've never experienced that wave,
that gentle surge, like I did when this strange boy stood across the

lake from me. Is that a vampire thing? Is that something we can do? My parents never told me about anything like that, but then again, they've kinda left out a lot of things about me. Oh well.

He whispered, and I heard every word.

"We had to make sure you were alone," he said.

"'We'?"

"There are others," he said, and those words . . . they thumped in my chest, pressed on my heart. "We've been watching you. Trying to find the right time."

The desert was silent around us. His voice was deep, so soft, his words a thrumming rhythm in my ears.

"The right time for what?"

"To make contact."

And then he was right next to me. "I'm Kwan," he said. "And you're not the only one."

I flinched, took a step back. The surge pushed against my body, like invisible hands were pressing on my chest. I heard it all: The beetles toiling in the dirt. The snake slithering underneath a bush to the west. The gentle lapping of water at the edge of the lake. Was that a coyote howling? I turned my head in its direction but could not see it. How far away was it? Fifty miles? A hundred? How could I possibly hear at that distance? I focused on Kwan's face, shutting out the sudden invasion of sounds.

"It's new, isn't it?"

His voice was confident. When had I last spoken to someone other than my parents? The words coming out of his mouth terrified me. Thrilled me. He was so beautiful, with smooth skin, sharp cheekbones, dark eyes, his hair jet-black and silky.

I wanted him. It was as simple as that.

"What's new?" I asked, resisting the urge to press my lips against his. Why? Why was this happening?

"The feeling you get," he said, and he smiled, flashing his teeth at me. They were sharp like mine.

"What is it?" I breathed my words, like an exhale I had been waiting a lifetime to release.

"It's what happens when we are together. People like us."

I swallowed down my desire. "Who do you think I am? Like *what?*"

"We were all born just like you," said Kwan, and he stepped closer. I held my ground. "We shouldn't exist, but we do."

"How did you find me?"

He smiled, his lip curling up on one side. "Dude, you have a *blog*."

I winced. "Wait, really? That's how?"

He nodded. Stepped closer.

"It's weird to see you again," Kwan said. "Even after that first time, I didn't want to believe you were real."

He raised a hand.

When his fingertips grazed over my cheek, I trembled. An electricity passed from him to me, and I could see so far, could hear so much, could feel the energy from my last feed growing within me.

"We have been trying to find you for weeks."

His index finger ran along my jaw.

"We have something you want."

Then it was on my bottom lip.

And he was so close.

His hand moved to the curls on the right side of my head.

"They're shorter on this side," Kwan said. "Did you know that?"

I laughed. I *knew* I was right!

His eyes went wide.

A *whoosh*.

He was gone.

I held my breath, and then I heard a crackling behind me.

Papi.

Mami trailing behind.

"Cisco?" she called out, and I tried to pretend like my whole life hadn't changed.

"Aquí, Mami," I said.

She gracefully dodged the cacti and ocotillo bushes. "What are you doing out here?" She was worried again, and her gaze was piercing.

So I told her the truth.

(Well . . . *a* truth.)

"This place," I said. "It makes me feel better. And a little less alone."

Papi joined her side, and he scowled. Maybe I shouldn't have said that. Maybe I should have kept it to myself. But I could see from the pain on their faces that they believed it.

And if they believed me, they wouldn't question why I was at the lake in the first place.

Mami played with her long hair for a few moments. "Do you really feel alone?" she finally asked.

Tears pricked my eyes, and I had to turn away. Wasn't it obvious? Wasn't it so crystal clear that I was completely isolated, that I was desperate for *anything* outside the life they'd made for me?

"Sometimes," I said, offering them a concession of sorts.

"I'm sorry you had to see . . . you know . . . what you saw, mijo." Mami laced her fingers with Papi's and continued, "I know we haven't *really* talked about it. We just don't want any harm to come to you."

"I know," I said. Wanted to say something more. I let the words perish. There was no need to justify this to them. They wouldn't get it. "I just need some time to myself every day. Not long. Is that okay?"

"Te amamos, Cisco," Papi said.

That's the worst part. I'm sure they probably do. But how do you tell someone that their love suffocates you?

NoOneKissesLikeGaston: Whew, my face is burning.
MiseryBusiness: Welcome back!
BrujaBorn: This has to be real. It just *has* to be.
298 Notes

invisiblebOy
July 18, 2018

Just after midnight, I made for the lake again. I knew I had a couple of minutes before my parents returned. They had left me alone to go hunt, and so I broke their rule without hesitation. They had hunted without me, so technically . . . they broke their own rule?

I made for that shimmering water.

Called his name.

It rang out over the water and he came to me, a burst of wind, and then he froze at my side. I stared into those eyes again.

"You're real, aren't you?"

He nodded.

"How are there others?"

"We don't know." He ran a hand down the full length of my left arm. I shivered, not from any chill.

"My parents . . ." I paused, let my eyes wash over his body, over the way his T-shirt fit across his chest, his round stomach. "They said I was the only one."

He smiled. "Definitely not true."

"But why?" My voice was not a whisper anymore. "Why would they lie to me?"

A frown twisted his face. "That's a question for them, not us."

"What else is true?"

Kwan tilted his head to the side. "About us? About what we are?"

I nodded.

"I don't know what else they told you," he said. "What I should say about what we are."

"I want to know it all," I said.

About me. About us. About *him*.

"I know you do, but . . ." He turned his face away, scrunched it up. "I don't know if I should be the one to tell you."

I put my hand on his chest. Didn't even think about it. I just wanted to feel that surge again, and his power—if that was what you could call it—rushed forward, spread into me.

But it wasn't enough. It seemed so unfair to experience this only once in a while, always unplanned, never sure when the next jolt would be. I needed *more*.

"I don't know if I can come back," I said. "If I can keep this up. My parents are going to catch me."

He turned to leave but paused. "You could come with us."

"I can't," I said, more of an instinct than an objection. "How could I do something like that?"

"We all did it," he said, and there was no hesitation there. In that, he revealed so much.

There were others.

Their parents had most likely lied to them, too.

And they had left.

"You just . . . went out on your own? But *how*?"

"Just . . . think about it."

Then Kwan disappeared as quick as he arrived.

And his words were all I thought about as I stretched out on the roof ten minutes later, staring into the night sky. Papi joined me, asked me what I was doing.

"Dreaming," I said.

He stood there for a few moments, and he couldn't have known that my body was humming with energy, the residual effect of being near Kwan.

"Am I really the only one?" I asked. Aloud. To him. To the sky.

He used the tip of his boot to scratch at the roof. It was an unconscious reaction to being nervous, and I sat up, holding myself with my elbows.

"The only one," he said, smiling at me. "Eres especial."

He walked back into the house without another word.

Did they know? Was Papi certain in that claim, or was it just another lie they told me to keep me safe?

I began to consider what Kwan had said, and the act twisted up my stomach, set my heart afire in panic.

He told me to think about it.

So I did.

NoOneKissesLikeGaston: Is it weird that I want you to go?
    Because I want you to.
NoOneKissesLikeGaston: (Wow, I'm talking to you like you're
    real. Are you real?)
924 Notes

invisibleb0y
July 19, 2018

The sun had just set when Mami came up from the cellar, her face fixed with a scowl. "Cisco, have you been reading those conspiracy blogs again?"

I had a book in my lap, my back pressed against the wall. My stomach lurched as I looked up at her. She was *serious*. "What are you talking about?"

"Your Papi said you asked him something strange yesterday," she continued, using a towel to wipe blood off her hands. "About being the only one."

I closed the book. "I was just curious, that's all."

But she wasn't buying it. I could see it written in her pained expression.

"You can't believe everything you read online, mijo," she said. "We are just trying to protect you."

"Protect me from *what*? Is someone coming to get me?"

"Well, *no*," she said, her shoulders drooping. "But that's because we've kept you safe."

I shook my head, then rose. "You're always saying that, Mami. But you never explain what I'm safe *from*."

"We can't let the other clans find you," she blurted out. "Ever. It's just too risky."

"What could they *possibly* do to me?!" I shouted. "I'm a vampire! I can just run away or you can fight them off or *something*. Instead we just *hide*? Are we nothing but cowards?"

"Don't speak to her like that." Papi's voice sliced through the tension in the air.

That's the thing with us vampires; we can sneak up on each other really well, and he strode right up to me. I had never seen him like this. Papi wore his fury like a mask, like an adornment for war. His mustache twitched as he spoke, and he pointed a straight finger at me. "Do you know what we gave up for you? What was asked of us?"

I shook my head.

"We lost our *clan*," he seethed. "We lost a community. A home in *one* place. We gave it up because we loved you, long before you were born. Can't you appreciate our sacrifice?"

"We would have chosen something different if we could have," Mami added, and she came to Papi's side, caressed his back, up and down. "Anything else. But this is what we had to do."

It took a moment. They presented such a unified force, but Papi didn't even realize what he'd said. "What do you mean?" I asked him. "What was 'asked' of you?"

The masks broke.

The facades cracked.

And for a second—if even that long—their expressions betrayed them. Told me everything I'd wanted to know.

As quickly as they'd broken, their faces became stony again. But it was too late. I'd already seen what I needed to see: They had been lying to me. My whole life.

"You said you left on your own," I said, tugging on that loose thread. "You said as soon as Mami was pregnant, you escaped in the middle of the night."

Mami hesitated. Just a moment. Just enough for me to know that the next words out of her mouth weren't true.

"We had to leave," she said, and uncertainty crossed her face again. "We had to keep you safe."

"Then why can't you just tell me the *truth*?" I shouted back. "What am I? Why did we have to leave?"

"Someday," said Papi, his eyes pleading as much as his voice. "We will tell you *everything*. But just trust us that you were unsafe, and so we did what we could to make sure you were protected."

They smiled at me. It was hollow, empty, an attempt to placate me, to keep me complacent.

I smiled back. My offering. My peace.

But I'm telling you now, Kwan. I hope you're reading this. I can't do this anymore. I have to know what I am.

Tomorrow. Meet me at the lakeside. 3:15 a.m.

Please. Please, tell me who I am.

FireOfTheSea: lol what is happening. why is this so INTENSE.

FireFromTheGods: first

FireFromTheGods: ah, damn

NoOneKissesLikeGaston: Oh, Cisco, I hope you find what
   you're looking for. I believe in you. So much! I already ship
   you and Kwan <3

941 Notes

invisibleb0y
July 19, 2018

I killed my first human when I was eight.

We store blood below the house. You never know when the population is going to wither away, or when people will move too far for us to hunt. My parents have tried to prepare for every possible scenario. When we hunt, we drink, and we take another to keep belowground just in case. I can go three months at most without feeding, but every so often, it's too hard to find a new meal. So it's the same in every home: We move in. Mami and Papi get to digging, and soon, we have a storage room below the earth, one that is cool, one that can protect what we need to survive.

You'd be surprised how long all of you humans can last with just a little food and water: months. Once we kept someone for a year and a half, and the only reason he didn't last longer is because a bad drought made it impossible for us to hunt. It sent people out of the desert that year, not into it.

I was eight the first time my parents led me down the stairs of our home to feed. I don't remember what state we were in. No matter. It was some nondescript place, in the middle of nowhere, in the heart of nothing.

I never knew who he was. But I remember him. I heard him whimpering. His hair like straw, matted against his forehead, his eyes wide as we descended, the way he tore at his restraints over and over again, ripping his wrists with new wounds, and then I smelled him. I smelled the fresh life spilling from where he'd rubbed himself raw.

And suddenly, I knew there had always been someone in our basement. My parents used to bring fresh blood to me in a ceramic bowl, and it was always warm. I put it together that first time: It was warm because it had just been drained from the body.

But that night, Papi pushed me toward the man. "Estás listo," he told me. "Tómalo."

Mami clutched my hand tightly. Then she released me.

Instinct took over. I plunged forward, and it was like I knew exactly where to bite, where on this man's body would provide the most blood in the least amount of time. My mouth clamped down on his leg, right on his femoral, and his warmth, his life, filled me up.

He fought.

It was futile.

He finally went lifeless beneath me. When I looked up at Mami y Papi, the man's blood dribbling down my chin, they gave me pride. Happiness. Joy.

"Lo hiciste," Mami said. "This is just the start, Cisco."

"Soon you'll come with us," added Papi. "Outside. To hunt."

I wanted to run away from that cellar right then, despite being full, despite not needing to feed. The urge nearly overpowered me.

It's been nine years. That urge hasn't gone away.

This isn't a joke. Or some weird cry for attention.

I'm going to leave.

I'm going to find a way out.

NoOneKissesLikeGaston: You don't really kill people. You're
  probably just saying this to seem tough.

TrueAnneRiceFan: Yo, he's a vampire. What did you expect?

NoOneKissesLikeGaston: You don't really know him like I do.
  I've been following this since the beginning.

1,285 Notes

invisibleb0y
July 20, 2018

This is it.

This is the last time you'll hear from me.

I crept out of the house just after three. I told Papi y Mami that I was going back to the lake for a few minutes before the sun came up. Papi made some terrible joke about how I was spending a lot of time there. I laughed but said nothing. I saw Mami exchange a look with him.

It filled me with dread.

Did they know?

I wasn't far from the house when I started to run, when I heard my name called behind me, when I knew they suspected that I had been lying. I ran faster than I thought possible, exhaustion pushing through my bones, begging me to stop, begging to feed. I began to sense other creatures, to feel their pulses as I rushed past, but I ignored them.

"Cisco!"

I couldn't stop.

"Cisco, ¡espera!"

I couldn't wait anymore.

"Cisco, *please!*"

I was done being protected.

I skidded to a stop at the edge of the water.

"Kwan, I'm here!"

Seconds later, my parents stumbled, fell into defensive positions.

There.

On the other side of the lake: Kwan.

"Cisco . . . ," he growled. My name in his mouth was raw with possibility. Was he warning me? Beckoning to me?

"I'm here," I said. "Take me with you."

"No!" Mami yelled. "You're not going anywhere!"

She reached out to grab my arm, but I flinched away from her, watched as disappointment and shock spread over her face.

"Please, Cisco," said Papi. "No puedes salir. We can't protect you if you do."

"We can."

Kwan was at my side. He placed his fingers in between mine, and he sent a shiver up my arm, into my whole body. His power caressed me, coursed through me, gave me strength. *How?* I thought. *How is this possible?*

"You're not alone," Kwan told me, then looked to my parents. "There are more of us, just like me, born like Cisco, and we have *survived.*"

They stepped out from behind the trees and bushes that surrounded the oasis. Five. Ten. Twenty. So many kids, all of them moving with the caution of those who know they can be hunted just as easily as they hunt others. They were tall. Short. I made eye contact with a girl whose skin was darker than mine, her hair braided tight against her head, and she nodded so slightly it was almost imperceptible.

And that wave was immense. Nearly overpowering. The energy I felt from Kwan in those early interactions was now multiplied twentyfold.

This. This was our power.

And it was amplified when we were *together*.

"How can you trust them?" Mami asked, her hands outstretched toward me like an offering. "They're just strangers!"

"Because of people like *you*," the girl spat out. "You kept us apart. You told Cisco he was *alone*."

I rounded on my parents, my mouth open in horror. "You *knew*? You knew this entire time?"

Papi was crying. "We would have told you," he said, his mustache twisting on his face. "Someday, we would have told you everything."

My body raged, but Kwan placed a hand on my chest.

The surge.

The power.

Our power.

"When?" I crossed over to Papi, stood nose-to-nose with him. "When was 'someday' going to come? When were you going to tell me that there were others like me?"

"When the clan told us to," he answered, his face quivering. "When they figured out what all of you could do when you were together, they were afraid! They were afraid of all of you!"

All of *us*.

I was not the only one of my kind. I wasn't *alone*.

Kwan squeezed my hand. "Cisco, I brought you something to prove that we mean what we say. That we know what you've been through. That proves that we *care*."

He let go. Reached into his back pocket.

I saw it flash in the low moonlight.

Papi cried out, and he made to move toward me, but he was surrounded moments later. I counted them: seven vampires, all young, all like me.

Strangers.

Strangers like *me*.

"Don't do it," Mami begged. "The rules are . . ."

But she didn't finish. What did the rules matter anymore? My parents had constructed them to keep me trapped, and now . . . Tears streamed from Mami's eyes. I was free. And she knew it. She could not put me back in the box I had lived in.

I had to believe. In *myself*.

I grabbed the mirror and held it up to my face as my parents' screams filled the desert air.

There I was.

Cisco.

Me.

The tears threatened to blur my image. My *clear* image. I wiped at them, and there I was.

My eyebrows were black. Thick. They nearly joined in the center. I used my other hand to trace down the bridge of my nose, to my wide nostrils, to my lips, then over my cheekbones. There was a dusting of facial hair across the lower half of my face. Would I have to start shaving? Did vampires *shave*? Papi had to cut my hair, so . . .

There was so much I didn't know. So many questions I had not thought to ask before.

But I had also never seen this.

This was *me*.

"You told me I would die," I said, speaking to my parents without looking at them. "You told me that if I didn't follow your rules I'd be taken away."

Papi started to say something. "Cisco . . ."

"What else is a *lie*?" I yelled. "What else isn't true?"

"You have to understand," said Mami. "We had to protect you."

"What else isn't true?" I repeated.

"It doesn't matter," Papi said. "Some of it. Enough that you'd trust us."

The irony. They lied to make me *trust* them.

"There's more," Kwan said. "So much more about us that you don't know. So much about *yourself*."

Papi stopped crying. Wiped at the remnants of tears. He stood straight, lifted up his chin, and examined me.

I wore it on my face: A declaration. A plea. *Please, I have to do this.*

He shook his head. "It's too soon," he said.

But then Mami spoke.

"Is it?"

And my Papi, who was always so certain, always so pleased by history, always in possession of the answer, had nothing to say to that. I could see words forming on his lips, but nothing came out.

Their faces were etched with pain.

And then . . . resignation.

Mami smiled at me.

Papi uttered a word.

"Hazlo."

Mami cried harder, but she nodded, too.

Almost imperceptibly.

I gave Kwan my hand.

Fingers looped around mine.

A desire bloomed there, not just born of our collective power, but of lust, too. When had a boy touched me like this? Never. I wanted that, too.

Do it.

He whisked me away, and I looked back at them, just once.

They smiled.

Was it a blessing? Perhaps. But they did not chase me. They did not follow.

They let me go.

We're in a car now. I've never been inside one before. Kwan said it'll get us to our next stop faster. We're picking up someone on the way.

Another one of *us*.

The battery on Kwan's phone is low. I gotta give it back.

You won't hear from me again.

I'm free.

CanIScream: Wow. Is this really over?

FireOfTheSea: What a story. Does anyone else think vampires are really real after reading this?

TrueAnneRiceFan: Fake. Entertaining, but . . . there's no way this is real.

NoOneKissesLikeGaston: Come back. Please! I can't go without my updates. Please come back, Cisco.

5,125 Notes

REFLECTIONS
Or But First,
Let Me Take a Selfie

Zoraida Córdova &
Natalie C. Parker

Mirrors are surrounded by superstition and lore. Narcissus loved his reflection so much he drowned in it. In many cultural traditions around the world, all mirrors and reflective surfaces are covered while a family mourns a death. Breaking a mirror supposedly comes with seven years of bad luck. Even the Evil Queen believes she can bewitch the truth from a mirror. And one of the oldest myths about vampires is that they cast no reflection at all. The root of this myth is exactly what Cisco discovers in this story: Most old mirrors were backed with silver, which, in some traditions, can harm or even kill a vampire. Thus, no reflections! This is such a well-known piece of mythology that it shows up again and again in contemporary stories about vampires, but the reasons evolve along with the tales. Another kind of reflection is how we see ourselves in stories, and who *gets* to see their lives and experiences reflected. Mark blends vampire lore with this question of who gets to have a reflection at all. Do vampires *really* cast no reflection, or is that merely the story Cisco's been told? The title of this piece is inspired by Dr. Rudine Sims Bishop's writing about children's literature.

In what ways do vampire stories reflect your life and experiences?

THE HOUSE OF BLACK SAPPHIRES

Dhonielle Clayton

They said the Turner women of the House of Black Sapphires were a little strange. That they were just *too* beautiful. That they were up to no good.

They said the Turner women were vampires.

And whenever that word appeared, it was time to go. The Turner firebird would start the mourning song from its window perch; it knew when too many were watching, whispering, and surveying the beautiful Black women who floated in and out of the peculiar apothecary-turned-house. Their ever-moving coffin of sorts.

Bea hated the word *vampire*, and whenever they arrived in a new city—just like now—she braced for it, for all the other immortal folks to lump them together when they were decidedly not the same.

Her entire family and their thirteen trunks clogged the mahogany seats of a New Orleans streetcar. Mama had said they were headed to the Eternal Ward, one of five versions of the city run exclusively by those like them. That *this* was home. One Bea had never seen before. One Mama wasn't sure she ever wanted to see again.

But as Bea looked around at all the humans scrambling about, she thought everything seemed normal here. The perfume of the mortals' sweaty skin and the sound of their beating hearts made Bea's serrated tongue flare; she was eager to feed after such a long journey. As they snaked down Canal Street, a sticky breeze clung to her, and she couldn't fathom that they were headed to a beautiful, stilted version of this place.

Bea's five sisters excitedly pointed out everything. Her oldest sister, Cookie, complained about how sloppy and unrefined everyone dressed. Sora wanted to wander into every perfume shop in the French Quarter, while Annie Ruth was on a hunt for the best bookstore. May talked about how she could put her paint set to work with all the colorful buildings and iron-lace galleries and balconies, and little Baby Bird's mind couldn't keep up with her tongue as she commented on every strange thing she spotted. But Bea was sad about leaving Charleston, South Carolina, behind. She'd grown fond of the sweet town, with its cobblestone streets and weeping trees and sweetgrass baskets, and kissing Reginald Washington hadn't been too bad, because his mouth always tasted like the peaches from the tree in his mother's yard. Her room there had had its own claw-foot bathtub, which never stained, even after so many blood baths. It had overlooked the Old Bethel Church. Who knows what she'd see outside the window in this next home. If it would be just as lovely. They'd been in Charleston for a good little while, almost fooling Bea into thinking the bird, their Honey, might not sing again and they'd stay put.

Maybe this time she'd find an eternal love.

She and her sisters used to make wagers about what city might be next and how many years or decades or millennia they might stay until the firebird's song would wake them, remind them that they must leave. Bea had stopped counting now. No more clocks. No more calendars. Mama forbade them, and it was just as well. The hourglasses were all they had, all they really needed.

She wished they'd head back to Paris. It'd been at least a hundred years or so. The window boxes would be blooming with pink geraniums this time of year, and it wouldn't be so hot. Maybe she could see Annabelle—the girl she used to bite and kiss when she was bored—see if she enjoyed eternal life, see if she might be Bea's great eternal love. They'd left too soon for Bea to determine.

"Stop should be coming up," Mama said. "End of the line."

"Doesn't look like anything," her littlest sister, Baby Bird, said, her long twists hanging outside the streetcar window.

Mama snapped her fingers. "Be still, baby."

Each time they went to a new town or a new city, Bea's questions changed, a deck of cards reshuffled, the newest one plucked becoming her current obsession. This time she couldn't stop thinking about love. This city was where her parents met. Where her mama bit her father long, long ago and they became eternal partners.

This was the place Mama fell in love.

She was determined to have that too. She would have a great love story here. Her wish drummed through her, determined to settle in her bones.

The streetcar stopped. The driver stood robotically and exited.

"The warden will come any minute now." Mama turned to face Bea and all her sisters. Bea's heart squeezed with anticipation. "This Ward is full of bad water and bad news. It's a place that breaks your heart." Her dark eyes landed on Bea, the heat of her warning caught in her searing brown gaze. The one lovesick Turner put on notice. "We'll bide our time, then move on."

This was a city Mama feared.

But Bea was determined to discover why.

A white man dressed in all black stepped into the streetcar.

"Who is that?" Bea's second-oldest sister, Sora, asked.

"A warden," Mama whispered. "Now hush. Not a word from any of you. Not until we pass on through." She stood, greeted him, and smoothed the front of her dress.

"Papers or key?" he asked.

"Key," Mama replied, handing him a curious bone-white skeleton key that Bea had never seen before. More questions bloomed inside her, but she put a hand over her mouth to keep them from tumbling out.

The warden inspected it. "The Turners. The Eternal Ward."

She nodded.

"Welcome home." He smiled and revealed the sharp points of his teeth.

He sat in the driver's seat and turned a series of cranks and gears. The streetcar oscillated left and right, breaking free of its cables.

Mama took a deep breath.

"It's going to be fine, Evangeline," Bea heard her father whisper.

The streetcar moved forward. Clouds swept in, darkening the sky. The day went to night. Water rose beneath them, slapping and sloshing against the sides of the streetcar. Bea gripped the wooden bench and her eyes grew wide with wonder. Lights illuminated the way ahead like a scattering of lightning bugs putting on a welcome show or performing a warning dance. Bea couldn't decide which. A jolt shot up her spine.

An iron gate rose from the water and flickered. Different versions of it appeared one after the other, turning from licorice black to velveteen violet to emerald green to a rich coppery gold, finally settling on a bloody crimson. Mama took a deep breath as the red gates opened and the streetcar sailed forward.

"There are so many gates," Annie Ruth whispered. "You think we'll get to go to the others?"

"Mama never told us about any of this," replied Sora.

"I want to go to all of them," Baby Bird exclaimed.

"Hush up, all of you," Mama ordered.

The questions inside Bea's head swirled as they entered the Eternal version of New Orleans. What were the other Wards like? Would she get to visit them? Why would her mama ever want to leave a place so deliciously wonderful? Why hadn't she told them every detail of this place?

Pastel-colored houses sat on iron pillars, resembling pots of blush on stacked tiers. Long piers stretched into the waters, inviting decadent boats. Black columns held gas lamps, and glittering cables crisscrossed overhead, pulling streetcar-boats that dropped off well-dressed passengers at long stilted promenades. A stew of salt and fish and spice smothered the air, its undercurrent the tang of fat and fresh blood.

"Close your mouth before you catch flies, Bea," her eldest sister, Cookie, commented; her voice sounded almost identical to Mama's—honeyed and cut with brown sugar. Figures as much since she was Mama's oldest and had been with her the longest. Bea never asked how old either of them was, for it was rude to inquire about a woman's age, even an Eternal woman. She and Annie Ruth had guessed that Mama had to be nearing four hundred years old, though she'd never appear a day older than forty, and even then, onlookers couldn't exactly be sure. Cookie appeared to be in her early thirties, she'd surmised, and Bea would forever be eighteen. That's when her heart stopped.

"Shut up, Carmella," Sora snapped back. "Have you ever seen anything like this? Didn't think so."

Bea winked at Sora, and added, "Yeah. Have you, Cookie? Have you?"

"Don't say 'shut up,'" Mama commanded. Even after hundreds of years, Evangeline Turner still liked her girls to be pillars of etiquette.

Their streetcar floated behind another, and the warden yanked a gear to attach their roof cables to the overhead lines.

Baby Bird jumped from her seat and into Daddy's lap. "When will we get there? Can we go shopping first? Who are all those people? What are they?"

Mama snapped her fingers. "Enough!"

Baby Bird slithered back into her seat.

Daddy handed the warden their address:

435 ESPLANADE AVENUE

PIER #6

New Orleans, LA

The warden navigated the canal streets.

Bea tried to take everything in: how brass bands spilled out of parade-boats, their instruments pointed at the sky and their thunderous music sending ripples through the water; how people followed in their own boats, dancing and waving handkerchiefs and colorful parasols; how the graveyard sat on platforms, the dead raised high above; how massive trees rose like giants out of the murky waters, with red-eyed bats hanging from their boughs. Signs warned folks against swimming because of the bayou gators. Vendor-boats shouted about the best blood mules and sugar-dusted sanguine beignets.

"Are all the Wards like this?" Bea asked her mama.

"No. Each one is unique based on who lives there," Mama replied.

"Is there always water?"

"No. Just in this one."

"Why?"

"A vampire pissed off one of the conjure women and she flooded it."

"How do you get to them all?" Bea pressed. "Can we visit the others?"

"Did you hear me before we left Charleston? You listening, child? Or you just like it when I repeat myself?" Mama snapped her fingers. "We won't be traveling to the other Wards. We will stay put until it's time to move on, and I hope Honey makes it quick. I never intended to ever return here, and I don't want no trouble."

But sometimes Bea wanted trouble. Anything that made her eternal existence a little more entertaining. Her stomach tangled with all the things she might unravel and uncover in this peculiar version of this peculiar city. But she knew one thing: She'd find eternal love here. An electricity crackled across her skin; the energy of certainty.

They turned off Dauphine Street, and Bea gasped. She knew immediately which house was their new home.

The primrose pink was the color of the blush Mama always wore. Window boxes spilled over with her favorite midnight roses and rimmed a double porch piped with iron-lace. Eight rocking chairs waited, one for each of them. Lanterns hissed, and all the big glass windows flickered warm beams of welcoming light. Through one of the windows, Bea spotted ceilings covered in flowers—an upside-down English garden—and glowing candelabras. A sign dangled above the cream white door—THE HOUSE OF BLACK SAP-PHIRES: BEAUTY APOTHECARY AND PHARMACY OF DELIGHTS.

A black tongue of a pier awaited them.

"This one is the most beautifulest ever," Baby Bird exclaimed.

"That's not a word," Cookie corrected.

Baby Bird scoffed. "It's *my* word. I can make them up."

"No, you can't."

"She can and it's called a neologism," Bea informed.

"Hush," Mama replied. "All of you."

The firebird perched on the porch railing, cooing and welcoming the Turners to their new home. Their new gilded coffin of delights. Bea's heart lifted at the sight of Honey, the hum of mischief lingering right beneath the brown of her skin, and her incisors elongated, ready to bite, ready for mischief.

◆

"The perfume atomizers go on the second shelf," Cookie ordered as the Turner girls prepared their beauty pharmacy and apothecary to open to the public tomorrow night.

The Eternal women and vampires of this New Orleansian Ward would be able to get everything they needed: from tonics to keep their complexions clear after starvation periods to drams to lure partners to their beds to sun salves to help protect those who couldn't tolerate it. The elixirs they bottled delivered on their promises, for there was no snake oil in these pretty containers. Only the Turner women knew the secrets hidden in each glass jar. A secret alchemy of blood and spices.

"Does it really matter?" Bea complained, but still placed one of the creams on its proper shelf.

"It's how it's been for the past three hundred years."

"So does that mean it always has to be?" Bea replied.

"Why you all of a sudden trying to change things up? Don't act brand-new just cause we're in a different city." Sora swept behind her and rearranged them. "No one wants to have to do this for you."

"I do my work," Bea snapped back.

"Biting folks Mama instructs you to don't count," Cookie challenged.

"None of you want to collect," Bea replied.

"You're stretching the truth. I *will* collect." Sora pivoted to face her. "I just prefer to tend to the blood vault. I'll do it when I have to."

"And I like biting handsome men." Cookie swayed and twirled. "Like Jamal Watkins from Detroit. Never been a better kisser than him. Should've turned him. He'd be my eternal partner now, and I'd have my own house and my own firebird. Maybe even a baby girl. Oof."

"Bea, you're the best at it," Annie Ruth added. "Have the sharpest teeth of us all." She flashed a crooked smile, exposing a set of perfectly pointed incisors. "And that weird tongue."

"And Mama's favorite." May's face twisted as she gazed up from her book.

"She loves me most!" Baby Bird protested with a stomp.

"You're too old for a tantrum." Cookie yanked one of her long twists. "But, of course, you're right. She does."

"None of this is true." Bea whipped around. Accusatory brown faces glared back at her. "Mama doesn't have favorites."

But they were correct that Mama took Bea most often to collect. Each of her sisters had a gift bestowed upon them by Mama after their hearts stopped. She'd kissed them, leaving behind a unique talent she'd handpicked. Cookie could charm any person out of their fortune or a kiss. With a mere sniff of her nose, Sora identified any talents hidden within someone's blood. If Annie Ruth hummed a certain type of song, she might make one dance until their death. At her command, May could reduce a person to laughter or tears with a look or the touch of her hand. And the littlest of them all, Baby Bird, remembered every detail, even those that happened before she'd been born.

"I'm not leaving this city without an eternal partner," Cookie announced.

A tiny whisper echoed inside Bea: *Me neither.*

"I've made a decision. I'm ready for my own firebird and my

own house. It's time for me to be on my own." Cookie smiled triumphantly.

"Does Mama know? Did you ask her?" Annie Ruth replied. "She's not going to say yes."

"You don't know that," Cookie said.

"If you'd stop being so picky." Sora swatted at her.

"If you ain't the pot . . . You complain about every man you meet," Annie Ruth said.

"They're never that interesting. Men rarely are until they're at least two hundred years old." Cookie hissed at her. "I just need to find someone like Daddy to turn."

"There are no mortals here," Sora challenged. "I can't even smell them. This place is full of other immortal folks."

"Maybe I'll get a vampire, then." Cookie pranced around, mimicking how white vampires walked as if they owned every place their ancient feet touched.

Baby Bird gasped. Bea bit her bottom lip. That would never be allowed.

"Mama doesn't want us mixing with them. You know the history." May climbed out of her chair like a house cat stretching. She nudged Cookie and Bea to the side so she could add price ribbons to the bottles.

"We all know she doesn't *like* it. Mama won't let us forget." Bea dusted the shelves to make the ever-watchful Cookie happy.

Each one took turns mocking the serious tone Mama adopted whenever she recounted how their bloodline had become Eternal—white vampire slavers biting their enslaved for sport—and how the ancestors sent the firebirds to save them from this worsening fate, transforming them into a different sort of immortal being: an Eternal.

"If you marry a vampire, you won't be able to have daughters. You have to marry a mortal like Daddy and then turn him after the last child. It's the only way," Bea reminded. "Or marry an Eternal man and have no children."

"How do we really know that's true? Mama just hates—"

The tiny *ping* of the doorbell ruptured through the room.

"How could we have visitors already?" Cookie headed for the window-doors. "No one even told the aunties where we ended up."

They all rushed to the lattice balcony and peered down. The water spread out left and right, choked with boats and water-coaches and floating streetcars headed in a hundred directions.

A young man in a black top hat held a red envelope in his white-gloved hands. A layer of sweat glistened on his brown skin like honey spread over pecans. It was too hot to wear what he wore, and the whole thing made him look out of place; a trinket from another time, much like them. They never advertised it, always trying to blend in as much as they could and maintain the classic refinement Mama always wanted. But he seemed so proud to stick out, as if he'd fallen through time and tumbled onto their new doorstep. He was even more peculiar than the peculiar sort in this Ward.

Mama stepped outside to greet him.

"She's nervous," May whispered.

Bea watched closely. Her sister May had the talent for sensing emotions, but Bea noticed how Mama gripped her hands tight to hide a tremble. Only a trained eye would've detected it, the tiniest flutters rippling through her fingers. Which made Bea even more curious as to the identity of this handsome young man.

"Who is it?" Baby Bird asked.

"Never seen him before," Sora replied. "But he reminds me of Tristan Hill. Remember him from when we were in Harlem? I used to love the way he'd kiss my neck before finding his way to my mouth. I should've chosen him for my eternal partner. I thought someone cleverer would come along and they never did. He's been dead a hundred years now. I missed out." She perched farther over the railing. "But I'd bite him."

"No, you wouldn't," Cookie said.

"How do you know? You're always trying to tell us what we would and wouldn't do halfway in between all the things you say we should and shouldn't do. Just 'cause you the oldest. Always acting like you Mama," Sora snapped.

Cookie slapped her leg, and Sora squealed. "That's a Shadow Baron, silly."

The young man lifted his sunglasses and glanced up. They all went silent. He smiled, tipped his hat, and sauntered down the pier and back into his boat.

Shadow Barons were the mortal enemies of Eternal women. They were Walkers of the roads of the dead, ready to pull those who had cheated death or lived a little too long with their canes. They were keepers of the crossroads.

Bea didn't take her eyes off him until he became as tiny as a black pepper grain in the distance.

But she wanted to know every single thing about him.

◊

"What kind of party is it, Mama?" Bea asked, as her three older sisters, Cookie, Sora, and Annie Ruth, stood at the edge of their house pier waiting for the water-coach Mama had hired.

"I told you exactly what you need to know," she replied, while inspecting each one of the dresses she'd handpicked for them to wear. "We're showing our faces. We always do this when we arrive in a new place. We'll be there an hour tops, so don't get comfortable."

"Who goes to a *ball* for that short a time?" Sora complained.

"We do, that's who." Mama adjusted the pearls on Cookie's collarbone and smoothed the satin neckline of her dress. "This isn't a friendly invite. It's a summons—and the Turner women will only oblige but so much. They operate by different rules here. It's Mardi Gras season. This fête brings all the Wards together. It's supposed to foster peace. Help all the peculiar folk of the world mingle."

"But—" Sora started.

"We don't know how long we'll be in this wretched place, so it's best to get on with a few folks here and be cautiously friendly. Everyone is all mixed up, and it requires a particular sort of manners."

Ever since the young man dropped off that invitation, Bea had wondered about what other sorts of immortal folk lived in all the versions of this city. When they'd arrive in other places, Mama would host a small dinner party, inviting other Eternal Black women—mostly her sisters if they were close enough—or hosting the Amaranthine if near their nations or any others. Mama would sometimes even invite a few carefully curated white vampires, sharing a decadent meal of blood-infused cocktails, richly beating hearts—collected by Baby Bird—and congealed blood puddings. Bea's favorite gatherings were blood-tastings, where Mama would have Sora infuse blood with spices and herbs. This unlocked their deep flavors and exaggerated latent talents and memories hidden in mortal hemoglobin, the result giving the most glorious high.

But they'd never been to a ball. Her stomach squeezed. Bea had only read about them in books. The dancing and champagne and pretty people. Lovers meeting in dark corners. Lovers talking until sunrise. Lovers kissing and out of breath. This would be the place where she'd look for it.

"Don't stare. Don't wander off. Don't ask intrusive questions. Mind your business. We don't need anyone minding us," Mama added.

The water-coach arrived and they eased into it as though sinking into a warm blood bath, careful not to ruin their beautiful gowns. Its lanterns bobbed left and right, scattering a constellation of light over Bea's mother and sisters. Bea thought she'd never seen them look so beautiful. Cookie was wrapped in white silk that hugged her, then flared out in a beaded mermaid's tail. She could've easily been en route to her wedding. Sora wore only black, always, and her gown rippled out in dark waves of tulle like she was a ballerina who'd escaped the underworld. Annie Ruth's mid-length gown revealed slivers of her perfect skin through its lacy pattern.

Their mother wore a velvet dress, a red ribbon curling itself around every curve of her hourglass frame. Her red lip told all that she'd bite; her teeth the sharpest. Bea felt like she'd never look as stunning as Evangeline Turner. Mama often dressed up, but never like this, as if she wanted to be seen, as if she wanted to be a storm, the boom of thunder and the crash of lightning in a room. Bea gazed down at the layers of her own dress, the yellow of sunlit honey, and wasn't sure Mama made the right choice.

The water-coach glided along, its glittering nose slicing through boat traffic as they made their way to the Garden District. The houses transformed into decadent tarts on a series of silver platters; some rosy red or robin's egg blue, and a few mint green or the indigo of a sunset. Garlands and window boxes frosted them like ornate icing.

Bea knew the house they were headed to before they turned onto St. Charles Avenue. An energy tugged at her bones as if cords had been tied to them, threatening to yank her forward.

A four-story midnight-black home stretched high above, three lattice balconies spilling over with the best-dressed people Bea had ever seen. Lavish water-coaches paused at a double pier, unloading pretty passengers.

"Do you feel that?" she asked.

"Feel what?" Annie Ruth replied.

"I feel it, too," Cookie said.

"Same," Sora added.

"When many immortal folk gather, it creates that pull. And the Barons are here," Mama said. "It's a warning."

A sensation made Bea jerk.

Cookie gasped. "But they're our enemies."

"I haven't forgotten," Mama replied.

Annie Ruth shivered with fear despite the thick heat, but Bea felt curiosity rise inside her. They'd always been told that the only thing that could kill an Eternal woman was the men who walked the roads of the dead and tended to the crossroads. Not garlic, not holy water, not the sun, not werewolves, not silver, and never any stakes.

Only the Shadow Barons.

But Bea had never seen what they looked like until that young man showed up on their doorstep earlier. In her head, a Baron was some disgusting creature, a boogeyman waiting to drag them to the layers of the land of the dead. After her hundredth birthday, when she was trusted enough to venture out on her own, Mama gave her the talk. "You'll feel real danger for the first time. You'll see the mark: the key to the crossroads branded on their deep-brown flesh."

"Why would the Barons be invited?" Annie Ruth asked. "Why would they bring the invitation in the first place?"

"They didn't consult me on the guest list, babies," Mama snapped. "It is the night the five Wards come together. All old grudges and grievances put aside for the moment. All to frolic and fellowship. I used to attend every year with my own mama before she petrified."

"Who else is in there, Mama?" Bea whispered.

"All the folk of the world. The conjure women will have their cauldrons, the fae their enchanted fruit, the soucouyants their fire, and more. This place is a tuning fork."

Bea had known that other types of peculiar folk roamed the world, but she rarely came across them. Some of her earliest memories included releasing a werewolf from a bear claw in their lawn at the Colorado house, spotting the boo hag Mama caught lurking in their wardrobe in the Lowcountry, and watching the conjure woman who came for blood to mix into her potions when they lived in Kingston, Jamaica.

The water-coach waited its turn to dock. A tuxedoed porter helped them out and onto the marble pier.

"You all stay close to me. I'll be saying hello to a few acquaintances and introducing you, then we'll be on our way. Our driver will be on standby," Mama instructed.

"All dressed up for five minutes," Sora mumbled.

"What was that?" Mama's eyes narrowed.

"Nothing." Sora glanced away. "Just saying how pretty you and my sisters look tonight."

"That's what it better be." Mama smoothed the front of her gown, stretched upright, shoulders squared, and turned on her heel. "Stick close. Especially you, my honeybee." Her eyes cut to Bea.

♦

The cavernous ballroom spilled over with the most beautiful people Bea had ever seen. They sauntered in and out of plush game rooms and decadent tea salons and balconies. At first glance, they all seemed exceptionally glamourous, but upon deeper inspection, she spotted their eccentric details: Many held goblets of blood and exposed their pointed teeth as they laughed and smiled; tipped ears peeked out from behind tall and festive headdresses; many faces flickered as they shifted back and forth through various forms, light fuzz coating the arms and necks of several; and some sauntered about with plates of party food floating at their sides. Bea made mental notes so she could tell May and Baby Bird every detail when they returned home.

Black-and-white lanterns hung above, dusting everyone in golden beads of light, and a brass band played music that made Bea want to dance and find someone to whisper all her questions to.

Mama stepped deeper into the room. The crowd started to part, eyes finding Mama and greeting her with nods of acknowledgement and respect and, if Bea wasn't mistaken, fear.

How do all these people know Mama? Bea wondered, as they sauntered down a path made just for them.

The bodies shifted into a long, wide lane, and one individual stood at the very end.

Fear tugged at Bea so hard she thought her legs might give out beneath her. The hair on her arms stood at attention. Her teeth elongated, ready to bite, and the spikes on her tongue protruded. Every part of her prepared to fight or run.

The man waiting for them wore the tallest top hat she'd ever seen, rimmed with writhing skulls. It was the richest and blackest velvet and matched his beautiful skin. The tails on his coat dragged behind him and a fat cigar sat in his very pink mouth, shrouding him in plumes of smoke. Her daddy would say he was casket-sharp, ready to attend the most glorious of funerals.

Bea felt the deep breath her mama took.

"Good evening, my greatest love," the man said through a puff of his cigar. "You are a sight for sore eyes. I reckon it's been about four hundred years."

Greatest love . . . who is this man? Bea inspected him. More questions blossomed inside of her.

Mama pursed her lips. "Maybe it should've been five hundred."

"And let you miss me? Never."

"Still full of empty flattery, I see. The years haven't clipped your tongue." Mama shifted her weight left and right, right and left. "And where might your wife be?"

"Tending to crossroads business while I'm away." He smiled, the cigar lifting with the curl of his lips, and his eyes found Cookie, Annie Ruth, Sora, and Bea. His dark eyes searing and intense. "Not all of us can cut loose."

"While the mouse is away, the cat will always play, it seems," Mama replied.

"And who do we have here?" The man turned his attention to Bea and her sisters.

Mama stepped aside. "May I present a few of my daughters. This is Annie Ruth, Carmella, Sora, and Bea. Girls, this is Jean Baptiste Marcheur."

"Back to formalities, my Evangeline?" he asked, then turned to them. "Most folks call me Smoke." Thick vapor rings billowed from his mouth, dancing in circles around them. His gaze intensified, searching their faces as if looking for something Bea couldn't quite discern.

"Beware of the charms of a Shadow Baron, my girls, for they are full of hot air," Mama said.

"So cold you are. Has your heart hardened so much without me?" He whipped around and tapped the shoulder of another person in a top hat. "While we're making introductions . . ."

The boy who'd delivered the invitation stared back at them. He wore a shorter top hat than Smoke's, but he shared the same hue of dark brown skin and lovely, mischievous eyes.

"My youngest son—Jacques Baptiste Marcheur," Smoke said with a flourish of his cane.

"Call me J.B." He tipped his hat. His eyes found Bea, and he looked like he had a secret. One Bea was desperate to know. "Good evening."

Smoke put a thick hand on his shoulder, then turned back to Mama. "It's a pity Anaïs isn't with us."

Mama bristled.

"Who is that?" Bea asked.

Smoke grinned, his eyebrow lifting. "Hmmm . . . I see you're still the same."

"Never you mind that," Mama said to Bea. "Smoke, a word in private?"

"Anything for you, chérie. It's been way too long."

Mama gritted her teeth, anger in her jaw, then faced Annie Ruth, Bea, Sora, and Cookie. "Stay put. I'll only be a moment, then we are leaving. Cookie, you're in charge until I get back. No mess, you hear?"

She waited for the chorus of *yes, ma'ams* before walking off with Smoke.

Bea turned left and right, itching to explore, itching to meet more of the Eternal men and women in the room. Well-dressed folk weaved through the crowd; strings of black pearls laced within a fascinating tapestry. Her sisters strode to a nearby table to retrieve champagne flutes bubbling with blood.

J.B. stared at Bea, and Bea stared right back. "What are you looking at?" she said.

"You," he replied with a smug grin.

She tried not to blush. "Why? There's tons of people in this room." Her eyes narrowed with mock annoyance, even though she was curious, too curious about him.

"But I've never met a more beautiful Eternal woman. My father says the Turners are the loveliest."

Bea tried to maintain eye contact, matching the intensity of his gaze, and willed herself to not look up at the wriggling skulls lining his hat. They opened and closed their mouths as if they had a message to impart. "I shouldn't be talking to you."

"You shouldn't be doing a lot of things. Probably shouldn't even be in this town. All everyone keeps whispering about are those pretty Black women in the house on Esplanade Avenue. The ones who have been away so long. Some want you here, and others not so much."

"I'm not afraid of you—or them," she bluffed.

He smiled. "I'm not afraid of you, either. Though my daddy says y'all steal hearts."

"Only our littlest sister, Baby Bird. But don't worry, I won't steal yours."

"What if I wanted you to have it?"

Bea's eyebrow quirked. "Why?"

"Why not? They say if you love an Eternal woman and get her to love you back, you have good fortune for a thousand lifetimes. That it'll allow you to cheat injury and death. One kiss can do it."

"You're a Walker. A Baron. You are death."

A smile played across his lips. "That's an unfortunate stereotype. Maybe I can tell you the truth and you can give me this eternal luck."

"I'm not a pair of shoes to try on for your test case."

"What if you love me back?" The cockiness in his voice sent a prickle across her skin. Did he know her secret? Did he know what she was looking for? What exactly could a Baron do—read minds and hearts?

"I've never loved anyone."

"Yet." He removed his hat, bowed, and disappeared into the crowd.

♦

Bea wandered through the party, watching as kissing couples slipped into closed-off rooms or sauntered through the halls of the great house. While her sisters mingled and tasted all the food, she explored, peeking into decadent rooms and climbing winding staircases until she found a room that satisfied her curiosity.

The walls boasted violets and turquoises like an anxious sky tumbling into nightfall. The ceilings bloomed in pinks and tangerines, a fruit bowl of the heavens. The doors were inlaid with ivory. Plush tabletops dotted the room, each displaying porcelain game boxes studded with gold, diamonds, precious gems, and the enameled décor of card suites. The ceiling arched in jutting curves and slopes. Chaises and high-backed chairs and claw-footed sofas circled game tables. Warm-weather curtains fluttered along the wall, exposing a set of doors carved from glass and the terrace they led to.

She glided past the game tables to see if they had her favorite, one called Carrom that she'd played with May when they lived in Bombay. She was pleased to find it, tucked in a far corner. Tiny red and black disks sat inside wells along the board's perimeter, and a beautifully drawn square held a circle in the center.

Her eyes cut to the door. She knew she should go back to the party. Her mama would be looking for her and she'd get a tongue-lashing for wandering off. But she started to clean each disk—they boasted little peacocks and doves and she couldn't help herself. She lined up the little Carrom chips on both sides as if May were standing across from her. Despite being younger than her, May had always won, landing her ten Carrom disks in the pockets first.

A servant pushed a chai cart into the room. "Care for tea?"

Bea nodded.

On the sandalwood tea table, the woman set out sticky, blood-soaked dates and a sanguine beignet doused in sugar. Lifting the kettle, she poured the steaming hot liquid into a small tumbler. She took out a vial. Blood. "Half or whole?"

"Whole," Bea replied.

The servant opened the spice box and dropped scoops of poppy, fennel, and nutmeg into the vial, meant to sweeten. She stirred the spiced blood into the liquid, and it went an inky black.

"Thank you." Bea took a sip, her tongue flaring as it extracted the blood.

The woman nodded and left the room.

One of the terrace doors opened.

"Well, well," a voice called out.

Bea glanced up to find J.B.

"I didn't know anyone was going to be in here," he said.

Bea eyed him suspiciously, the tug of his presence strong now that they were alone.

"Have you decided on my proposition?" he asked with a clever smile, revealing a set of dimples. He moved closer to the game board. The tea churned in Bea's belly. "Care to wager?"

"What you've heard about Eternal women is untrue," Bea replied. "It would be a waste."

"How do you know?" His eyebrow lifted.

"I've been one for two hundred years. I think I'd know about this."

"Are you sure?" He grinned, revealing the tiniest sliver of a gap between his front teeth. "How can you know everything?"

"How can you be so certain?"

"I'm never certain about anything." He took a seat opposite her. "Witnessing death does that to you."

All the things Mama had said about the Shadow Barons stacked one on top of the other, like the layers of a crepe cake.

"They will always pull the Eternal toward rest."

"They leave their mark."

"They aren't able to resist sweeping them away."

"You're afraid," J.B. challenged.

"I am not."

"Then let's play." He motioned at the board. "I win, we put it to the test. One kiss. You win, you can ask me a question. I can feel them humming through you."

Bea jumped as if he could hear the loop of questions spinning in her head. She nibbled her bottom lip. Her eyes cut to the door again, knowing she should return to the party, knowing her sisters and mama were probably panicked and looking for her. But her eyes found his again, his challenge glinting. "You must have dozens of women wanting to kiss you. Even other Eternal ones. You don't really need one from me."

"Maybe. But I've never had the chance to kiss someone who looks as beautiful as you do."

She blushed. "Your false flattery will get you nowhere."

"I've never had the pleasure of meeting a Turner woman before. Let alone getting a kiss from one. I have to take the chance."

"We're enemies."

"That makes it even more interesting." J.B. removed his top hat and his beautiful locs fell over his shoulders. "But I've never truly believed it. Yes, we exist on opposite sides of life and death. You should be dead. I can take you to the land of the dead at any moment. You can feel it."

Bea could, but she didn't want to admit it. Every few minutes that deep pull would tug at her. The warning drumming through her. She reached for her tea and gulped down a giant too-hot sip.

"But you can also affect me. One bite and I'm shut out. My abilities gone."

Mama had never told her this. Maybe she didn't know herself.

"The stakes are even, so do you accept?"

Bea knew she should say no. Her mouth opened to refuse, but her hand extended. "If you insist."

A full smile consumed his face. J.B. motioned for Bea to start first.

She thumped one of her Carrom chips easily into a near pocket and smiled triumphantly.

"Lucky," he said.

"You know it's possible that I could pocket all my men before you get to take a single shot."

"Yes," he said. "The perils of this game—not even getting a turn or chance to choose your own fate. But it's unlikely that you'll win that way. You're liable to get distracted or run out of blessings. My father said the Turner women are lucky, but he didn't say they are infallible."

"I have an ironclad focus when determined."

"I've been known to prevent a lady or two from doing what she's set her mind to."

"How much champagne was required?" Bea teased.

J.B. laughed, and she loved its deep, warm sound.

She felt the pull again. That deep tug and a headache that punched its way into her temples. The warning.

"My father was in love with your mother, you know?" he said.

"I didn't. Not until tonight."

He continued: "He was her first love. Despite the rules. Despite the hate from both Barons and Eternal folk. Wanted to marry her, but she didn't return to this Ward . . . or any others . . . after finding your father."

"They could've never been together."

"But they were for a long time."

Mama's secrets settled over her. She'd never imagined her with another partner outside of Daddy.

"Why would she even play around? Or come that close to death?" Her mama wasn't a gambling woman. "He could've killed her. You all always pull folks toward the crossroads. It's in your nature." Bea's stomach dropped as more questions added to the tornado of others within her. Mama had avoided all her detailed inquiries on the subject over the years, only giving them a single and sharp message—*Stay away from the Shadow Barons!*

"My father is very powerful. He has a lot of control."

Bea crossed her arms, confident this shouldn't take very long. She'd embarrass him and send him on his way. She circled the board and shot another disk into a pocket.

"Your turn *again*," he said.

Her fingernail throbbed from the plucking of the disks. She paused to suck on it.

"Need to forfeit due to pain?"

She scoffed. "You wish."

"Rather I want. I need to know if what my father said is true. He has a luck that all the Walkers dream of. That I want. He's charmed—and I think it's all because of your mother."

"Maybe he's lying. Maybe it's all a bluff."

"They may call him Smoke, but he doesn't blow it. There's something else."

Bea leaned over the board again to study her next move. She wondered what a kiss with him might be like. She'd had many over the years, but never one so dangerous. A kiss with an enemy. A kiss that could kill. She thumped another disk, but the tug of his presence sent sharp pain through her. She missed the pocket this time and cringed.

She felt his big smile and scowled.

"My turn," he said, flicking one of his Carrom chips into one of hers and landing two of his disks in opposite pockets. "Seems like we're tied already."

Bea grimaced. What would happen if she lost? Would she honor the wager? Her head said she should immediately return to the party. She was supposed to be mingling and meeting others, looking for someone who might turn out to be her eternal love. But her silly feet wouldn't move. She'd fallen into a strange bubble with J.B.; an electrified tether kept her planted in her chair.

J.B. took a second turn and easily landed another piece in a pocket. "That's three to two now."

"The game is far from over, so I wouldn't get cocky."

He didn't take his eyes off her as he sank every last piece with one flick of his finger.

She sat back, stunned. Her head spun with surprise.

"I won." J.B.'s eyes twinkled with delight. "A bet is a bet. You owe me that wager."

Just one kiss won't do anything, she told herself. Her own curiosity chipping away at her fears.

"I won't bite," he said.

She laughed.

He shifted closer to her. "And I won't pull."

She'd never kissed a non-mortal before.

"Do you promise not to bite?" he whispered.

"Yes," she replied.

"May I?" he asked, reaching for her.

The words hung between them like a series of fireworks ready to explode.

She nodded. His palms grazed the nape of her neck first. The feel of his skin on hers made her heart flutter. A tingle to his touch, a reminder of what it felt like before her heart stopped. Up close, Bea could see the rich tones of his brown skin. His eyes combed over her face, and she felt him taking in every detail. His heart thudded so loudly it was the only noise between them.

Looking at him was like discovering something new about the world she'd known so long.

He leaned forward.

She squeezed her eyes shut.

He pressed his lips onto hers, the most delicious curiosity guiding his tongue.

COFFINS
Or How Else Does
One Get Beauty Rest?

Zoraida Córdova &
Natalie C. Parker

You're probably familiar with the idea that vampires sleep in coffins. At least, *some* vampires—like, the father of vamps, Count Dracula himself—sleep in coffins. (Others prefer spooky old mansions or low-rent, basement apartments). In some cases, the vampire must sleep in their own coffin with their own grave dirt or they'll become weak and die. In others, it's a means of keeping away deadly sunlight. And nothing says "Hey, I'm totally undead" quite like the sight of a vampire crawling out of a coffin! Whatever the reason, the vamps who need their trusty death box are literally stuck with it. They cannot leave it behind even if they want to! In Dhonielle's story, she's reimagined the coffin in the most magical way—by transforming it into an apothecary that moves to a new location every few years. Bea is both bound to her family and anxious to strike out on her own, even if she has to burn to do it.

How far would you go to gain your independence?

FIRST KILL

Victoria "V. E." Schwab

I

[Friday]

Calliope Burns has a cloud of curls.

That's the first thing Juliette sees.

There are so many other things, of course. There's Calliope's skin, which is a smooth, flawless brown, and the silver studs that trace her ears, and the mellow rumble of her laugh—a laugh that should belong to someone twice her size—and the way she rubs her left fingertip back and forth across her right forearm whenever she's thinking.

Jules notices those, too, of course, but the first thing she sees every day in English, when she takes her seat two rows behind the other girl, are those curls. She's spent the last month staring at them, trying to steal the occasional glimpse of the cheek, chin, smile beyond.

It started with a kind of idle curiosity.

Stewart High is a massive school, one of those places where it's easy for change to go unnoticed. There are nearly three hundred people in their junior class, but this year, only four of them were new, introduced at the first-day assembly. Three of the transfers were boring and bland, two square-jawed jocks and a mousy boy who's never looked up from his phone.

And then there was Calliope.

Calliope, who looked straight out at the assembled school, as if rising to some unspoken challenge. Calliope, who moves through the halls with all the steady ease of someone at home in their skin.

Juliette has never felt at home in her skin, or in any other part of herself, for that matter.

Two rows up, the dark cloud of curls shifts as the girl rolls her neck.

"Ms. Fairmont." The teacher's voice cuts through the room. "Eyes on your test."

The class snickers, and Jules drops her gaze back to the paper, sluggish blood rising to her pale cheeks. But it's hard to focus. The air in the room is stale. Her throat is dry. Someone is wearing way too much perfume, and someone else is tapping their pencil, a rhythmic metronome that grates on her nerves. Three people are chewing gum, and six are shifting in their chairs, and she can hear the shuffle of cotton against skin, the soft *whoosh* of breaths, the sounds of thirty students simply *living*.

Her stomach twists, even though she ate breakfast.

It used to be enough to get her through the day, that meal. It used to—but now her head is beginning to pound and her throat feels like it's full of sand.

The bell finally rings, and the room plunges into a predictable chaos as everyone rushes to lunch. But Calliope takes her time. And when she gets to the door, she looks back, the gesture so casual, as if checking over her shoulder, but her gaze lands squarely on Juliette, and she feels her pulse turn over like a stubborn engine. The other girl doesn't smile, not exactly, but the edge of her mouth almost quirks up, and Jules breaks into a full-blown grin, and then Calliope walks out and Jules wishes she could crawl under the floor and die.

She counts to ten before following her out.

The hall is a tide of bodies.

Up ahead, Calliope's dark hair bobs away from her, and Juliette follows in her wake, swears she can smell the subtle honey of the other girl's lotion, the vanilla of her ChapStick. Her steps are long and slow, and Juliette's are quick, the distance between them closing a little with every stride, and Jules is trying to think of something to say, something witty or clever, something to earn one of those rare, low laughs, when her shoe scuffs something on the ground.

A bracelet, lost, abandoned. Something fancy, fragile, and Jules reaches down without thinking, fingers curling around the band. Pain, sudden and hot, slices across her skin. She stifles a gasp and drops the bracelet, a red welt already rising on her skin.

Silver.

She hisses, shaking the heat from her fingers as she cuts through the tide of traffic in the hall and ducks into the nearest bathroom. Her hand is throbbing as she shoves it under the tap.

It helps. A little.

She rifles through her bag, finds the bottle of aspirin that isn't aspirin, and dumps two capsules out into her palm, tips them into her mouth. They break open, a moment's warmth, an instant of relief.

It helps in the way a single breath helps a drowning man, which is to say not much.

The thirst eases a little, the pain recedes, and the welt on her skin begins to fade.

She glances up at the mirror, tucking wisps of sandy blond hair behind her ears. She is a watery version of her sister, Elinor.

Less striking. Less charming. Less beautiful.

Just . . . less.

She leans closer, studying the flecks of green and brown in her blue eyes, the scattered dots across her cheeks.

What kind of vampire has freckles?

But there they are, flecked like paint against pale skin, even though she's careful to avoid the sun. When she was young, she could spend a good hour outside, playing soccer or just reading in the dappled shade of their family's oak. Now, her skin starts to prickle in minutes.

Add it to the growing list of things that suck (ha ha).

Her eyes drop to her mouth. Not to her teeth, polished as they are, fangs tucked up behind her canines, but to her lips. The boldest thing about her. The only bold thing, really.

Her sister told her that good lipstick is like armor. A shield against the world.

She digs through her bag, draws out a blackberry shade called Dusk.

Jules leans into the mirror, pretending she is Elinor as she reapplies the lipstick, carefully tracing the shade along the lines of her mouth. When she's done, she feels a little bolder, a little brighter, a little *more*.

And soon, she *will* be more.

Soon—

The bathroom door crashes open, the room filling with raucous laughter as a handful of seniors barge in.

One of them glances her way.

"Nice color," she says, a note of genuine appreciation in her voice. Jules smiles, showing the barest hint of teeth.

Outside, the hall is empty, the bracelet gone, rescued by someone else. The tide of students has thinned to a stream, the current heading one direction—the cafeteria—and Jules is thinking of skipping lunch, or rather the performance of it, and curling up in a corner of the library with a good book, when Ben Wheeler comes crashing into her.

Ben, fair skin tan from a summer of running in the park, brown hair sun-bleached a tawny gold.

She hears him coming. Or maybe she feels him coming. Senses him the second before he knocks his shoulder into hers.

"I'm wasting away!" he moans. "How is a growing body supposed to make it between breakfast and lunch? The hobbits had the right idea."

She doesn't point out that she saw him scarfing down a bag of animal crackers between first and second period, a granola bar between second and third. Doesn't point out that he's clutching a half-eaten candy bar in one hand even as they make their way to lunch. He's a distance runner, all sinew and bone and wolfish hunger.

She leans against Ben as they walk.

He smells good. Not bitable but likable, pleasant, homey.

They've been friends for ages.

In seventh grade, they even tried being more, but that was right around the time Ben figured out he preferred guys and she realized she preferred girls, and now they joke about which one turned the other.

Gay, that is. Not vampiric. Obviously.

Nobody turned her, either way. She was born like this, the latest in the honorable line of Fairmonts. And as for the whole blood gift, or curse, Ben doesn't know. She hates that he doesn't know.

Has thought a hundred thousand times about telling him. But the what-ifs are too big, too scary, the risks too great.

They reach the cafeteria, all scraping chairs and shouting voices and the nauseating scent of stale and overheated food. Jules takes a deep breath, as if diving underwater, and follows him in.

"Cal!" calls a girl, waving to Calliope across the room.

Cal. That's what Calliope's friends call her. But Cal is a rough word, a heavy hand on your shoulder, a gruff sound in your throat. Juliette prefers Calliope. Four syllables. A string of music.

"Here's a wild thought," says Ben. "Instead of silently pining, what if you just admit you have a crush on her?"

"It's not a crush," she murmurs.

Ben rolls his eyes. "What would you call it, then?"

"It's . . ." Juliette looks at the other girl, and she is back in the kitchen that morning, trapped between her parents, wishing she could crawl out of her skin.

"We're not trying to pressure you," said her dad, one hand sliding through his hair.

"It's just, one day you're going to find someone," added her mom. "And when you do——"

"You're making it sound so important," he cut in. "It doesn't have to be."

"But it *should* be," Mom said, shooting him a warning look. "I mean, it's better if it is . . ."

"Oh no, not the talk," said Elinor.

Her sister drifted through the kitchen like a warm breeze, on her way in instead of out. Her porcelain cheeks were flushed, a sleepy glow on her skin that always seemed to follow her home. "Firsts are just firsts," she said, reaching for the coffeepot. She poured herself a cup, the contents dark and thick. Juliette watched as she added a shot of espresso. A "corpse reviver," she called it.

Juliette crinkled her nose. "How can you drink that?"

Elinor smiled, soft and silver as moonlight. "Says the girl living on capsules and cats."

"I don't drink cats!" she snapped, appalled. It was an old joke, gone sour with age.

Her sister reached out and ran a perfect nail along her cheek. "You'll know when you find the right one." Her hand dropped to the space over her heart. "You'll know."

"Hurry up and bite someone."

Juliette blinks. "What?"

Ben nods at the lunch buffet. "I said, hurry up and buy something." The line is getting restless behind them. She scans the selection of sandwiches, pizza, fries, doesn't know why she bothers. But that's not true. She bothers because it's what a human girl would do.

She grabs a bag of chips and an apple and follows Ben to the end of an empty table at the edge of the room.

Ben eyes the mountain of food on his lunch tray like he can't decide where to start.

Jules tears open the bag of chips and offers him one before dropping it on the table between them.

Her mouth hurts. The pain is a low ache running through her gums. Her throat is already dry again, and she is suddenly, desperately thirsty in a way no water fountain is going to fix. She tries to swallow, can't, dumps two more capsules into her palm and tosses them back dry.

"You're going to give yourself an ulcer," says Ben as the capsules burst in her mouth, blossoming on her tongue. A moment of copper warmth, there and then gone.

The thirst eases, just enough for her to swallow, to think.

The pills used to really work, to buy her hours instead of minutes. But the last few months, it's gotten worse, and she knows that soon the pills won't be enough to quench the thirst.

Jules presses her palms against her eyes. Keeps them there until the spots come and then go, leaving only black. A merciful, obliterating dark.

"You okay?"

"Migraine," she mumbles, dragging up her head. She lets her gaze drift two tables over and one down, is surprised to find Calliope looking straight back. Her pulse gives a little jerk.

"You could talk to her," says Ben.

"I have," she says, and it isn't a lie.

There was a moment in English last week, when she told Calliope she'd dropped her pen. And that time in the hall when Calliope made a joke and Juliette laughed even though she wasn't talking to her. And once, in the second week of school, when it was *pouring* outside and Jules offered her a ride home and she was just about to take it when her brothers pulled up in their truck and she said thanks anyway.

"Well, you'll have your chance."

Juliette's attention snaps back. "What?"

"Alex's party. Tomorrow night. Everyone's going."

Alex is a varsity football player, a "steel-jawed fox," and Ben's current crush, which is unfortunate, since by all accounts Alex is straight.

Ben waves his hand whenever she mentions that.

"People aren't straight," he says. "They just don't know better. So, party?"

Jules is about to say she doesn't do parties when she catches a warped reflection in Ben's soda can, a blank canvas, a pair of blackberry-colored lips.

"What time?"

"Pick you up at nine," says Ben. "And *you* better make your move. Calliope Burns won't wait forever."

II

[Saturday]

Juliette hovers outside her sister's room.

She's about to knock when the door swings open under her hand and Elinor appears, obviously on her way out. She looks Jules up and down, taking in the starry tights, the short black dress, the polish on her nails already smudged because she can never seem to wait for it to dry. "Going somewhere?"

"Party," says Juliette. "Could you, I don't know . . ." She gestures down at herself as if Elinor has some transformative magic instead of just good taste. "Help me?"

Elinor laughs, a soft, breathy sound, doesn't check her watch. Reggie will wait. She motions toward her vanity. "Sit down."

Jules lowers herself onto the cushioned stool in front of the well-lit mirror, examining the line of lipsticks balanced along the back edge as Elinor hovers behind her. They both show up, of course; she's never understood the logic behind that myth. Juliette studies her sister in the reflection—they're three years apart, and, side by side, the differences are glaring.

Elinor's hair is silver-blond, her eyes the deep blue of summer nights, while Juliette's hair is a dingier shade, more straw than moonlight, her eyes a muddy blue. But it's more than that. Elinor has the kind of smile that makes you want to smile back and the kind of voice that makes you lean in to listen. She is everything Jules wants to be, everything she hopes to become. After.

She remembers Elinor before, of course; it's only been a few years, and the truth is, she's always been delicate; beautiful. But there's no question that now she's *more*. As if that first kill took who she was and turned up the volume, made everything sharper, stronger, more vibrant.

Juliette wonders what she'll be like with the volume turned up, which parts of her will get loud. Hopefully not the voice in her head, doubting everything, or the nervous energy that seems to steal across her limbs. That would be her luck.

Elinor's fingers slide through her hair, and she feels her shoulders loosen, her tension melt. She doesn't know if this is a vampire power or just a sister one.

"El," she says, chewing the inside of her cheek. "What was it like?"

"Hm?" her sister says in that soft, cooing way as she touches a curling iron, testing its heat.

"Your first kill."

The moment doesn't slam to a halt. The world doesn't stiffen or still. Elinor doesn't stop what she's doing. She simply says, "Ah," as if everything about Jules is suddenly clear.

"Is it really so important?"

Elinor considers, a slow shrug rippling through her. "It's as important as you make it." She twists Jules's hair, pins a piece of it out of the way. "Some believe it's just the doorway, that it doesn't matter which one you pick, as long as you go through." She works her magic, taming Jules's hair into ribboning curls.

"Others think the door determines the place beyond. That it shapes you."

"What do *you* think?"

Elinor sets the curling iron aside, turns Jules toward her, one finger lifting her chin.

"I think it's better if it means something."

A soft brush slides along her cheekbone.

"It didn't mean anything to Dad," says Jules, but Elinor clicks her tongue.

"Of course it did. He took his best friend."

Her stomach turns. She didn't know that. "But he said—"

"People say all kinds of things. Doesn't make them true." Elinor dips a small brush into a pot of liquid liner. "Close your eyes." Jules does, feels the tickle of the line along her eyelid. "Mom went a different route," continues Elinor. "She took a guy who wouldn't take no for an answer. It was the last word on his lips as he died." She laughs a small, soft sound, as if telling a joke.

Juliette opens her eyes. "What about you?"

Elinor smiles, her perfect red lips parting a little. "Malcolm," she says in a dreamy way. "He was beautiful, and sad." She looks past Jules in the mirror. "He didn't struggle, even toward the end, and he looked so peaceful when it was over. Like a sleeping prince. Some people want to die young." She blinks, returning to herself. "Others put up a fight. The most important thing is never to let them get away."

Jules looks down at the array of lipsticks on the vanity, starts to reach for a coral, but Elinor shifts her fingers two tubes right, to a deep shade, neither red nor blue nor purple. She turns over the tube, reads the label on the bottom.

HEART-STOPPER.

Elinor takes the lipstick and applies with it an expert hand. When she's done, she pulls back, head tilted like a marble sculpture. "There."

Juliette studies her reflection.

The girl in the mirror is striking.

Hair falling in pale waves. Blue eyes ringed black, the sharp cut of the outer edge making her look feline. The dark lip, something more feral.

"How do I look?" she asks.

Her sister's smile is all teeth.

"Ready."

♦

There's a sign on the door that says COME ON IN, but Ben still has to pull her over the threshold.

Parties are everything Juliette hates.

They are loud music and crowded rooms, food she can't eat and booze she can't drink, and all the trappings of the normal life she'll never have. But she drank a full cup from the coffeepot before leaving, and at least the sun's gone down and taken the worst of her headache with it. The world is softer in the dark, easier to move through.

Still, the only thing that makes her go inside—besides intractable, impossible Ben—is the idea, the fear, the hope that Calliope is somewhere in this house.

But there's no sign of her.

"She'll show up," says Ben, and she wants to believe him, and she wants to go home, and she wants to be here, and she wants to be more, and she wants to take a shot from the bar, wants to do something, anything to calm her nervous heart.

She purses her lips, tasting the dark red stain called Heart-Stopper, and agrees to stay. Maybe she will find someone else, maybe it doesn't matter, maybe a first is just a first.

Ten minutes later, a dozen of them have migrated to an upstairs room and Ben is leading a game of Truth or Dare, and she doesn't know if he's doing it for her or for himself, because he looks pretty sad when Alex picks truth, and then *he* picks dare, and now he's drinking a beer while doing a handstand, an act that defies the laws of physics, and Jules is laughing and shaking her head when Calliope walks in.

And when she sees Jules, she smiles. It's not the bright smile of friends meeting in a crowd. It's something sly and quiet, there and then gone, but it leaves her heart pounding.

She stops a few feet away, so they're on the same side of the room, side by side, and that's better because Jules doesn't have to look at her, doesn't have to weather the force of the other girl looking back.

Ben finishes and holds up his hands like a gymnast dismounting to a room full of applause.

And then he looks at Jules and smiles.

"Juliette," he says, eyes dancing with power, and she knows what he's going to say, knows the shape of it at least, and she wills him not to, even as her heart pounds.

"I dare you to spend sixty seconds in the closet with Calliope."

The room whistles and whoops, and she's about to protest, to make some quip about not being in the closet anymore, that if he wants them to kiss, they can kiss right here, in front of everyone, in the safety of the light. But there's no time to say any of that, because Calliope's hand is already closing around hers, pulling her forward out of the crowd.

"Come on, Juliette."

And the sound of her name in the other girl's mouth is so right, so perfect, she follows, lets Cal lead her into the closet. The door swings shut, plunging them both into the dark.

Dark. It's a relative thing.

Light spills beneath the bottom of the door, and Juliette's eyes steal the sliver, use it to paint the details of the crowded closet. The coats taking up 90 percent of the space, a pile of boxes around their feet, the hangers knocking into the back of her head, and

Calliope—not the back of her head or some stolen sideways glance but right here, the slope of her cheek and the curve of her mouth and those steady brown eyes, somehow warm and sharp.

"Hi," she says, her voice low and sure.

"Hi," whispers Juliette, trying to sound like her sister, with her airy confidence, but it comes out all wrong, less like a breath and more like a whistle, a squeak.

Calliope laughs, less *at* her, than at this. The crowded closet. The closeness of their bodies. And, for once, the other girl seems nervous, too. Tense, like she's holding her breath.

But she doesn't pull away.

Jules hesitates, thinks they should either be closer together or farther apart.

Ben never said what they were supposed to do.

Sixty seconds isn't much time.

Sixty seconds is forever.

Calliope smells good, of course she does, but it's not her lotion or her ChapStick.

It's *her*.

Jules's senses flare and narrow until all she can smell is the other girl's skin, and her sweat, and her blood. Blood—and something else, something she can't place, something that sends warning bells ringing dully through her head.

But then Calliope kisses her.

Her mouth is so soft, her lips parting between Jules's own, and there are no fireworks. The world doesn't stop. She doesn't taste like magic or sunshine. She tastes like the grapefruit soda she was drinking, like fresh air, and sugar, and something simple and human, and people talk about the world falling away, but Juliette's mind is racing, is here, aware of every second, of Calliope's hand on her arm, of her mouth on her mouth, of the coat hanger digging into her neck, and she doesn't understand how people simply kiss, how they live in the moment, but Jules is so painfully *here*.

There is the subtle ache in her mouth, the shallow longing of her teeth sliding out. And in that moment, between the fangs and the bite, she thinks of how she'd rather go to a movie, rather enjoy the scent of Calliope's hair, the murmur of her laugh, rather stay in this closet and keep kissing her.

Just two human girls tangled up.

But she is so hungry, and her mouth hurts so much, and she is not human, and she wants to be more.

Juliette's mouth drops to the other girl's neck.

Her teeth find skin. It breaks so easily, and she tastes the first sweet drops of blood before she feels the tip of a wooden stake drive up between her ribs.

I

[Friday]

Juliette's mouth is a work of art.

That's the first thing Cal noticed.

Not the canvas, exactly—the way her bottom lip curves, the twin peaks of the top—but the way she paints it. Today at school, her mouth was the color of blackberry juice, not quite purple, not quite pink, not quite blue. Yesterday, it was coral. Last week, Cal counted burgundy, violet, and, once, even jade.

The colors stand out against the stark white of her skin.

Cal knows she shouldn't spend so much time looking at the other girl's mouth, or at least not at her lips, but—

A dinner roll hits her in the side of the head.

"What the hell!" she snarls.

"Dead," announces Apollo.

Theo points his knife. "Just be glad it wasn't buttered."

Cal scowls at her older brothers as they go back to shoveling food. She's never seen anyone eat the way they do. But then again, they're built like the gods they're named after. Built like heroes. Built like Dad.

He's on the road, on a long haul—that's what they call a distance hunt. He's a trucker, too. It's good cover, but she misses him. His broad arms, his bear hugs. The way he can still pick her up, like he did when she was little. How safe she feels surrounded by his arms. Cal used to trace the black bands that wrapped his forearms, feeling the raised skin beneath her fingers. One for every kill. Used to draw lines on her own arms in Sharpie, imagine earning her first mark. First kill.

She doesn't like it when he's gone this long. She knows there's always a chance—

This time she sees the roll coming, plucks it out of the air and winds up to throw it back, but Mom catches her wrist. Calliope looks at Mom's right forearm, wrapped in delicate threads of ink.

"Not at the table," she says, plucking the roll out of Cal's fingers. And Cal doesn't bother pointing out one of her brothers threw it first, because she knows that doesn't matter. *Rule #3: Don't get caught.*

Theo winks at her.

"Where's your head at?" asks Mom.

"School," says Cal, and it's not a lie.

"Settling in?" asks Mom, but Cal knows she means "blending in," which is a totally different thing. She knows that moving around is part of the job; she's been to a dozen schools in half as many years, and every time, the warnings are the same. Just blend in. But in high school, the two feel contradictory.

Blending in, it's standing out. It's knowing yourself, and owning yourself, and Cal does, but thank god they're too old for show-and-tell because she's pretty sure the sharpened stick and the strands of silver in her bag wouldn't go over well.

"Cal's got a crush," says Apollo.

"Do not," she mutters. Jules isn't a crush; She's a target. And okay, maybe the first thing that caught her eye were those lips, the color of pomegranate seeds. Maybe there was, for a brief moment, the beginnings of a crush, but then she noticed the way the girl stuck to the shade, cringing away from the merest glimpse of sun between clouds. The way she picked at her food without eating. Last week, she found the bottle of capsules in the girl's bag, cracked one open in the bathroom sink and watched the dark red substance ribbon into the drain. And today, in the hall, she dropped a silver bangle, waited around the corner and watched as the girl reached to grab it, then recoiled when the silver met her skin.

And now she's sure.

Juliette Fairmont is a vampire.

Theo rises to clear his plate. "Eat up, stick," he says, kicking her chair.

"Don't call me that."

"A ghost passing gas could knock you over."

Cal's fingers tighten around her knife.

"Theseus Burns," warns Mom, but Apollo's up now, too, and Cal can feel the shift in the room, the energy winding tight as wire. "Where are you going?" she asks.

"Hunt," answers Theo, the way someone might say *drugstore* or *market* or *mall*. As if it's nothing. No big deal. Just another night.

Cal's heart quickens. She knows better than to ask if she can come. A question begs an answer, and the answer is usually no. Better to stick with statements.

"I'm coming with you," she says, already on her feet, fetching her boots from the hall. She's learned to keep a set of gear downstairs. Last time she jogged up to her room to grab her stuff, they were already gone.

"You finish your homework?" asks Mom.

"It's Friday."

"Not what I asked."

Cal doesn't stop lacing her boots. Her brothers are walking out the door. "Math and physics, yes, English, no, but I'll do it first thing in the morning." Her mom wavers. The front door swings shut. Cal shifts from foot to foot.

At last, her mom sighs.

"Fine." And she says something else, something about being careful, but Cal doesn't catch more than a glimpse as she surges out the door. An engine revs, and she half expects to see the taillights on the pickup, two red eyes gleaming as the truck drives away.

But it's there, idling, in the drive, and Cal beams, because they waited.

"Wipe that grin off your face," says Theo. "And get in."

♦

Up front, Theo raps his fingers on the steering wheel, and from the safety of the back seat, Cal stares at the tattoos that wind around his right forearm, mirrored by the bands that circle Apollo's bicep. Cal runs a fingertip along the inside of her elbow, counting down the weeks until she turns seventeen.

Apollo was fifteen when he made his first kill, took down a shape-shifter with a crossbow at thirty feet.

Theo was *twelve*. She'll never forget the sight of him, smiling through a sheen of oily gore as he trailed Dad back to the campsite on a family trip. They'd gone off, just the two of them, to study marks on the trail and had come across a full-grown wendigo. He and Mom had a big fight about it after, but Theo just kept grinning as he held aloft a monstrous claw, a prize Dad made him toss into the fire. He has a strict rule about keeping things like that. The only trophies he approves of are the black tattoos, anonymous reminders of victories past.

Their bodies read like a map. A ledger.

And hers is still blank.

"Wake up, stick."

Cal blinks as Theo cuts the engine, kills the lights. She squints into the dark and suppresses a low groan at the sight of the cemetery gates.

They're parked outside a graveyard, which rules out the wilder monsters that show up in woods or bars, places with plenty of food. Not a nest of vamps, either—they're more likely to hole up in mansions than mausoleums.

No, a graveyard means they're hunting *ghouls*.

Cal hates ghouls.

She's really not fond of dead things in general. Zombies, specters, wraiths—it's the emptiness, the hollowness that unnerves her. Theo says they're easiest to hunt because they don't beg. Don't plead. Don't trick you into caring.

But they also don't stop.

They are voids, insatiable, relentlessness. They don't feel pain, or fear. They don't get tired. They come, and they keep coming.

Cal wishes they were going after werewolves, or changelings— hell, she'd rather go up against a demon than a dead thing, but it's not like picking a college major.

Hunters don't specialize.

They hunt what needs hunting.

What, not who, her dad's voice booms in her head. Never think of them as *who*. Never think of them as *them*, only *it*, only the target, only the danger in the dark.

They climb out, and Theo tosses her a flak jacket and a pair of elbow pads, the hunting equivalent of wearing kid floaties in a pool. Then it's time for gear.

Shovels, timber, steel spikes—those can be stored in the bed of the truck, passed off as ordinary farm gear.

The rest of the tools they keep in a hidden compartment under the bench.

The seat comes away like a coffin lid, revealing silver crosses and iron chains, a steel garrote and an assortment of daggers, things you can't exactly pass off as yard equipment. She balances on the footboard, staring down at the cache.

Cal's been building her own kit, stashed in the hatchback of her beat-up five-door, an old tool chest hidden under a pile of reusable shopping bags, because if Dad taught her one thing, it was to always be prepared. Hunters carry a whiff of the work on them, a spectral signature that some monsters can scent.

The more you hunt, the more the things you're hunting start to notice you.

Which is fine, if you're using yourself as bait in a trap, but it's less ideal if you're not on a job.

They each take a walkie-talkie. Theo chooses a samurai sword, while Apollo goes for an ax that looks massive, even in his grip, then tosses Cal a tire iron.

It hits her palm hard enough to bruise, but she doesn't wince.

"The last time I checked," she says, "the only way to kill a ghoul is a head shot."

"Right."

"Yeah, well, a tire iron isn't exactly designed for decapitation."

"Sure it is," says Apollo. "If you swing hard enough."

"The iron's just a precaution," says Theo, handing her a pair of binoculars. "You're on watch."

Watch. The hunter equivalent of *stay in the car.*

"Come on, Theo."

"Not tonight, Cal."

Apollo grins. "Hey, if you're good, we'll let you do a dead check."

"Gee, thanks," she says dryly, because who doesn't love pulping skulls with a steel bar. She grabs a dagger from the kit, slips it into her back pocket, and trails after them, feeling like a puppy biting at heels as they head for the entrance. Apollo picks the lock in seconds, and the iron gate swings open with a faint groan.

Cal's mind does this thing where it pulls away from her body, zooms out until she can see the whole scene from a distance, and she knows it doesn't look good: three black teenagers clad in makeshift armor, marching into a graveyard with spikes and swords.

No, officer, everything's fine. We're just out here hunting monsters.

Dad has a contact at the sheriff's department, a family friend he saved on a camping trip when they were kids. But memory's a weak bond in the face of trouble, and no one wants to test the current strength of that old thread.

"Cal," snaps Theo, who can always tell when her mind's wandering. "Get some height."

She hoists herself up onto a grave marker, one of those massive angels people get when they want to stand out from the shallow tide of tombstones.

Like climbing a tree, she thinks, hooking her leg over the wing. She straddles the old stone sculpture as her brothers fan out and wait for her to scan the dark. It's a windless night, and the cemetery stretches out, gray and still, and it's only a few seconds before she catches sight of motion to her left.

A grisly shape sits on the edge of an open grave, gnawing on a human calf, the leg still wrapped in suit cloth.

Cal wishes she'd skipped dinner.

A second ghoul comes into sight, shuffling between the graves.

It looks human, or at least it looks like something that used to be human, but it moves with the staggered stride of a puppet on uneven strings. The ghouls look like corpses, tattered clothes clinging to withered forms—but of course they aren't wearing clothes, just strips of skin, flesh and muscle ribboning off old bones.

Call whispers into the walkie-talkie. "I see them."

Theo's voice crackles. "How many?"

She swallows. "Two."

She guides them forward, each to his target. One row over, two graves down, like a game of battleship, holds her breath as her brothers close in. They get close, but ghouls are sharper than they seem. The one feasting twitches upright. The one searching turns, the motion jerky but impossibly fast, and the fight begins.

Theo swings his sword, but the ghoul twists out of its path and surges forward, gnarled hands and snapping teeth. Several rows over, Apollo slashes out with his ax, but he's off-balance, and the blow is low. It passes through the ghoul's stomach, lodges somewhere around his spine. No—the tombstone behind it. He twists the blade free, falls back with the force of the motion, and rolls up into a crouch.

She watches her brothers, marveling at Theo's grace, so at odds with his size; at Apollo, a blur of speed and force. But then a flash of movement catches her eye. Not from her brothers or from the ghouls they're fighting. The motion comes from the graves to her right.

A ragged shape moving too quick through the dark.

And Cal realizes she was wrong. There aren't two ghouls in the graveyard.

There are three.

The third is twice the size of the others, a rotting mess of limbs and teeth.

And it's heading for Theo.

Theo, who's too busy trying to carve up his own monster to notice.

Cal doesn't think.

She jumps from the angel's wing, hits the ground hard, pain lancing up her ankles as she runs.

"Hey!" she shouts, and the ghoul turns just as she swings the tire iron at its head. It lands with a crack, the creature's face jerking a little as the bar glances off its skull. And for a second—just a second—Cal's blood races in the best of ways, and she feels like a hunter.

But then the ghoul smiles, a horrible, open-jawed grin.

Cal dances back, away, out of its grip, and remembers the dagger. She pulls it from her pocket, rips the sheath off with her teeth as the ghoul shuffles toward her.

She drives the blade into the creature's neck, but the dagger is barely long enough to cut its throat. It gets stuck somewhere around its collarbone, tearing out of her grip as the ghoul's fingers scrape her skin.

She scrambles backward, but her boot catches on a broken grave and she goes down and the ghoul is on top of her. Up close, it reeks of rot, sickly sweet, and the fear is sudden, wrenching. It slams into her like a wave and she has to fight the urge to scream.

It gnashes, making a terrible chattering sound as it snaps its jaw. She drives the iron bar up between its teeth, forcing its head back and away as its bony fingers claw at her, leaving trails of its latest meal. She kicks out, trying to drive it back, but it's strong, impossibly strong for something made of sinew and bone, and the fear is a high whistle in her head, a fever in her blood, and her hands slip on the bar and she is going to die, she is going to die, she is going to—

Theo's sword slices through the monster's neck, the blade so close Cal feels the breeze on her face.

The ghoul's head rolls into the weedy grass.

The rest of the ghoul collapses into a heap of sinew and bone, and then her brothers are there, kneeling before her, walls blocking out the horror of the world beyond. Cal grips the bar hard to stop her hands shaking.

"You're okay, you're okay," Theo's saying, low and rhythmic.

Apollo rises, hefting his ax, and ambles over to the ghoul's severed head.

Cal swallows.

"Of course I'm okay," she says, as Apollo drives the ax down into the monster's skull. It bursts like a rotting pumpkin under the blade.

Cal doesn't puke. It feels like a victory.

It feels like a failure.

Pathetic. Absolutely pathetic.

Apollo kneels to collect Cal's dagger from what's left of the ghoul's throat.

"Should have given me a sword," she mutters as Theo hauls her to her feet.

◆

Her brothers buzz all the way home.

They're wound up, riding high in the aftermath of the hunt, and Cal is buzzing, too, but for all the wrong reasons. For missing the third ghoul in the tally, for taking on a dead thing with a five-inch knife and an iron bar, for tripping, for scrambling, for getting twisted up in fear.

Apollo doesn't give her shit. Theo doesn't lecture. They don't chew her out. They don't say *anything* about it, and maybe they're trying to make her feel better, but they don't. It makes her feel like a kid thrown into time-out, and she spends the whole ride wondering, just like a kid, if they're going to tell Mom.

She's waiting for them in the living room. "How did it go?"

And Cal waits for them to rat her out, to say it was fine until they had to save her sorry ass, but Theo just nods, and Apollo grins and says, "Ghouls old fun," because he can't resist a shitty pun, and then Mom looks right at Cal, as if she can read the truth in her face, but Cal's learned that truth is something you don't just go around showing.

"All good," she says, the words like a stone in her stomach.

And Mom smiles and goes back to watching her show, and Cal heads for the stairs, her brothers on her heels. She's at the top when Theo catches her elbow. "You okay?"

It's all he's said. It's all he'll say.

"Of course," she says, trying to sound bored as she pulls free, slips into her room.

A few moments later, she can hear the buzz of the tattoo gun down the hall, the laughter her brother uses to cover up pain.

She frees the straps and clasps of the makeshift armor, grimaces when she sees the tear in her favorite jeans. It's her fault, she should have changed, should have worn something she didn't care about losing. Cal strips, searching for broken skin, signs of injury, but there's nothing but a few scrapes, the beginning of a bruise.

Lucky, she thinks.

Fool, she answers, staring down at her hands, the grave dirt lodged deep under her nails. She goes into the bathroom, tries to scrub the cemetery from her skin. The water runs, and in the white noise she replays it all again, scrambling backward over the weedy ground, heart pounding, the fear, the panic, the shock of shoulders hitching up against stone and the urge to throw up her hands, not to fight but to hide, to get away.

Her stomach turns, bile rising in her throat.

The Burns are hunters, and hunters don't run.

They fight.

Cal's hands are raw by the time she shuts off the tap.

Her dagger lies discarded on the comforter, and she knows her mother would give her hell for leaving weapons out, so she picks it up, sinks to her knees beside the bed, and draws out the leather chest she keeps beneath. She drops the dagger in among the silver crosses, the needle-thin blades, the collection of wooden stakes.

Cal runs her hand over these, pausing at one on the end, a drum stick sharpened to a wicked point. She lifts it, brushing her thumb over the initials she carved into the wood.

JF.

Juliette Fairmont.

Down the hall, the tattoo gun stops buzzing. The laughter dies away with it, and Calliope spins the wooden stake between her fingers and decides she's ready to earn her first mark.

II
[Saturday]

There are monsters you can kill from a distance, and there are ones you have to face up close.

Cal tells herself that's why they're here, in the closet. Tells herself that's why she's tangled up in the other girl's arms. Why she's kissing Juliette Fairmont.

Juliette, who is not a girl at all, who is a monster, a target, a danger in the dark.

Jules, who tastes like summer nights and thunderstorms. The crackle of ozone and the promise of rain. It is one of Cal's favorite things. That's the idea, she's sure, the trick. Because it isn't real; it's just another way to catch prey.

Which is how Juliette sees her.

Prey.

Remember that, Theo warns.

This is a hunt, adds Apollo.

And she really doesn't need her brothers' voices in her head right now, not when Juliette is pressed against her, as warm as any living thing. Her heart pounds, and she tells herself it's just the high before the kill and not the warmth of the other girl's mouth or the fact she has dreamed of both these things.

Of killing Juliette.

Of kissing Jules.

And even as her fingers curl around the stake, she wonders what would happen if they stopped here, if they left this closet hand in hand. If they went back to the party. If, if, if. She doesn't have to do this. It's not a sanctioned hunt.

Her family will never know.

They can just—what? What is she supposed to do? Take Juliette home for dinner? Introduce her to her family?

No. There is no future here. Not for them.

But there is one for *her*. One where she gets her first tattoo. Where she earns her place between her brothers. Where her father comes home from his hunt and sees the thin black band below her elbow and knows he doesn't have to worry anymore.

And then the other girl's mouth drops to her throat, and there it is, the subtle press of teeth, the bright flash of pain, and Cal's bones know what to do. She draws the stake and drives the tip between the vampire's ribs.

She hears the soft, audible gasp of Juliette's breath catching, and Cal falters. Just for a second, but it's enough time for the vampire's hand to fly up, for her fingers to catch the wooden stake.

Juliette pulls back, her mouth open in surprise, and even in the dark, Cal can see teeth.

"Time's up!" calls a voice, and the door flies open.

They pull apart, a slash of space carved between them by the sudden light, and Juliette's fangs are gone, and Cal presses the wooden stake back against her forearm, and she does the only thing she can.

She runs.

The room is filled with whoops and cheers as Cal surges out of the closet, past the crowd and into the hall, her pulse pounding in her ears.

Shit, shit, shit.

The first rule of hunting, the one that matters most, is finish what you start. And she didn't. The one thing she had was the upper hand, the advantage of surprise.

But now Juliette knows.

She *knows*.

♦

Jules doesn't know what just happened.

She squints in the sudden light, but by the time she can see again, Calliope is gone.

Calliope, who just tried to kill her.

She can still feel the wooden tip of the stake between her ribs, the sharpness of it like a rock through the smooth glass of their kiss. The kiss. And just a taste of blood.

And now Cal's gone, and her sister's voice drifts through her head.

Never let them get away.

Shit.

Jules strides out of the closet, one hand pressed to her front to hide the tear in her shirt, the other hovering over her mouth even though her fangs have already retreated. The room is filled with whistles and laughs, and beneath the raucous sound, she can hear blood. Blood, pulsing inside them. Blood, pounding like a drum inside her head. Cal's blood, rushing beneath the surface of her warm skin, so close Jules could taste it, could taste her—

And now she's getting away.

And she knows Juliette's secret.

She *knows*.

"I have to go," she says, pushing through the group.

"But it's your turn!" calls Ben.

But Jules doesn't stop, can't stop. She's out the door and in the hall, on the landing, looking down at the wave of students on the first floor, she's scanning the clustered heads, searching for that cloud of curls, and—

There.

There she is, heading for the front door. She's got her hand on the knob, one foot across the threshold when she stops and looks back into the house. Juliette grips the wooden rail as the girl's gaze rises up the stairs and finds hers.

And holds.

And for a moment, the sound of the party drops away, and all she hears is blood. Hers, slow and stubborn, and Cal's, thundering and quick. For a moment, they are back in the closet, a tangle of lips and limbs, before the whole thing tipped, before kiss became kill.

Cal stares up at her across the gulf of space. Jules stares back, holding her breath, and she knows the other girl is holding hers, too, knows they are both waiting to see who will break, who will move, who will run, who will chase.

Calliope's mouth pulls into a crooked grin.

And Jules stares back, smiles back, and thinks—

Let the hunt begin.

KISS / MARRY / KILL
Or The Villains We Love to Love

Zoraida Córdova & Natalie C. Parker

While not all vampires can claim to be charming (take, for example, the decaying form of the Nosferatu), the romantic allure of vampires is a tale as old as time. They are powerful, dark, dangerous, and while their bite can kill, it can also entrance. They might just be the original bad boys. It's kind of difficult to imagine building a romantic life with someone who might never age or who might, totally by accident, drink your mom or something like that. Still, romance with vamps is a popular part of the mythology. But as often as we see a romance played out between a vampire and a human, or a vampire and a slayer, it is super rare to find one with a happily ever after. Slayers, like humans, usually come to the relationship with too little power, but here, Victoria is complicating the idea that the vampire is the natural villain by introducing a slayer with a strong family tradition, putting them on equal—and deadly—footing.

What do you think? Who is the real villain: the slayer or the vampire?

Acknowledgments

This anthology wouldn't be possible without the MVPs of the night: Vampires, who live in the minds, hearts, and imaginations of so many. But they can't take all the credit. That is why we would also like to thank:

Lara Perkins for being an incredible advocate and agent.

Our editor, Weslie Turner, for sharing our vision for the project and approaching every stage with impeccable grace and insight.

The phenomenal Imprint/Macmillan teams who continue to support this work, including: Erin Stein, Hayley Jozwiak, Kayla M. Overbey, Cynthia Lliguichuzhca, and many more.

Adriana Bellet aka Jeez Vanilla for cover art that exceeded our wildest hopes.

Our authors: Tessa, Dhonielle, Mark, Laura, Julie, Victoria, Samira, Heidi, Rebecca, and Kayla. Your stories are *everything* we wanted when we set out to put this collection together.

Most importantly, to you, dear reader, for sharing in our love of the undead.

Cheers,

Zoraida & Natalie

About the Authors

SAMIRA AHMED is the *New York Times*–bestselling author of *Love, Hate & Other Filters*, *Internment*, and *Mad, Bad & Dangerous to Know*. Her short stories and poetry have appeared in anthologies including *Take the Mic*, *Color Outside the Lines*, *Ink Knows No Borders*, *Who Will Speak for America*, *This is What a Librarian Looks Like*, and *Universe of Wishes*. A graduate of the University of Chicago, Samira has taught high school English, worked in education nonprofits, and spent time on the road for political campaigns. She was born in Bombay, India, and grew up in Batavia, Illinois, in a house that smelled like fried onions, spices, and potpourri. She has lived in Chicago, New York City, and Kauai, where she spent a year searching for the perfect mango. Visit her online at samiraahmed.com and on Twitter and Instagram @sam_aye_ahm. Samira's problematic blood-sucking fave is Spike.

DHONIELLE CLAYTON is the coauthor of the Tiny Pretty Things series and the *New York Times*–bestselling author of The Belles series. She grew up in the Washington, DC, suburbs on the Maryland side and spent most of her time under her grandmother's table with a stack of books. A former teacher and middle school librarian, Dhonielle is cofounder of CAKE Literary—a creative development company whipping up decidedly diverse books for a wide array of readers—and COO of the nonprofit We Need Diverse Books. She's got a serious travel bug and loves spending time outside of the USA but makes her home in New York City, where she can most likely be found hunting for the best slice of pizza. Visit her online at dhonielleclayton .com and @brownbookworm on Instagram and Twitter. Dhonielle's favorite vampire is Count von Count from Sesame Street.

ZORAIDA CÓRDOVA is the author of many fantasy novels for kids and teens, most recently the award-winning Brooklyn Brujas series, *Incendiary,* and *Star Wars: Galaxy's Edge: A Crash of Fate*. She is the co-host of the podcast *Deadline City*. Zoraida was born in Ecuador and raised in Queens, New York. When she isn't working on her next novel, she's planning a new adventure. Visit her online at zoraidacordova .com. Her favorite vampire will forever be Angel . . . but Damon Salvatore is a close second.

TESSA GRATTON is the author of adult science fiction and fantasy novels *The Queens of Innis Lear* and *Lady Hotspur*, as well as several young adult series and short stories which have been translated into twenty-two languages. Her most recent YA books are the original fairy tale *Strange Grace* and *Night Shine*. Though she's lived all over the world, she currently resides at the edge of the prairie with her wife. Visit her online at tessagratton.com. Tessa's favorite vampire is Gilda, from *The Gilda Stories* by Jewelle Gomez.

HEIDI HEILIG is the author of the acclaimed Girl From Every-where series, as well as the Shadow Players series. Her books have made the Indies Next List and both the Andre Norton and Locus Recommended Reading lists and she has a past life as a musical theatre writer. Visit her online at heidiheilig.com or on Twitter @heidiheilig. Heidi's favorite vampire is the Titular character in *The Rime of the Ancient Mariner* by Samuel Taylor Coleridge.

JULIE MURPHY lives in North Texas with her husband, who loves her, her dog, who adores her, and her cat, who tolerates her. After several wonderful years in the library world, Julie now writes full time. When she's not writing or reliving her reference desk glory days, she can be found watching made-for-TV movies, hunting for the perfect slice of cheese pizza, and planning her next great travel adventure. She is the author of *Side Effects May Vary*, *Ramona Blue*, *Dear Sweet Pea*, *Faith Taking Flight*, *Puddin'*, and *Dumplin'*, which was adapted into a film on Netflix. You can visit Julie online at imjuliemurphy.com. She can be found on Twitter and Instagram as @andimjulie. Julie's favorite vampire is Edward Cullen and she's not even a little bit ashamed.

MARK OSHIRO is the award-winning author of *Anger Is a Gift* and *Each of Us a Desert*. When not writing, editing, or traveling, they run the online Mark Does Stuff universe and are trying to pet every dog in the world. You can visit them online at markoshiro .com or @MarkDoesStuff on both Twitter and Instagram. Mark's favorite vampires are Blade and Angel.

NATALIE C. PARKER is the author and editor of several books for young adults including the acclaimed Seafire trilogy. Her work has been included on the NPR Best Books list, the Indies Next List, and the TAYSHAS Reading List, and in Junior Library Guild selections. Natalie grew up in a Navy family, finding home in coastal cities from Virginia to Japan. Now she lives with her wife on the Kansas prairie. Find her online at nataliecparker.com. Her vampire queen is Caroline Forbes.

REBECCA ROANHORSE is a *New York Times*–bestselling author and winner of the Hugo, Nebula, Locus, and Astounding awards.

Her novels include *Trail of Lightning*, *Storm of Locusts*, *Star Wars: Resistance Reborn*, and the middle grade novel *Race to the Sun*. Her latest adult novel, *Black Sun*, comes out Fall 2020. Her young adult short fiction can be found in *Hungry Hearts*, *A Phoenix First Must Burn*, and *A Universe of Wishes*. She lives in northern New Mexico with her husband and daughter. Find her online at rebeccaroanhorse .com or on Twitter @RoanhorseBex. Rebecca's favorite vampire is Jean-Claude from the Anita Black: Vampire Hunter series, but the Blood River Boys are an ode to her teenage faves, Michael and David from *The Lost Boys*.

LAURA RUBY writes fiction for kids, teens, and adults, including the young adult novel *Bone Gap*, a finalist for the National Book Award and winner of the Printz Medal. She is on the faculty of Hamline University's MFAC program. Visit her online at lauraruby.com and on Twitter and Instagram @thatlauraruby. Laura's favorite vampire is the girl from *A Girl Walks Home Alone at Night*.

VICTORIA "V. E." SCHWAB is the #1 *New York Times*– and Indie-bestselling author of more than twenty books, including *Vicious*, the Shades of Magic series, and *This Savage Song*. Her work has received critical acclaim, been featured by *Entertainment Weekly* and the *New York Times*, been translated into more than two dozen languages, and been optioned for TV and film. The *Independent* calls her the "natural successor to Diana Wynne Jones." Visit her online at veschwab.com and follow her on Twitter @veschwab. Victoria's favorite vampire is obviously Lestat.

KAYLA WHALEY is an essayist and novelist living outside Atlanta. Her work has appeared in *Catapult*, The Toast, and *Michigan*

Quarterly Review and in the anthologies *Here We Are: Feminism for the Real World* and *Unbroken: 13 Stories Starring Disabled Teens*. She holds an MFA from the University of Tampa and was formerly senior editor at Disability in Kidlit. Visit her online at kaylawhaley.com and follow her on Twitter @PunkinOnWheels. Kayla's favorite vampire is Claudia, especially as played by Kirsten Dunst.